CAPE COD PROMISES

Love on Rockwell Island
Book Two

Bella Andre

&

Melissa Foster

ISBN-13: 9780986135842

Cover Design: Natasha Brown

BAYSIDE BOOKS, LLC
PRINTED IN THE UNITED STATES OF AMERICA

Note to Readers

We love hearing from our readers and have been so excited about your response to our Love on Rockwell Island books! Creating the island and all of our sexy characters is so much fun, and we're thrilled to bring you Trent Rockwell and Reese Nicholson's love story. Watching them fall back in love has been an emotional journey well worth the wait, and we hope you love them as much as we do!

Happy reading,
Bella & Melissa

Chapter One

CROUCHED ON THE worn hardwood floor beside the shelf he was building, Trent Rockwell sat back on his heels, turned the hammer over in his palm, and listened to the sounds of the island. Crickets, tree frogs, and occasional distant voices snuck in through the open windows of the old gristmill, bringing back great memories of growing up on Rockwell Island with his four younger siblings. The familiar sounds of his youth had nearly been erased by the constant noise of New York City, where he'd been living for the past ten years. He'd been back on the island just shy of two months, returning after his stodgy grandfather, Chandler Rockwell, demanded that Trent and his siblings take over management of the prestigious Rockwell

Resort.

It had been a blessing in disguise. Trent had been contemplating returning to the island for quite some time, but finagling a way to do so without losing his successful law practice had kept him from making the move. Now that his grandfather was in his mideighties and had suffered two heart attacks in recent years, Chandler Rockwell had needed to make a drastic change. Trent wondered if his grandfather had somehow known that his grandchildren had needed a change, too.

While two of his younger siblings, Ethan and Sierra, had made the island their home after college, Trent and his other siblings, Quinn and Derek, had built their careers on the mainland. But in the weeks since they'd returned to take over the resort, Quinn had already fallen in love with Shelley Walters, who had been vacationing on the island—and she'd fallen so deeply in love with Quinn *and* the island that she'd never left. They'd moved in together, and Shelley had bought the old gristmill, where she was opening an organic coffee shop called Shelley's Café. After weeks of renovation, which Trent and his brothers were handling, her café was almost ready for its grand opening.

Trent's life had also changed drastically since coming home. After watching Quinn and

Shelley fall madly in love, he had begun to take stock of his own life and reclaim aspects that had been missing for too long, like time off from work to enjoy being with friends and family. After years of grueling hours sitting behind a desk with his mind entrenched in legal jargon, he no longer pored over legal documents until all hours of the night. Instead, he once again found relaxation and enjoyment in working with his hands, preferring to come to the gristmill and work late in the evenings, long after his other siblings had called it a night.

Scents of Cape Cod Bay swept over Trent's bare chest like a caress, stirring memories that had kept him up at night long before he'd moved back to the island. His mind drifted to a summer ten years earlier, when in the space of six short weeks, he'd met, fallen in love with, and married Reese Nicholson. She'd been just nineteen years old to his twenty-six, with hair as blond as spun gold and gorgeous brown eyes that were like windows to her enormous warm and loving heart.

Without the distraction of overtime hours, the questions Trent had been asking himself for a decade kept rising to the forefront of his mind: If he hadn't worked seventy hours a week, if he'd paid more attention to Reese's needs and slowed down enough to put her first—above his career, above the need to socialize in the circles that had secured his rising to the top of the practice—would they have split up six months after their wedding? Or could they have made their relationship work?

He rose to his feet, trying to push past the familiar tightening in his chest. But he never could escape thoughts of Reese for very long, and since coming back to the island, it felt like she was everywhere—even though she'd been in Oregon helping her sister with her new baby ever since Trent had returned.

Still, her absence hadn't stopped the memories from assaulting him at every turn. It didn't help that her gallery was right across the street from the gristmill. Hell, Trent couldn't even pass the local beach without seeing the image of Reese, looking angelic in her wedding gown. He still heard her sweet laugh in the brushing of the leaves in the wind. And even now, as the breeze wrapped around his chest again, it was *her* fingers he felt trailing along his skin.

Who was he kidding? He hadn't been able to escape thoughts of her since he'd come home to the apartment they'd shared in New York City ten years ago with a diamond bracelet and a bottle of champagne on their six-month anniversary...and found the *Dear Trent* note that had ended their marriage.

I never thought I'd write you a note like this, and I know it's—

No. He couldn't go there again. Being back on the island always served to sharpen the rough edges of those memories, and he forced himself to push the painful thoughts away. The sound of a car door closing helped bring his mind back to the present. *No sense in wallowing in what was...or what could have been.* He wiped his brow with the shirt he'd tossed aside and picked up the hammer again. He'd pound her out of his head. One nail at a time.

He brought the hammer down and missed the nail. Uttering a curse, he tightened his grip on the hammer and tried again, missing his thumb by a hair. Now, more than ever, he could use the release another few hours of manual labor would provide. But if he kept thinking about Reese, he was sure to nail his thumb to the floor. He set the hammer on the old grinding stone and looked around for his painting supplies, figuring he couldn't do much damage with a paintbrush.

Realizing he'd left his brushes in the car, Trent blew out a frustrated breath and headed outside. He couldn't see a darn thing with those overgrown bushes lining the front yard. He'd have to remember to ask Shelley if she wanted them trimmed, or at least cut a pathway so people didn't have to push through them, just like he was doing right—

He smacked head-on into a soft, curvy form, instinctively putting his hands around the woman's waist to steady her at the same moment that her hands clutched at his chest. Whatever she had been holding crashed to the ground, but he held her steady so that she wouldn't also stumble and fall.

His hands and body recognized the feel of her curves immediately, even before his brain had a chance to kick in. His brain still wasn't fully functioning when her name—"Reese"—slipped from his lips, soft and familiar.

"Trent?" Her body went rigid. "I...I was just...I wanted to welcome Shelley to the neighborhood."

He knew he should let her go, but for this one perfect moment, he couldn't keep from drinking her in instead. She felt so good, so warm and sweet, even after all these years.

"At eleven at night?" Somehow, he managed to force his hands back down to his sides.

She looked away, but the moonlight caught the rosy blush on her cheeks. "I wanted to leave her a gift basket as a surprise for when she gets here tomorrow. And I didn't think anyone would be working this late."

Trent followed her gaze to the street below—and her car parked at the curb. The one with the Rockwell Island lighthouse he'd given her the week they'd first met still hanging from the rearview mirror.

* * *

WITH HER HEART in her throat, Reese bent to pick up the contents of the gift basket she'd brought for Shelley. She'd known Trent had been back on the island for nearly two months—her best friend and employee, Jocelyn Steller, had called her the minute she'd heard about the Rockwell siblings taking over the resort. But Reese thought she'd have time to prepare before running into Trent.

Now, as she tossed the items she'd brought for Shelley back into the basket, she was a trembling mess, and the way he was looking at her in the moonlight as he helped her pick up the gifts was only making her more nervous. Especially after she'd all but admitted she'd come late to avoid seeing him.

"You don't have to help me pick everything up," she said, wishing he would leave but aching at the thought of him walking away. He smelled like hot, sweaty, *yummy* man...and it brought back a thousand sexy memories she couldn't let herself think about. Lord knew she did enough of that late at night, when she was alone with the memories of him touching her, holding her—

"It's okay, Reese," he said as he set a bottle of lotion back in the basket.

Oh Lord. She'd forgotten how deep and sexy his voice was and how when he said her name, it vibrated all the way through her.

Even after all these years, he still had the ability to turn her inside out.

As he picked up the driftwood on which she'd painted a scene for Shelley and drew his dark brows together as he studied it, Reese couldn't resist making a quick visual inspection of her own. The line of his jaw had sharpened over the years, and the peppering of dark whiskers gave him an edgier feel than the suit-and-tie Trent she'd remembered from their life in New York.

Did he still have to be so darn good-looking? So gorgeous that her pulse didn't have a chance of staying steady when he was this near to her.

She'd caught only brief glimpses of him a handful of times over the past few years when he'd been in town for short visits with his family, and she'd certainly never allowed her eyes to linger the way she was now. Allowing that was probably a huge mistake, given the way her stomach was fluttering like crazy.

His dark hair was slightly longer, reminding her of how he'd looked when they'd first met. His eyes were still as serious as they'd always been, but something was different about them—the longer he looked over the painting, the more they softened. And—*holy cow*—how had she not noticed until now that he was bare-chested? He was broader, thicker, more manly than he'd been when they'd shared a bed. A deliciously wild and sexy bed.

Breathe, Reese. Breathe.

He lifted his eyes from the driftwood she'd painted and his lips tipped up in a smile. "This is beautiful, Reese. The detail in the waterwheel really brings it to life, and the brook is so well done that the water practically flows off the wood."

Hearing Trent's praise brought back such good memories. Trent had not only been the first person to support her artwork outside of her family, but he'd also understood in a way no one else had how it fulfilled her and set her free at the same time.

She opened her mouth to respond with a *thank you*, but the urge to kiss him—to thread her fingers into his hair and pull his mouth down over hers so that she could see if he still tasted as good as he used to—was so strong it stunned her.

Reese snapped her mouth closed, more than a little surprised by the desires that her ex-husband had so quickly reawakened. Trent set the wood in the basket, and their fingers brushed, sending a shiver of heat up her arm, before he rose to his feet and reached for her hand.

Oh no. If I take your hand, I'll want to be in your arms, and I can't get hurt again.

She had to get out of there. *Now.*

She pushed to her feet and managed to find her voice. "Can you be sure Shelley gets the basket?" She took a step backward. "I've got to run."

"But you just got here," he said as she headed for the sidewalk.

She stumbled over her own feet as she hurried away, afraid that if she looked back at him again, her resolve to keep her distance until she could handle seeing him without going all squishy inside would simply dissolve.

She needed a few days.

Or months.

Or a year.

Or maybe it was going to take a lifetime to figure out how to get over Trent Rockwell.

Chapter Two

THERE WEREN'T MANY things that made Reese happier than sitting atop her favorite spot on the dunes and painting in the early hours of the morning, when the sun spread its beauty over the bay. Hues ranging from peach to vibrant orange melted into the fray of the blue-gray sky. Reflections of clouds danced off the water, broken only by boats and buoys and their liquefied shadows.

It was also where she and Trent had first met.

She'd spent years avoiding this very spot after their divorce, and hadn't set out this morning with the intention of ending up here. But as if her legs had a mind of their own, it was where she'd ended up. And now she remembered just how spectacular this view of the beach and the bay was. She could even see the tips of the resort's roofs off to her right. She'd always thought that this was the most beautiful location on the whole island.

Reese tucked a lock of hair behind her ear and inhaled the salty sea air, trying not to think about last night and how good it had felt to be back in Trent's arms. But being here, in the very spot where she'd first set eyes on him, it was impossible *not* to think about him.

She'd spent ten years moving past their marriage. Ten years trying to forget the summer they'd fallen in love, when every day had held such wonderful promise and every night had sparked with the flames of their insatiable passion. She'd even stopped drinking her favorite smoothie, which she'd concocted out of fruits and yogurt the first night she and Trent had made love. They'd both been ravenous after hours of lovemaking but too revved up to eat. Trent had made a joke about surviving on the glory of passion, and their Passion and Glory smoothie was born.

She'd been so naive, thinking that an island girl like her could ever be happy in a big city like New York. They'd had such big hopes and dreams, and they hadn't been worried about making things work—not when they'd been sure that true love would trump any obstacles in their path.

But while it turned out that true love hadn't actually been able to make their marriage or life in New York work, Trent's love *had* inspired Reese so deeply that her artistic abilities had surged while they were together. She'd been inspired by him in a way that she'd never been again—not until today, when her painting of the sunrise over the bay seemed almost effortless. Her brush had taken on a mind of its own this morning, moving over the canvas in long, quick swipes, creating arcs and mixing colors in new and beautiful ways. All because of how thrilling it had been to be in his arms again and to look into his deep blue eyes. Reese set her paintbrush down on the tray of her wooden easel with a sigh. No matter how much she wanted to deny it, she knew exactly why she'd gotten up before dawn and come to her old favorite spot; she had been hoping to catch a glimpse of Trent running, just like she used to so long ago. She'd dated a few guys since their divorce, but not once had she felt the explosive creativity—or soul-deep passion—that Trent stirred in her with just the whisper of her name.

She shivered, thinking of the way her name had rolled off his tongue with familiarity that went beyond an old friend. And his hands. *Good Lord, his big, strong hands.* The way he'd caught her by the waist and held on tight... It was as if he'd zapped a magic wand and erased all the years of hurt with just one touch.

Ohmygod. No. No, no, no! I cannot get wrapped up in him and be hurt all over again.

She began packing up her painting supplies, lifting her eyes at the sound of seabirds sweeping down to the beach, where they gathered and pecked at a fish that had washed up onshore.

Was that what she was doing? Pecking at something that was long gone and should be left alone?

Leaving Trent had been the most difficult thing Reese had ever done. She'd thought they had the type of love that could never be ignored or be broken. But after six months of Trent coming home long after she'd gone to bed, seven days a week, she'd realized that she wasn't anywhere near the top of his priority list. Work came first. And then networking. And then sleep, when he could fit some in. A wife barely made the list, especially one who never managed to say the right thing at his important networking events and who just couldn't find her footing in such a big city, no matter how hard she tried. She wasn't happy, and she knew he couldn't possibly be happy either. Splitting up had seemed like the only way forward for either of them—so that he could give his all to his career without anyone holding him back and she could head back home to the island to paint.

Leaving had been horrible. *Beyond* horrible. But the worst part about it wasn't just that she'd felt there was no option left but to leave. No, the very worst part was that instead of saying goodbye in person, she'd left him a note. She'd sobbed the entire time she'd written it, her hands shaking, her stomach roiling.

Dear Trent,

I never thought I'd write you a note like this, and I know it's unfair to leave this instead of talking with you in person, but no matter how hard I've tried to say these things to you face-to-face, I always lose my nerve. We've grown so far apart, and I miss us terribly, but I know it would be worse to let things keep going like they have these past six months. You are doing everything you hoped you'd do with your career, and I'm lost here in New York. I'm sorry I couldn't become what you needed, or what you deserve. You don't need me holding you back, which is why I'm going back to the island today. This is the hardest thing I've ever done, but I still know I need to do it. For both of us.

I'll always love you.

Reese

She still cringed to think of how it had all

played out. But the truth was that if she'd looked into the eyes of the man she adored, there was no way she would have been able to leave. And then they both would have only grown more and more unhappy together.

He'd come after her, of course. Trent Rockwell wasn't the type of man who let something he wanted slip through his fingers. But his attempts to get her back had been rationalizations, not remedies. He'd told her *why* he needed to work late hours and *why* his career had to be his top priority, without even so much as an offer to try to spend more time with her or to pay more attention to their marriage.

As a seabird picked up the fish carcass and flew away, she realized that was exactly what she'd done a decade ago. She'd picked up her broken heart and returned home.

Only now, after having been in Trent's arms again, she knew that no matter how much she tried to fool herself, she had never really left her deep feelings for him behind.

She was bending to finish packing up her supplies when she spotted a tall, broad figure jogging toward the steep wooden steps that led to the top of the dune. Her pulse quickened, and she knew she was playing with fire. Testing herself. Could she see him again without her heart going crazy?

As Trent came clearly into view down below the dune, Reese scooted back so he couldn't see her. But even just that quick peek sent a pang of longing through her chest, chased by a world of hurt.

No, she thought as she made herself look away. She wasn't going to do this to herself. She *couldn't* do this to herself. Not now. Not after spending two months helping her sister, Sarah, and her wonderful husband, James, care for their adorable new baby. At twenty-nine, Reese was finally ready to move on with her life. And after holding that tiny little boy in her arms, she longed for more.

She hadn't even realized that she'd been holding herself back. But obviously she had, because when she'd watched Sarah and James together with their new baby, she'd felt all the hopes and dreams she'd packed away ten years ago come rushing back. She was finally ready to fall in love and get married again, and start a family. This time, with a man who wouldn't dream of putting her last on his list.

But no matter how hard she tried, she couldn't stop herself from peering down again at Trent while he ran up the steep stairs, looking devastatingly handsome—and dangerously threatening to her heart.

But her future children deserved more than a father who worked twenty-four seven.

And she deserved a husband who would be a true partner.

Reese grabbed her easel and supplies and hurried toward the parking lot. She couldn't—and wouldn't—keep wishing things had gone differently between them.

It was time to move on. Once and for all.

* * *

DEALING WITH CHANDLER Rockwell was never comfortable. But today, as Trent prepared to walk into his grandfather's office, he struggled not only to steel himself against Chandler's cold nature, but also with the incessant questions and unfamiliar feelings he'd been plagued with since running into Reese last night. It was difficult enough to pull his shoulders back and put on his lawyer face with his grandfather on a normal day, but it was even harder to be strong when his insides felt like they were twisted into knots.

"You going to stand out in that hall forever?" Chandler grumbled.

Trent lifted his chin as he walked into Chandler's office. "Good morning, Grandfather."

His grandfather's dark eyes tracked him as he crossed the room. Chandler's narrow-eyed stare, coupled with the firm press of his lips, gave him an ever-present look of disdain. He was dressed in a blue button-down shirt and silk tie, and his frail hands clung to the arms of the wheelchair, his thick, black brows drawn into an angry slash. Trent wondered how anyone could live in a paradise like Rockwell Island and continually seem disgruntled. But he knew better than to let those questions show on his face—steady eye contact, a professional smile, and a nod always did the trick with his grandfather.

Trent smiled warmly at Chandler's private nurse, who was standing dutifully beside his wheelchair. "Good morning, Didi."

"Good morning, Trent." Didi's Mediterranean accent made her answer sound as regal as she looked in a sea-green dress, her long blond hair pinned up in a bun.

Up until a few months ago, Chandler had gone through nurses like others might go through tissues, but Didi had proved to be as strong-willed as his grandfather. Trent sensed that she'd somehow managed to gain Chandler's respect, as well. Lord knew, she had Trent's respect for being able to put up with the man the way she did without losing her self-respect.

Chandler nodded toward the leather chair across from his massive desk. "This won't take long."

Then you should have just called me instead

of taking me away from my work to come to your private wing of the resort.

But Trent knew that wasn't how things worked with his imperious grandfather. Chandler beckoned, and everyone jumped.

Chandler leaned slightly forward and shifted his eyes to the door as if he expected someone to walk through before saying in a hushed but stern tone, "I need you to track down the deed for the resort."

"That should be easy enough. I'll go through the files and have it sent up to you shortly."

Chandler had mandated that Trent and his three brothers give up the businesses they'd spent a decade building to return to the island full-time and run the resort for a year—something they'd all balked at. But Chandler's threat of selling the resort to a large conglomerate that would have fired the loyal staff and left hundreds of island residents without employment was enough to make Trent and his siblings accept the proposition with a few caveats. Trent and his brothers had stood firm in an all-or-nothing stance—include their sister, Sierra, and their father, Griffin, as well, or they all walked away—and Chandler had met their demands. Most importantly, their grandfather had agreed to keep his hands out of all business dealings.

Which was why Trent wanted to know, "Why do you need the deed?"

But Chandler simply sat back and waved his hand in the air as if the reason weren't important. "Just bring it to me." He turned to Didi before Trent could ask any further questions. "I'm not feeling well this morning. Please take me back to my room now."

Trent rose to his feet with a frown. He knew enough about his grandfather's machinations over the years to wonder just what the hell Chandler was playing at now.

* * *

TWO HOURS LATER Trent had gone through most of the files in his office but was no closer to finding the deed than he was when he'd begun looking. After placing a call to the courthouse and learning that the transfer of the deed was never filed after his great-grandfather's death, he had to redirect his search and look for the original transfer paperwork.

At least he'd been distracted from thinking about Reese for a little while.

"Knock, knock."

His younger brother Quinn walked into his office. He had become so relaxed since falling in love with Shelley and moving to the island that he actually looked like a different man. Especially today, his blue eyes shining with curiosity.

"So?" Quinn sat down on the leather couch and crossed an ankle over his knee. "I hear there was a basket from Reese in Shelley's café this morning that wasn't there last night when we left. Want to tell me how it got there?"

"Not really." Talking about Reese would only make Trent think about her again.

"So we're going with the basket-elves theory? That's what Shelley thought you might want to do, too."

"Quinn." Trent ran his hand roughly over his face.

His brother's teasing expression shifted to concern. "Was it that bad seeing Reese again?"

"No. It was that *good*." Trent had been tortured all night long by how good it had been to have Reese back in his arms.

"I ran the old route to the dunes this morning," he admitted. He hadn't run that route since they'd split up, but after bumping into her last night, it was like his legs had carried him in that direction without any thought.

"And?"

"I still can't get her out of my head. I know it's over and she's moved on. I've seen her very briefly on and off over the years, but last night..."

Trent paused, searching for the right words to describe how blown away he'd been by the intense feelings that had consumed him the second he'd realized it was Reese in his arms— and how awful it had been to realize just how badly she'd wanted to get away from him. She had all but run from him.

"Last night outside Shelley's café, when I realized Reese is even more beautiful, even more talented than she was before, something hit me. Hard."

"You mean the fact that you're not really over her?"

Yes.

The lightning-quick answer inside his brain stunned him silent. Most of all, because he knew it was true.

"What did you think was going to happen?" Quinn asked after letting Trent stew for a few moments. "You two never really hashed everything out. Don't you think that has to happen at some point, given that the island's too small for you two not to keep being thrown together?"

Trent knew his brother was right. Ten years ago Trent had explained to Reese that as a burgeoning lawyer he was expected to work long hours and attend the highbrow social events that even he never really cared for. But she hadn't wanted to hear it. She'd told him that she was *last* on his priority list—not even just second to his job, but seventh or eighth, after his workday, parties, office events, and whatever else might lead to his success. She'd also said she didn't even recognize him anymore. Right before he returned to New York, his mother had said something that still rang in his ears today. *When your heart is ready to commit, you'll know. Until then, you just have to do the best you can to move on.*

And moving on was what he thought he'd accomplished. Although, now that he was thinking about it, it *had* taken him a long time to sign the divorce papers. Even after he'd followed Reese back to the island and she'd made it clear that it was really over, he still hadn't been able to sign the damn things. Mostly because he'd kept thinking, kept hoping, that somehow it would all work out. That *they* would still work out. His attorney had hounded him for weeks until Trent had finally lost hope and signed them. He still had the bottle of perfume she'd left behind and every love note she'd ever scrawled on napkins and slips of torn paper. Hell, he'd never changed his aftershave because she'd loved it so much. All of that should have clued him in to his inability to really move past Reese. Instead, he'd done what he was best at—he'd tried to work thoughts of her away. But it had never really worked, had it?

"You're right," Trent said slowly. "We never did hash things out. Not really. Not like we should have."

His brother was looking at him with concern now as he said, rather apologetically, "I didn't just come to razz you about Reese. We've also scheduled a meeting tomorrow morning at ten to discuss the community project."

Sierra had come up with the idea of hosting a project at the resort that would represent the close-knit community and the warmth of the island. The last time they'd discussed it, they'd narrowed it down to a couple of front-running ideas, but they hadn't made any firm decisions yet.

"I'll be there."

"Good." Quinn looked at all the files and papers strewn around Trent's normally meticulous office. "Although between Reese and whatever mess you're dealing with right now, you look like you could use a break. Shelley's going out with Sierra tonight, so I'm meeting Ethan and Derek for a drink. Want to join us?"

A drink—*or three*—was exactly what Trent needed to chase thoughts of Reese out of his head. Otherwise, it was bound to be another long and sleepless night.

"Absolutely."

Chapter Three

REESE WAS STANDING on the widow's walk in front of her easel, her emotions howling and gusting inside her like a brutal storm as she painted, when she heard the glass doors to the loft slide open behind her and Jocelyn's careful footsteps approach. Jocelyn had been there when Reese had fallen head over heels in love with Trent a decade ago. She'd been Reese's maid of honor at their wedding. And then she'd been there to help Reese pick up the pieces of her broken heart after she and Trent had broken up.

"Reese? Are you okay? You've been up here for hours." Jocelyn was tiny at five one and barely a hundred pounds soaking wet, but she was no wallflower. She could be as tough as a drill sergeant or as sweet as a preschool teacher—all skills Reese had heavily relied on ever since Jocelyn began running her gallery a few years ago.

Reese clearly heard the testing of the waters in her friend's tone. *Are you upset enough to need a hug, or do you need a swift kick in the butt, instead?* Reese was so used to pushing away painful thoughts of Trent that she automatically said, "I'm okay, thanks."

Jocelyn peered over Reese's shoulder at the painting and arched a finely manicured brow. Her auburn hair tumbled over her shoulders as she narrowed her bright hazel eyes. "Actually, it looks like you're still reeling over bumping into Trent."

"I thought I was totally over him," Reese suddenly blurted out, "and then, after all these years, he knocks me to my knees in five seconds flat. Tell me I'm an idiot."

"You're an idiot." Jocelyn embraced her in a quick hug. "Of course, you know that if you change your mind about him, I'll be right there saying you're brilliant."

"Joce..." Reese had been wrestling with her feelings for Trent all day, and the only way to deal with them and keep her sanity was to paint.

"What? That's what friends are for, isn't it?" Her friend sat on a deck chair, and as she kicked her feet up on the railing, she said,

"Don't give me that look. Mae is running the gallery. I'm on a helping-a-friend-in-need break. I'm allowed one a day. It's in my contract."

"You must have a really great boss," Reese teased as she put her feet up beside Jocelyn's and tried to relax.

"She's the best. Oh, before I forget, Tami Preston called to remind you that she's showing her artwork at the flea market on the other side of the island the day after tomorrow and you promised to go."

"I'm glad she called. I've been so distracted that I probably would have forgotten. At least I remembered that I'm heading to Bay's Edge tomorrow." Reese taught painting classes for senior citizens at Bay's Edge Assisted Living Facility.

"And Sierra called, as well, to let us know that she has a late meeting to go to before she joins us for our girls' night out."

Every few weeks Reese and Jocelyn enjoyed a girls' night with Sierra Rockwell and her cousin Annabelle, who owned a clothing shop in town. Tonight Reese *really* needed the girls. Only...things suddenly seemed far more complicated than usual.

"Do you think it'll be weird between me and Sierra now that Trent's back in town for good?"

"Sierra has always been careful not to talk

too much about her brother," Jocelyn replied. "Why would it be any different just because he's living here now?"

Reese eyed her painting, as if it held all the answers.

"Is it because you're worried that she'll see how conflicted you are? You do look a little on edge, but if I didn't know you so well, I might think it was because of work or any number of things other than Mr. Hot and Delicious's hands on your hips again."

Reese tipped her head back and closed her eyes against the setting sun with a groan. She'd always worn her emotions on her sleeve, which was one of the things that had made it even harder when Trent had become too entrenched in work to notice. When they were living on the island, he'd noticed practically every breath she'd taken. But in New York, he'd barely noticed her at all.

And now she had no idea how to gain control of the emotions he'd unearthed with nothing more than a quick touch and a few words. She obviously hadn't been able to paint them away today.

The only thing she knew for sure was that she was not over Trent Rockwell.

But at the same time, she definitely couldn't let herself get hurt again. It had been a real test of strength to survive the deep, dark ache of missing him for the first few years after she'd left him. So even if managing her feelings for Trent was going to be the biggest uphill battle of her life, she knew she had to find a way to do it.

Because she'd never survive losing Trent twice.

Jocelyn rose to her feet and squeezed Reese's shoulder. "Just remember one thing—if you can't drink it away, cry it away, paint it away, or eat enough ice cream to drown it, it just might be too real to be forgotten. After all, you do still have that lighthouse he gave you ten years ago hanging from your rearview mirror," Jocelyn pointed out before she walked back inside the gallery.

The lighthouse. He'd given it to her on their third date.

And as she glanced at the painting she was working on and the two other canvases propped against the railing beside her, she realized she'd painted that lighthouse into every single picture.

* * *

TRENT FOUND HIS parents talking with his brother Derek in his father's office.

"Am I interrupting?"

"Never, honey." His mother, Abby, hugged

him. "We're just going over our options for hiring a marketing company to handle the resort."

"Well, that sounds like more fun than the wild-goose chase I'm on. Chandler asked me for the deed to the resort."

"What on earth does he need the deed for?" Derek asked as he rose from his chair.

Although Derek had agreed to be a part of the resort takeover and to live on the island for one year, he still hadn't fully embraced the situation. His resentment toward their grandfather was evident in his stormy dark eyes.

"He wouldn't tell me. And when I called the courthouse, I learned that the deed transfer giving Chandler ownership of the resort was never filed. I called his office to find out what the hell is going on, but his assistant told me he wasn't available. Dad, do you know where the legal documents might be?"

His father, Griffin, frowned. "As far as I know, the deed should have been kept with the rest of the legal documents. Abby, honey, you're better with names than I am. Who was the resort's last legal counsel?"

Trent's parents had always been openly affectionate, with each other as well as their children. They'd also always been integral parts of each other's lives on every level. *Just like*

Reese and I once were.

"Robert Faison was the last person to run the department. You remember him," Abby answered. "He was a heavyset, balding man. He passed away unexpectedly from a heart attack about... Could it have been eight or nine years ago now?"

"That sounds about right," Griffin said.

"He worked for your great-grandfather for many years, and stayed on after Chandler took over," Abby explained to Trent. "Griff, after he passed away, weren't a number of his files archived to the basement with the reorganization?"

Griffin kissed the back of Abby's hand. "I can always count on you to remember everything."

He turned to Trent. "Ask Irene about it. She manages the archives. I'm sure she'll know where those files are."

Thoughts of the deed went out the window as his parents' unrelenting commitment sent his mind spiraling back to Reese and the promise they'd made on their wedding day.

I promise to always love you. Forever.

It was a promise that sounded so simple. However, in the wake of their painful divorce, he'd ended up believing it was actually the most difficult promise in the world to keep.

But now that he'd held Reese in his arms

again and had gotten lost staring into her beautiful brown eyes, he finally realized the truth: It was a promise that he'd always kept.

Because he still loved her.

And he'd love her forever.

Chapter Four

THE HIDEAWAY WAS one of the most happening spots on Rockwell Island. Owned by Sierra Rockwell and decorated with local artwork, it was also one of the friendliest gathering places in town. The interior boasted wide-planked hardwood floors, rough wood walls, high ceilings with iron chandeliers, a cherrywood bar, and a covered patio with gorgeous bay views.

"I am so glad I moved to the island," Shelley Walters said. "Every day is like an adventure, with the changing tides and the tourists coming and going."

This was Shelley's first time joining them for girls' night, and she instantly fit in. She was vivacious, funny, and easy to talk to, not to mention stunning, with a mass of dark, curly hair and a bright outlook.

Reese had never imagined Trent's younger brother Quinn, who had always worked at least as many hours as Trent, would change his workaholic ways. But now that she'd gotten to know Shelley a little better, she understood why he had. Shelley's energy and positive outlook were contagious.

"In fact, one of the things I was most hoping for here was girls' nights out. When did you guys start doing them?" Shelley asked.

"Jocelyn, Annabelle, and I were in the same graduating class at Rockwell High," Reese told her, "and Sierra was a year behind us. We used to be really good about getting together every week, but life kind of got in the way, so now we do it as often as we can. Of course, when we were younger, we had study dates, not drink dates."

"Studying boys, maybe," Annabelle said. "My grades definitely would have been a whole lot better if we'd actually studied our books more often back then."

And yet even though Reese and Sierra had been good friends in high school, because of the age gap between them and Trent, it wasn't until the summer after Reese had graduated, when Trent had come back to the island after finishing law school, that she'd finally met him. Just thinking about the first time she'd seen him jogging toward the steps on the dune made her pulse quicken. At twenty-six he'd been broad-chested and ripped, and from the very moment his iridescent blue eyes had met hers, the sexual tension between them had been inescapable.

At nineteen, raised by parents who were a decade older than the parents of all her friends, she'd spent more quiet evenings at home with her close-knit family than out partying. So when Trent introduced himself and his voice alone sucked the air from her lungs, it was so foreign a feeling, and so incredibly intense, that it had intrigued and embarrassed her at once. Trent's eyes had gone dark and serious when he'd seen the picture she was painting, and they'd ended up spending two hours talking about her love of art and his love of literature.

By the end of the night, they'd both fallen head over heels in love.

"I can't imagine what it must have been like to grow up here," Shelley said, breaking Reese out of her Trent trance. "Everyone is so close, and you can always get out on the beach or a boat."

"And the men," Jocelyn said as she lifted her glass. "Don't forget the men. Let's just say that summers on Rockwell Island have always been *really* easy on the eyes."

Reese could all but hear the other women's

questions—especially Sierra's—even though everyone had been careful not to say a word. But she refused to let anything come between her and her friends. Not when they'd been the ones to pick her up and put her back together after her marriage had failed.

Taking a deep breath, she made herself say, "I ran into Trent last night when I dropped off your basket, Shelley. Just literally smacked right into his bare chest."

At first Sierra looked surprised by the way Reese had brought up her brother to the group. Quickly, however, Sierra's surprise turned to curiosity, her brow rising as if to say, *And?*

Trent had been an elephant in the room between them for way too long. Besides, he had made his priorities clear long ago, and no matter how much she had wanted them to be different, they weren't.

After her divorce, she'd quickly learned that she couldn't draw strength from the bottom of a bottle or a heavily frosted piece of chocolate cake. But she could draw strength from the bond of friendship surrounding her. Even Shelley, whom she'd only recently met, seemed to care deeply about what Reese had to say. There was no judgment around this table, no pity, only unconditional support and love. And right now, when Reese was battling old wounds, she needed their support more than she needed oxygen.

"I'm not going to lie to you guys," Reese said, putting a hand on Jocelyn's arm to let her know everything was okay. Even though it wasn't. "It felt really good—and even more confusing—to be in his arms again and to hear him say my name in that way that always made my knees go weak."

"I get it every time Quinn calls me *Shell*," Shelley said.

"I wish I knew that feeling," Sierra said with a laugh. But then her eyes sobered. "Is it hard seeing him again, Reese?"

"Harder than I thought it would be," Reese admitted.

"I remember the day you met him." Jocelyn leaned across the table. "I'd never seen you so caught up in anyone before in my life. You said he breathed new life into you, remember?"

"I was nineteen. How much old life could I have had at that point?" Reese laughed, but the truth was that he'd sparked desires and wonder in her that were too enticing to ignore. Before meeting Trent, she'd acted like she'd understood when the girls talked about how certain guys made them *so hot*. But she had never truly felt anything like that until she'd met Trent.

"At nineteen?" Shelley frowned. "I was full of rebellion against my cold, stuffy parents."

"By the time I hit nineteen and was finally away at college and out from under my brothers' thumbs, I barely knew what to do with myself," Sierra told them. "I was thrilled and lost at the same time. I had to trust myself and my decisions for the first time ever. Because, suddenly, there was no one there to keep me from making mistakes."

"Your brothers would always be there for you no matter how many miles separated you," Reese assured her friend.

It was one of the things she had most admired about Trent—the way he was always looking out for his family. Even when they were in New York and he was so busy with work, he used to call home all the time to check in with his parents and his siblings. She'd almost forgotten about that protective side of him.

"I know they'll always be there for me just like I'll always be there for them," Sierra replied, "but back then, as much as I wanted to get out from under their overprotective thumbs, it was disconcerting to be off the island." She touched Reese's arm. "I know you can relate to that, since you're a total island girl, too."

Trent had been so wonderfully encouraging at the start of their relationship that she'd let herself get swept up in the excitement of getting her work into New York

City galleries and building a life in a new city with him. But once they'd moved to New York, he was always working, and she'd found the city overwhelming and scary. She'd felt like Dorothy in Oz, afraid she didn't fit in with the fast-paced, übertrendy New Yorkers. It had been a culture shock of the worst kind.

"Do you know what I missed most when I was living in New York?" Reese said. *Besides Trent.*

"Me, of course," Jocelyn chimed in.

"Exactly. I missed *this*. Being with friends who really knew and cared about me. Knowing that I could walk to Jocelyn's or call Annabelle or Sierra, and in a few minutes, we could all be together. I also missed seeing my parents every Sunday morning for breakfast."

"I missed you guys and my family, too, when I went away to school." Sierra sipped her drink. "But I always knew I'd come back, so for me those four years were just a blip in time."

A blip in time? Reese thought about all the wonderful days—and nights—she and Trent had had before things had gone bad. She mulled that over for a moment and corrected herself. Their relationship hadn't really gone bad. They hadn't fought or said hateful things. *Lonely* was a better word. Distant. Whatever the word for it, they'd had too deep of a connection to demean their relationship as a *blip in time*.

Everything about their love had been bigger than life, which was probably why, during the good times, it had been so much more than a blip—and during the unhappier times, it had felt so much worse.

"But you didn't plan to come back from New York City, did you, Reese?" Sierra asked.

She and Sierra had never really talked about her marriage—or divorce—so plainly before. And even though it hurt to revisit old wounds, Reese couldn't help but feel that it was long past due.

"No. I thought I'd only come back to visit. Because I knew Trent's life needed to be in the city. At least, I thought that's where he'd always be. But now he's back. I can't imagine how badly he wishes he could return to the city."

"Actually," Sierra said, "I don't think he plans to go back at all."

This time, Reese was the one looking at her friend in shock. "Why? I thought he loved it there."

"Maybe he did, but now that he's back on the island, he's working half as much as he did at his practice."

"Why do you think that is?" And, Reese had to wonder, why *now* instead of when she'd begged him to work less all those years ago, when they might have been able to save their marriage?

"Actually," Shelley said, "Quinn was just saying yesterday how much he thinks Trent has changed since coming back to the island. He thinks maybe it's because he's watched our relationship develop and finally started to realize everything he gave up by being a workahol—" She suddenly stopped speaking, as if she'd just realized that she might have waded too deep into things. "I'm sorry, Reese. I don't mean to stir things up for you. Sometimes I talk too much, especially when the drinks are flowing."

"Don't worry," Reese said as she picked up her own glass, "things were already stirring before any of us got together tonight."

But for how long? Had they been stirring only since last night, when she'd run into Trent again? Or was the truth—a truth she didn't want to face—that they'd been stirring for *far* longer than that? Say, ten years or so.

Plus, even though a part of her wanted to believe that he was learning to relax and enjoy life in a way he'd never let himself when he was practicing law in the city, she simply couldn't believe it was true. Because if it *was* true, then what could have possibly been a strong enough force to make him change his approach to life?

Lord knew her love hadn't been anywhere near strong enough...

Darn it. She'd come here tonight to have

fun with the girls, not fall deeper into her *Do I still foolishly love Trent Rockwell?* hole. But before she could change the subject, Jocelyn nodded toward the front window.

Trent and his brothers were walking into the restaurant. When they entered, Reese's ability to think evaporated with the night breeze that followed them inside.

Chapter Five

THE HIDEAWAY WAS supposed to be the perfect place for forgetting about Reese for an hour or two while hanging out with his brothers. But the moment Trent walked in and saw Reese sitting with Sierra, Shelley, Annabelle, and Jocelyn, he couldn't tear his eyes away from the woman he still loved.

The amber-colored blouse she wore set off her wide, surprised eyes, and her hair was loose and carefree, the way Trent had always loved. The din of the restaurant fell away, and all that remained was the pulse of energy blazing a path between them.

"Go on." Derek gave Trent a gentle nudge.

Reese was watching Trent with the same mix of confusion and interest as she had last night, while he was hit with such longing for the woman he'd once called his own that he wasn't sure he could handle a single drink.

"What are you doing here?" Shelley asked, clearly thrilled to see Quinn as she rose to kiss him.

"Kissing my girl."

"Hey, guys." Sierra smiled up at them rather than asking why they were crashing her girls' night. "Pull up a seat."

Trent tore his eyes from Reese long enough to catch a glance between Sierra and Quinn that he couldn't read. Had Quinn known they were going to be here? Had he and Sierra planned this to try to push him and Reese back together?

But by the way his brother pulled up a chair beside Shelley, draped an arm over her shoulder, and whispered something in her ear that made her flush, Trent figured it was far more likely that Quinn simply couldn't stand to be apart from Shelley—rather than that he was setting his hand at matchmaking. The guy was so damn happy it was sickening. Great for Quinn and Shelley, but nauseating all the same.

Ethan and Derek pulled up chairs from another table and sat beside Jocelyn and Annabelle, leaving only the space beside Reese for Trent. As he reached for an empty chair from the table behind Reese, he couldn't help but wonder about his siblings again. They'd never done any matchmaking before. And yet...

"Do you mind if I join you?" he asked Reese.

Though she shook her head, she shifted uncomfortably in her seat. He could see the pulse beating fast at her throat—and when their eyes met, the breath caught in his throat.

It had been ages since he'd seen that look in her eyes, but it was one he'd never forget. It was the look she'd gotten seconds before they'd ripped each other's clothes off in the bathroom of another restaurant ten years ago...or on the golf course late at night...or on the beach under the stars...

That look surprised the hell out of him, though it shouldn't, because he knew he was giving her the exact same one.

Suddenly, her eyes widened, and she looked away.

Apparently she hadn't realized she was giving him *that* look, either. Not until he looked back at her with it mirrored on his own face.

That turned him on and worried him at the same time. Their sparks were definitely still there. It hadn't been his imagination the other night. But her reaction just now, turning away, fighting the connection—that made his stomach twist.

"I'll bet the five of you got quite a few glances tonight," Ethan said in his easy way.

Trent clenched his jaw against the idea of

any other guy looking at Reese, even though he knew it happened all the time because she was so damned beautiful. Damn it. He'd better get a grip on his emotions, or he'd end up tangling his hand in her hair and kissing her like he'd been aching to do since he'd bumped into her at Shelley's.

He knew from their history—and from that *look*—that they wouldn't stop there.

He stole another glance at her, and when she caught him looking, her lips parted on a silent gasp. Their knees brushed under the table, and heat seared through him. As their eyes held for another beat, he longed to tell her so many things.

You look incredible.

It's so nice to be near you again.

I'm so sorry for everything I did wrong.

I'm dying to kiss you.

Knowing he had to put space between them before he did something stupid, Trent rose to his feet and shoved his hands in his pockets to keep from touching her. "I'm going to the bar to get a pitcher of beer."

After Trent ordered the pitcher, he watched from the bar as Reese frowned and fidgeted nervously with her hands in her lap. Just as he was returning to the table with the pitcher and glasses, Reese pushed back her chair and made a beeline for the door.

"Reese?"

She stopped and looked over her shoulder. It felt as if she were looking at him for the very last time and wanted to memorize every detail. Then, without a word, she turned and walked out the door.

Trent set the pitcher and the glasses on the table. "Where's she going?"

"She said she had to take care of something," Annabelle answered.

More like get away from me. Had he read her wrong last night? Had there been a spark of connection between them like he'd thought? Or was she completely and utterly over him? And was it better if she was, since he'd hurt her so badly the first time around?

Trent had to know for sure.

He ran out the door and into the brisk evening air, catching up to her as she hurried across the parking lot. He reached for her hand to stop her from leaving.

"Reese, please wait."

When she turned, there was no denying the conflicting emotions in her eyes, or the quick squeeze of her fingers around his, as if for a fleeting second she didn't want to let him go.

But then she dropped her eyes to their hands, gently moved hers away, and said, "What do you need, Trent?"

You, he thought. But he said instead, "I'm

sorry for everything that happened between us. I know I hurt you deeply, and..." He paused to try to wrap his mind around his thoughts, but his emotions were so close to the surface that he was afraid telling her he was still in love with her would only push her farther away. "I'm sorry," he said again. "For everything. Please stay?"

She stared at him for a long moment, her eyes searching his, her chest rising and falling with each heavy breath. "I can't," she finally said, so softly he almost didn't hear her. The sadness that filled her eyes nearly tore his heart from his chest. "Me and you...the divorced couple trying to act normal while making everyone else feel uncomfortable. I can't even begin to process what's going on between us. So how can we expect our friends and your family to deal with it?"

Trent stepped in closer again, wanting to touch her, but resisting the urge for fear she'd pull away again.

"It doesn't have to be uncomfortable. We've bumped into each other before," he reminded her, even though the truth was that they'd only ever seen each other briefly across a parking lot or in a grocery store.

"It's different now." She took a step back, and the confirmation that she needed space between them stung.

"You mean because I'm living here?"

She nodded, the difficulty of whatever she was about to say written in her wrinkled brow and the rising of her shoulders. "I'm trying to get used to the idea that we'll be seeing each other a lot more now that you're back. It's a lot to take in, don't you think?"

"Couldn't that be a good thing?" *Please tell me it is.*

"I don't know. That's something I'm still trying to figure out. And I'm going to need some space to do that." She paused long enough for the words to settle in before saying, "Good night, Trent; have fun with everyone tonight," and walking to her car.

He fought the urge to go after her, because even though he wanted to beg her to stay and talk things through, he'd already hurt her once. Regardless of whether there was hope for something more between them again or not, he still wanted to apologize for all the pain he'd caused her. But right now he didn't need to push her or make her relive the past.

Giving her space was the least he could do, but hell if it didn't feel like he was losing her all over again—before he even had a chance to make things right.

Chapter Six

REESE HAD BEEN teaching painting classes at Bay's Edge Assisted Living Facility since shortly after returning from New York. What had begun as a way to keep herself distracted from thoughts of her failed marriage had turned into one of the things Reese most looked forward to. She'd thought that teaching the elderly to paint might brighten their days with something new and exciting to look forward to, while offering a sense of creativity and accomplishment. But what she'd found was comfort of her own. She'd met a host of insightful, caring friends who'd embraced her and helped her through some of her toughest moments.

As she walked through the front door juggling a box of paints and a bag of paintbrushes, she thought of her students—friends—who had passed away over the years. The ache of every loss hit her hard. And then a new, bright face would take the empty seat in her class, and a new relationship would develop.

That cycle of loss and moving forward had helped Reese move on after her divorce. At least she'd *thought* she'd moved on.

"Good morning, Reese," Kathleen Torrence, the front-desk receptionist, greeted her, breaking her out of her thoughts about Trent.

Kathleen was a spunky brunette who had gone to school with Reese's mother. Kathleen's mother was living at Bay's Edge, and every time Reese walked through the doors, she couldn't help but wonder if one day she'd be visiting her own parents there. It was the only assisted living facility on the island, and it had a stellar reputation for treating the residents on all levels—mental, physical, and emotional.

"How's your mom today?"

Kathleen put her hand out and wiggled it from side to side. "Fair to middling. Thanks for asking."

Reese tightened her grip on the heavy bag on the verge of slipping out of her hands, and Kathleen said, "You'd better go put that bag down. Looks heavier than usual. And watch out for the Rickenbachers. They were in rare form at breakfast," Kathleen called after her.

Reese grinned as she headed into the arts and crafts room. The Rickenbachers were in their late eighties, but they acted like teenagers, so openly frisky with each other.

They reminded her of how she and Trent used to be.

Used to be?

Last night when he'd walked into the Hideaway looking like sex on legs, the room had heated up about a hundred degrees. Especially when he'd looked at her the way he used to. The way that made her heart melt and her insides rev up. All she'd wanted was to pull him into a back hallway and devour him in one big, delicious gulp.

The bag dropped from her fingers, and paintbrushes scattered across the floor. "Darn it." But when she turned to set down the box of paints, she missed the edge of the counter, sending them scattering, too.

"My, oh my, missy. You sure are flustered today, aren't you?" Tilly Carlson said as she walked into the room toward Reese.

Reese looked up at the elderly black woman who was smiling down at her and realized she'd forgotten to bring the book she'd promised to loan her. "A little flustered, yes. And unfortunately, I forgot your book, too. But I'll bring it later. I promise. How are you doing today, Tilly?"

Tilly always took the time to put on makeup in the mornings and style her short hair, which she wore pushed back from her face with a pretty fabric headband. Even mapped with wrinkles, Tilly's skin looked soft and youthful, despite her advanced age. When she'd first joined Reese's class two years ago, she'd told Reese that the key to good skin was a smile.

Glancing down at her walker, Tilly said, "Every day I can still push this baby around is a good day."

Reese put the paints back in the box. "You look nice today. Is that a new outfit?"

Tilly lowered herself into a chair, then smoothed the brown zip-up jacket she wore over a flowered shirt. "You don't think it's tacky, do you? I'm not used to wearing tracksuits."

"A beautiful woman like you could never look tacky," Morris Rickenbacker said as he came into the room with his wife, Norma.

Tilly rolled her eyes. "You're such a flirt."

"That he is," Norma said, leaning over to peck her husband's cheek. Her gray hair was brushed away from her face in a layered style. She had a slight overbite, and always looked like she was smiling. She stopped just short of Reese, who was still gathering the brushes from the floor. "Goodness, Reese. What happened?"

Reese put the last brush in the box, hoisted it to the counter, then pinned a picture of an oak tree to the corkboard on the wall. "Just a little mishap. How are you this morning, Norma? Morris?"

"I feel so good, I think I'm growing hair." Morris rubbed his palm over his bald head.

"You wish, sweetie." Norma sat at a table. "That's a wonderful outfit, Tilly. Did your daughter send that to you from Los Angeles?"

After Tilly nodded, Reese asked, "Is she going to make it up to visit before winter?" Tilly's daughter rarely visited, unfortunately.

"I think that's why she sent the outfit, to let me down easy. She's writing a screenplay and apparently it's an all-day, every-day endeavor." Tilly's voice was thick with disappointment.

"I still say you should tell her to get her butt up here," Morris said. "She hasn't visited you in months."

"Morris. That's enough. You're going to make her feel bad," Norma chided him.

"I'm sorry, Tilly," Reese said as she began laying out the supplies for the class. "I'm sure she misses you."

"She's got a man now, and I know what love does to a woman's head. I miss my daughter, but not like I miss my Ritchie." Tilly passed a paintbrush to Norma. "He was my first and only true love."

"You'll see him again," Norma said, patting Tilly's hand.

"Norma was my first love," Morris said.

His wife squeezed his hand. "We both know I was your second, but I'll take that over not being your love at all."

"You are my *forever* love," Morris said.

"Yes, I know. But Sadie got something I'll never have," Norma said without a hint of resentment but with longing in her eyes instead. "She got to see what first love looks like in your eyes, and felt it in your touch. What a devastating loss that she died at twenty years old."

Morris leaned forward and whispered, "I was eighteen with Sadie, and it hurt so much to lose her so young. But you and I, my love, we have depth you can't find in youth."

Was that true? Reese wondered. Was adult love even deeper than youthful love?

Trent had told her that he'd never been in love before they'd met, and she'd seen that in his eyes and had felt it in his touch. Their love had been so powerful that every time they came face-to-face again she felt as if she were reliving all of her firsts with him. The feel of his palm against hers that very first day. The soft press of his lips to hers. And, *oh God,* the first time their bodies came together with such insatiable passion that they couldn't even make it to the bedroom.

The tape dropped from her trembling hands.

"Goodness," Tilly said, obviously startled by the clack of it hitting the floor.

"Sorry." Reese crouched to pick it up and pressed the tape against her stomach to keep the others from seeing it shake in her hand. "Tell us more about Ritchie, Tilly."

"I was twenty-seven when I met him," Tilly said, looking past Reese out the window, as if she were watching a scene unfold before her. "He was thirty-four. He'd been around the block a few times, but I hadn't dated much. He was a policeman on the other side of the island, and he tried to give me a ticket for jaywalking."

"Jaywalking? Can you get a ticket for that?" Morris asked.

"I'm pretty sure it was his way of getting my name and number," Tilly said. "The minute I laid eyes on that man, I knew that he was *the one*. He was big and burly, not like most men these days, who shave their chests and Lord only knows what else." She laughed. "My Ritchie was all man, with a deep voice and eyes that looked right into my soul, and when he held me...I knew I'd never find true love like that again."

Everything Tilly said Reese could have said

about Trent. She gripped the chair so tightly her knuckles turned white.

"What about you, Reese? Have you found true love?" Tilly asked as she turned back from the window.

None of them knew about her and Trent. But this morning something inside her broke open, like she'd been holding part of herself closed for so long it suddenly cracked, and the words tumbled free.

"I was in love once, and he was *everything*." She pulled out the chair and sat beside Tilly. "Like you and Ritchie, I could feel his love in his touch, see it in his eyes. And when we were together"—she sighed a dreamy sigh—"nothing else existed except this cloud of happiness."

"Oh, girl, you have been touched by love." Tilly touched her arm. "And what happened with this man?"

"I'm not really sure. I think he got a little lost." She paused for a moment, then added, "We both did."

Tilly patted her hand. "Well, honey. You know that old saying, 'If you love someone, set them free'?"

"Yes." That was just what she'd done when she'd left ten years ago. Tried to set them both free because she'd been sure there was no other way.

"Well, sweetie, if you ask me, love doesn't

get set free. Love lingers. Love haunts. Love consumes." Tilly leaned in close and her tone grew even more serious. "Love isn't easily dissuaded. It doesn't go away when one of you dies, and it certainly doesn't go away when one of you moves away. It's like a boomerang. No matter how many times you toss it away, it always comes back."

Chapter Seven

TRENT SAT IN the basement of the Rockwell Resort meticulously sorting through archived legal documents. There were at least a dozen boxes spread across the floor. He'd been at it for two hours, and he'd found documents dating back several generations, but what he hadn't found was the paperwork to transfer the deed. The cold concrete walls and the scent of musty old papers was a world away from where he'd been a few months ago, when he'd have sent an assistant to search through files. He didn't mind doing the grunt work, however. Especially not today, when he needed some time to really think about Reese. He could swear that last night in the parking lot, when she'd squeezed his hand, he'd seen so much emotion in her eyes. Regret. Longing. Desire.

All the same emotions he was feeling for her.

He rubbed a crick in the back of his neck and decided that he needed to talk to Reese. The last thing he wanted was for her to be uncomfortable, but if she was uncomfortable because she still had feelings for him, that was a lot different from being uncomfortable because of bottled-up resentment. Last night, one look from her in the bar had made it clear that she still wanted to rip off his clothes—but however good sex could be, it didn't equate to love. That Trent knew all too well. Over the years he'd tried to fill the gap Reese had left in his heart, but no one ever came close to her. None of them felt as good in his arms, or made his body hum with a whisper across his skin. No one saw in him the man Reese had once seen. The man who had somehow gotten lost in overtime and ladder climbing.

He placed the file he was holding in a box, wishing he hadn't gone so many years without reaching out. But the truth was that he hadn't been ready before now. When Reese had left him ten years ago, he'd been too caught up in making his mark and then in building his own practice. But after spending more time with his family these past weeks, and watching Quinn and Shelley fall in love, he'd finally realized that he was still empty inside.

Trent breathed deeply, trying to clear his mind and feeling as though he'd been duped—by his own damn self. He shook his head with the painful realization, and man, was it hard to accept that this all came down to him. He'd tricked himself into thinking that he was *something*, and sure, he was the best attorney in his field, but what did that really mean in the long run? He came home to an empty house and distracted himself with work from the only thing—the only person—who could ever really make his world complete. *Reese.*

He couldn't blame her for needing space. But what if that was just her way of pushing him away again? What if it was time for them to finally sit down and talk face-to-face about everything that had happened in the past—and everything that was brewing between them now—even if it was uncomfortable?

A memory suddenly flashed through his mind of the day he'd come home and found the note Reese had left when she'd gone back to the island. Because she couldn't even look him in the eyes and tell him she was done.

Obviously clear communication was something they'd needed to work on in the past. Then again, they were just kids back then, weren't they? Could they do better now as adults who had some life lessons and experience under their belts?

As a lawyer, Trent had honed his ability to separate truth and facts from obtrusive issues. He'd thought he'd been equally as good at interpreting his relationship with Reese.

But he'd been wrong. So wrong that he'd lost the person most important to him in the world. The only woman he'd ever loved.

Trent rose to his feet, running a frustrated hand through his hair as he mentally prepared for the biggest case of his life. His plea for Reese's forgiveness—and a second chance with the woman he'd loved since she was nineteen years old.

* * *

AN HOUR LATER, Trent was sitting in a conference room at the resort, meeting with his family. His father never sat at the head of the table, and today was no different. Griffin and Abby sat side by side, holding hands, and his parents' ever-present love and their respect for each other made Trent long for Reese even more.

"We should be able to finish the little we have left to get Shelley's café ready to open over the next two weeks, then bring in a painting crew to finish up, which shouldn't take more than a couple days at most," Quinn said. "The opening is in less than three weeks, and assuming everyone's work is on schedule, we should make it with a day or two to spare."

"I'm almost done with the shelves. One more night is all I need," Trent said.

"Derek and I will finish the attic work this week, too." Ethan was Trent's youngest brother, and with his dark hair tousled from his early-morning fishing trip, he looked a hell of a lot more carefree than the rest of them.

"Shelley and I have curtains we want to put up," Sierra said, "but of course that will wait until after the painters come in."

"And since I'm having lunch with Darla this week," their mother added, "I'll have her put Shelley's grand opening on Chandler's calendar." Darla Collins was their grandfather's personal secretary, and she and Abby had been friends for a long time.

"You think Chandler will come to Shelley's grand opening?" Derek asked. "Isn't that a little bit beneath him? Making time for a celebration?"

All of them had a complicated relationship with their grandfather. Mostly because he was a prickly, stern man who rarely smiled and always seemed to be trying to control everyone and everything.

"Derek," Abby said, "I know Chandler isn't the easiest man in the world to get along with, but he is your grandfather, so please show a little respect. He cares about this island, and I'm sure he'll want to celebrate with Quinn and Shelley."

"Cares about the island?" Derek didn't look the least bit chastened by their mother's uncharacteristic lecture. "He was going to sell the resort and didn't care that the new owners would fire the local staff, who rely on the income to survive. The locals *are* the island, Mom."

As Griffin spoke, Trent found himself comparing his warm and loving father to his cold and distant grandfather. Even after all these years, he had a hard time putting Chandler and Griffin together as father and son. Griffin was just as shrewd a businessman as Chandler, but he treated every person he met as if they were as important as the next, no matter what their social status.

Griffin was the type of man Trent had always striven to be, but the truth was that he'd acted more like Chandler during the decade he'd lived in New York. He'd been aggressive and competitive, and the cost had been the highest he'd ever pay—losing the love of his life. Only he'd been too consumed with succeeding to see it. He hadn't even seen their separation coming. And then, over the next ten years, instead of spending time relaxing with his family over the holidays, he'd come home for a mere two or three days, then rushed back to work.

How had he gotten so far away from the man his father had raised him to be?

"Before we all head out," Quinn said as he set a folder on the table, "we still need to discuss the community-outreach program."

Trent gazed out the window behind Quinn, where sunlight glistened off the inky water and a sailboat made its way across the bay. In his mind he saw himself and Reese sharing a boat ride all those years ago. Back when she looked at him like he was the only man on earth she could ever love. His heart ached with the memory. Was Reese looking out at the same view and painting it? And was she thinking of him the way he was thinking of her?

He'd never believed in love at first sight—not until he'd seen her painting at the top of the dune during his morning run ten years ago.

He'd run up the dune steps faster than he ever had before, hoping that she wasn't going to pack up her things and leave before he reached her. When he'd finally made it to the top, she'd looked like an angel dropped from a cloud just for him. And when she'd turned to look at him, her eyes had gone wide and her paintbrush had dropped to the sand.

He'd closed the distance between them, introduced himself, quickly learning that she was not only smart and funny, but also a passionate and talented painter. When he'd picked her up for their first date that night, they hadn't been able to keep their hands off each other. They'd made love right there in the foyer of her apartment. It had been breathless. Reckless. Sexy as hell.

And perfect. It had been *perfect.*

Had he known he was going to be her first lover, he would have taken his time and made sure everything was romantic for her. Hell, he hadn't planned to make love to her that first night, on their first date. But they'd never been able to keep their hands off each other—not for a minute, much less enough time for him to plan something like that. Two nights later they'd sailed out to the middle of the bay, anchored the boat, dove in, and made love in the water. He could still hear Reese's sweet giggles as he'd kicked his powerful legs to try to keep them afloat while their bodies moved together with youthful exuberance.

"Honey." His mother touched his arm. "What do you think about Quinn's question?"

Trent looked around the conference table at his family and realized that they were *all* waiting for his response. "Sorry. I'm a little distracted today." Trent forced himself to focus on the discussion again. "What were you wanting to know?"

"Quinn was saying that Reese is going to be painting the mural," Sierra told him as Quinn slid the folder with the information about the community-outreach program toward Trent. "She is such an amazing painter that we know she'll create something beautiful to represent our close-knit community and the magical feel of the island. We want to know if you'll manage the project."

Trent opened the folder and his heart flipped in his chest as he scanned the project details.

Rockwell Resort Community-Outreach Project

Title: Island Mural

Location: South wall of the resort

Artist: Reese Nicholson

Trent set the folder down. Even when Reese was nowhere near him, she was *everywhere*.

"Yes, I'd be happy"—*thrilled*—"to manage the project."

Sierra and Abby exchanged smiles, while Quinn laughed. The knowing look in his brother's eyes told Trent that he'd been hoping for this decision. He obviously wanted Trent to be just as happily in love as he was.

"Are you sure about this?" Derek clearly felt compelled to point out that, "You two have history, and after the way she hightailed it out of the Hideaway last night, things didn't look so amicable."

"I'm sure." Trent left no room for negotiation. Not when it came to Reese. Not when this might be his chance to finally get her to stick around at least long enough for him to apologize to her for everything he'd blown in their relationship. There was no way he was going to give up a chance to be with Reese.

"I think it's a wonderful idea, honey," his mother said, patting him on the shoulder. "Who better to work closely with Reese than you?"

My thoughts exactly.

Chapter Eight

REESE'S GALLERY WAS decorated in a bright and airy theme, with white walls and pale yellow trim, accented with shades of green. Throughout the interior she had painted dandelions in various stages of growth. Parachutes of fluff floated up the walls, while newly sprouted green buds anchored the lower trim and dandelions in full bloom peeked out from corners and from behind paintings. Now she measured and planned from her perch at the top of a stepladder, preparing to hang a painting between a dandelion in full bloom and dandelion fluff.

"I'm pretty sure you're not going to be able to avoid him forever," Jocelyn said as she handed Reese a hammer.

Reese took the hammer and leaned one

hand against the wall for balance as she thought about Trent—and how avoiding him was the last thing she wanted to do. Her mind traveled back to the summer they'd met. They'd walked down this very street hand in hand, talking about the future they'd been sure they'd have. *One day your name will be in all the galleries in New York, and we'll think back on how fun the journey was. We'll laugh at how hard you thought it was when we were going through it. I've got faith in you, Reese. Your talent is bigger than the island.*

She smiled to herself, remembering how important Trent had made her feel. How his faith in her artistic abilities had surpassed any praise she'd ever received. He'd been so sure of everything back then. And it had been that faith that she'd carried back to the island with her when she'd left New York, that faith that had given her the confidence to open her own gallery.

"I'm not sure I actually do want to avoid him," she said as she sat down on the top of the ladder with the hammer in her lap and rested her chin on her palm. "Which might be an even bigger problem than both of us living on the island again." She and Jocelyn had been discussing Trent on and off all morning, and while she'd thought that she'd have her feelings figured out by now, she wasn't even close.

"Are we taking a break?" Jocelyn asked.

"We're taking a...moment."

"To do?"

Reese peered down at her friend. Jocelyn wore a long cotton skirt and a pale green tank top with a cute pair of sandals. Her hair was secured at the nape of her neck with a wide clip.

"To admire your sexy librarian look," she teased.

"That was exactly the look I was going for," Jocelyn said with a grin. "Now, back to Trent and all that not-avoiding you're thinking about doing."

Reese picked up the hammer again. "Hold the ladder. I need to get this painting hung so that the whole day doesn't end up being a write-off." She appreciated that her friend simply gripped the sides of the ladder and waited for her to collect her thoughts. Thoughts that were zinging back and forth in her head like a ball in a pinball machine. "I thought I was over him," she said as she began hammering the nail into the wall. "But every time I'm near him, I get all mushy inside, and all those feelings I thought I had dealt with come rushing back."

"Maybe that's not a bad thing?"

Reese clutched at the wall, nearly tumbling off the ladder at the sound of Trent's deep voice asking her if getting mushy over him ten years after their divorce was a bad thing. The next thing she knew, he was standing behind her and settling his big hands on the sides of her thighs—simultaneously stabilizing her and sending her even *more* off-balance.

"Careful," he said in a soothing and far-too-sexy tone that made Reese's stomach flutter as she tried not to focus on the heat of his hands. Or the strength of them.

Or, most of all, just how good she knew they would feel moving over every inch of her, head to toe, while she begged him for *more, more, more!*

She turned to glare at Jocelyn, knowing her best friend would clearly understand her message—*Why didn't you warn me he was walking into the gallery?*

From behind Trent, Jocelyn mouthed, *Sorry. I didn't see him!*

"What are you doing here, Trent?" Reese didn't mean to snap, but she was really embarrassed that he'd heard her talking about him in such intimate detail. It didn't help that he was standing way too close as he helped her down the ladder, looking way too hot and smelling way too delicious.

This was not good. Not good at all.

Or maybe the problem was that he was *too* good.

Oh God.

"I wanted to come by to give you the good news in person," he said with an easy smile. "The two of us are going to be working together on the community-outreach project."

"The mural?" Reese smoothed her jeans to give her hands something to do besides reaching out to touch him. "What do you mean we'll be working together?"

"I'm managing the project." His piercing blue eyes never wavered from hers. "I came over to set up a meeting so we can talk about the details."

How the heck had *he* been the person at the resort chosen to work with her on this? How was she going to work with him when she couldn't even talk to him? Didn't anyone realize they were divorced? And that divorced couples shouldn't spend a bunch of time together...especially when they had a knack for wanting to rip off each other's clothes?

"Are you free tonight?"

His easy smile hadn't changed, but the air between them sizzled. Even though he wasn't asking her on a date, that was exactly what this felt like to her crazy, lust-befuddled brain.

"Tonight?" She tried to think up an excuse to buy a little more time to prepare herself. But when she opened her mouth, all that came out was, "Sure."

His smile broadened. "Great. How does six o'clock in the resort conference room on the second floor sound?"

The resort conference room? Okay, maybe all this heat is just in my head. "That sounds fine."

He glanced at his watch, then said casually, "I'm meeting my mother and Sierra for lunch. I'd better run."

"You're taking lunch off?" She was a little embarrassed that surprise rang loudly in her voice, but the Trent she'd left in New York wouldn't have taken off time in the middle of the afternoon to have lunch with anyone but an important client. In fact, she could count on one finger the number of times they'd had lunch together on a weekday.

"Things have changed, Reese." His smile was gone now, and he was looking at her with an intensity that seared through her.

"Have they?" She hadn't meant to ask the question but, again, the words were out before she could stop them. Before he could answer, however, and make the quicksand between them any deeper, she said, "Please tell them I said hello."

"I will. And I'm looking forward to hearing your ideas for the mural tonight."

With that, he headed out the door while Reese stood there with her hand covering her heart.

"See?" she said to Jocelyn. "Every time he talks to me, or touches me, I'm nineteen all over again. This is so freaking ridiculous."

"Honestly, you were a bit of a bumbling mess. Adorable, but bumbling."

"Thanks, Joce. You could have at least lied to me." Reese put her face in her hands and mumbled, "What am I going to do?"

"Him," Jocelyn said.

When Reese lifted her head from her hands, she tried to look shocked at the suggestion that she hop back into bed with her ex. But it wasn't easy to pretend she hadn't been wanting just that from the moment she'd tumbled into Trent's arms outside Shelley's café. Even if she knew opening that door with Trent was dangerous. They were *too* drawn to each other. It was too easy to get lost in him, and if he put his hands on her? She'd be a goner for sure.

Still, she made herself say, "You've got to be kidding."

"I've known you my whole life," Jocelyn said. "And what I just witnessed has only happened once before—the last time you fell head over heels for Trent Rockwell."

The last time? "What am I going to do?" Reese felt more twisted up and confused than she ever had before. "A week ago I was ready to leave the past behind and finally move on."

"Or maybe you had your life on hold because you were still in love with Trent."

"This can't be good. Even if he is taking off to have lunch with his mother and sister today, I'm sure he still works too much and puts work ahead of everything else in his life."

"Although you did have all those awesome marathon sex sessions," Jocelyn pointed out with a laugh.

"Stop." Reese laughed, too, but her body shivered in the most delicious way with the memory of Trent's big hands on her. And his mouth. *Oh God, his mouth.* "It's been ten years. Ten years without anything even remotely flirty. We never even had any real closure after our divorce, and now *this*? This sudden—insatiable—desire to connect with him on every level again."

"I swear I'm not taking his side," her friend said, "but I can't help wondering if maybe, just maybe, that isn't such a bad thing. Because when the two of you are in a room together..." Jocelyn fanned herself. "I'm not exaggerating when I say I've never seen chemistry like what you two have. Both then *and* now. What if he *has* changed his life for the better?"

Reese shook her head, trying to separate her emotions from her desires and think clearly, but they were all muddled together.

Then again, when it came to Trent, they always were. There was no sex without emotion. There was no sex without love. From the very start, the physical and emotional had been tangled together so completely they'd blended into one.

"Okay," she finally admitted. "He's having lunch with his mother and sister, and he walked here when he could have made a phone call instead, and that's all different from the way he was in New York. Still, that doesn't mean the man who worked ninety hours a week is gone."

Reese looked around the gallery, remembering how much work it had taken to drag herself back into life after their divorce, much less get up the gumption, and the desire, to open her gallery and actually fulfill her dreams. But she'd done it, and if she jumped right back into Trent's arms, she was risking everything she'd worked so hard to achieve. Her brain turned to mush around him, *even after all this time*. It was a little unsettling—and equally as exciting—to feel the effect they still had on each other. But this time she knew she needed to slow down and think things through. She needed to make herself, and building up the trust between them, as a priority over her raging hormones and secret daydreams about having Trent's love again.

Drawing upon the strength she'd honed all

those years ago, she silently renewed the commitment to herself and the life she'd built. They'd take it slowly, like the older, wiser adults they were.

At least they would if she could figure out how to keep her lips off his...

Chapter Nine

THE CONFERENCE ROOM had seemed like a stellar idea when Trent had suggested it. It was a professional environment that shouldn't be the least bit seductive, which dinner in a dimly lit restaurant might have been. It was also located on the administrative floor of the resort—nowhere near his suite, or any other bedrooms for that matter. But as Trent watched Reese study the architectural outline of the resort, her brows knitted together and her lips pursed in that adorable way she had when she was concentrating, he realized it wouldn't matter if she was sitting in the middle of a boardroom or the center of his bed.

He was even more captivated by her than he had been ten years ago.

When Trent shifted in his seat and his leg

accidentally brushed hers, Reese lifted her eyes to his, reminding him of how easily he had always gotten lost in them. She blinked up at him through thick lashes, her eyes full of desire, but as she shifted her knees away, he could see that it was underscored with confusion.

After ten years of conflicting feelings, I'm suddenly not conflicted at all.

Trent finally knew exactly what he wanted—another chance with Reese. He badly wanted to clear the air between them and let her know how sorry he was for their divorce, but he was so worried about short-circuiting the small steps they were taking that he wasn't yet sure how to do it.

As her eyes moved over his face, lingering around his mouth, Trent suppressed the urge to lean in and kiss her. Being with her was so natural, so comfortable—for *him,* at least. As if no time had passed since their last kiss the morning he'd gone to work...and she'd gone packing.

But Reese's brows were knitted tightly together and she was nibbling nervously on her lip, and his heart ached to apologize, even if he wasn't sure of the right way to do it.

Would there ever be a right time?

Trent wasn't an indecisive man, and trying to refrain from it all—the apology, touching Reese, telling her about his burgeoning emotions—was just too damned hard. "Reese, we should talk. About us. About our divorce. I really am sorry for everything, and I'd like to—"

She put up one hand to stop him, clutching the table with the other as if she were bracing herself. "Please, Trent. Don't do this. Not when we're going to have to work together on this mural."

But he couldn't just give up. Not when it suddenly felt like giving up was exactly what he had done ten years ago. "There must be some things we can get out in the open."

Her eyes roved over his face again, and he was almost positive that the wall she'd erected was starting to crumble away. He held his breath, waiting for her to finally talk to him—or at least to hear him out. But before either of those things happened, she turned away from him and focused intently on the drawing again.

"How much of the wall am I allowed to paint?"

"There are no boundaries put on the space. You can use the entire wall if you'd like." He tried to sound nonchalant, professional even, and knew by the way the tension in her shoulders began to melt that he'd hit his mark. He leaned over the documents to get a better look, and their shoulders brushed.

She licked her lips, driving him even crazier, and when she stole another quick glance at him, the cooler air that had come with her shutting down his apology heated and sparked again.

He and Reese had never been good at cooling things down. Their connection had always run too deep—and apparently still did. *Thank God.*

"No boundaries," she said just above a whisper.

His heartbeat quickened. "Do you have any idea"—*what you're doing to me?*—"what you're going to paint?"

"Not yet." She wouldn't look at him as she added in a softer voice, "I'm still trying to decide."

Trent had lived with her long enough to guess that she wasn't just trying to figure out the mural, she was also trying to figure out *them.* He didn't want to push her so hard that she'd run, but he couldn't hold back the hope that he was reaching her at least a little bit. "Reese, can we talk about us? Please?"

"How can we when this is exactly what we lost?" she asked. She turned to face him, and a lock of hair fell in front of her eyes. "Not just talking to each other, but listening. Really *listening.*"

As he'd done so many times before, Trent reached up and tucked the lock behind her ear. He hadn't forgotten how silky her hair was and how smooth her skin felt, but it stunned him nonetheless.

"You're right. We screwed up. In the worst way possible. But we can try to fix it now."

Her eyes were full of both desire and restraint as she shook her head. "I don't know if we can."

Even though he knew he shouldn't, he couldn't resist stroking his fingertips gently over her cheek. He had missed touching her so much, and she always felt so warm, so good. So *right*.

"Trent," she whispered, desire taking the lead now as she reached up to touch the back of his hand, and her lips parted. When her tongue swept across her lower lip again, his restraint shattered.

"We did lose track of how to talk to each other, but we sure as hell never lost this."

Trent sealed his lips over hers and slid his hand to the nape of her neck. He kissed her gently at first, testing the waters, half expecting her to push him away. Instead, she gripped the sides of his head and deepened the kiss, sliding her knees between his as she moved closer, the same way she always used to.

She tasted sweet, hot, and so damn familiar it was hard for Trent to think. But he didn't need to think. All he needed was *Reese*, and he didn't want to stop with just one kiss. Their tongues moved with familiar passion and longing so thick it threatened to pull him over the edge.

But just as quickly as she'd deepened their kiss, now she was pulling away with the same speed. "You kissed me!" She covered her mouth with a trembling hand, her eyes wide with surprise.

Desperate to kiss her again, Trent couldn't stop the truth from pouring out. "Maybe I should be sorry I kissed you, but I'm not. How can I be when you're the only woman I've ever wanted to kiss like that?"

"Trent. I'm not sure...I don't think..." She shifted her knees away, her hand still touching her lips.

He knew how conflicted she was, could hear it loud and clear in the tone of her voice. But the way she'd kissed him, how greedily she'd claimed his mouth and held him so tightly, told him that she wasn't completely over him.

And that gave him hope. More hope than he'd had in ten years. All he wanted was to pull her into his arms and love the conflict in her eyes away, but he knew he should give her time to think.

"You don't need to figure this out tonight, Reese." He put his fingertips beneath her chin and gently tilted her face up to his so that he could look into her eyes. "But I need you to know something."

"What do you need me to know?" Her words were barely above a whisper, almost as if she'd been trying to get herself to keep from asking the question.

"I never broke our promise."

* * *

OUR PROMISE.

The words they'd spoken to each other a decade ago rang in her ears as if they'd just vowed them. *I promise to always love you. Forever.* She could see the truth of Trent's confession in his dark eyes and hear it in the tone of his voice. Reese knew each of Trent's tones by heart—serious, professional, playful, loving, sensual—and now they were all rushing back at once. His touch had melted the tenuous wall she'd worked so hard to erect around herself for their meeting.

"I should go." *Because if I sit here any longer, I'll kiss you again.*

She saw the disappointment in his eyes that she hadn't reacted to his confession, but she was too flustered to even try to respond. She wanted to kiss him and to yell at him all at once. Ten years was a long time, and now they'd just crossed a line that not only made it hard for her to see where the past ended and where the present began, but even harder to process and remember the reasons she *shouldn't* kiss him.

She rose to her feet and he also stood, automatically placing a hand on her lower back like he'd done so many times before. One tiny movement was all it would take to turn in to his arms, go up on her toes, and kiss him again.

One more delicious kiss.

Just one.

Her knees were already wobbling and her heart was racing when she finally remembered—she couldn't do this. She couldn't just jump into a relationship with Trent the way she had when she was nineteen. She wasn't a girl anymore. She was a woman who needed to know where she stood with her own emotions.

The lure to go further with him was too strong. The desire to allow his strong arms to hold her, to feel his heart beating against hers, to hear his seductive whispers in her ear, was too enticing. She had to get away before she pulled him down by his shirt and ravaged that incredible mouth of his. Again.

Reese picked up her purse and scrambled to gather the papers in her arms as she valiantly fought the urge to give into her desires. She took a step away, torn between running out the door and running into his arms.

"I...Um...Thanks, Trent. I'll—"

He smiled that easy smile that made her pulse quicken. "I'm really glad we're working together on this, Reese."

"Okay," she said too breathlessly as she took a step toward the door.

"Good night."

Oh God, that voice...

A nod was all she could manage, before she hurried from the room and toward the exit. A few moments later, she pushed through the doors and inhaled a lungful of the crisp night air. Then another. And another.

As she drove down the quiet streets toward her cottage, an unfamiliar feeling washed over her. So startling was the sensation filling her chest, so overwhelming, that it took her a few long moments to recognize it as relief. Her entire body felt lighter as it washed over her, through her.

Despite desperately *wanting* Trent's apology, she wasn't fully ready to hear it yet. But at least she was finally allowing the thoughts and emotions she'd been suppressing for so many years to sail freely through her mind.

And now, for the first time in forever, Reese felt like the heart she'd locked down so tightly during the past decade was finally allowed to feel again.

Chapter Ten

REESE POPPED OUT of bed at five the next morning, feeling better than she had in a very long time. Her mind was spinning with ideas for the mural as she showered and dressed, filled a mug with coffee, and headed down to the resort to scope out her new canvas.

Mornings had always been her favorite part of the day. She loved to watch the sun roll in over the water and listen to the crows as they cawed their messages from high in the pitch pine trees. She pulled her gray cashmere knit cap on and shivered in her thick cream-colored sweater, glad she'd thought to wear her favorite boots to ward off the September-morning chill. She set her messenger bag down on the grass and pulled out her sketch pad, then stood back, assessing the wall of the resort.

She wouldn't paint the entire wall. It was massive, and besides, Reese didn't like boundaries. She often left her paintings free-floating in the center of her canvases, leaving the edges unconfined.

Last night Trent had said that she'd have no boundaries. Had he said it because he remembered that about her? Because he sure remembered how to kiss her.

There were kisses you wished had never happened. There were kisses that left a woman feeling no different from the way she'd felt before she'd experienced the kiss. There were kisses that made a woman's skin go hot and her stomach flutter with anticipation. But Trent's kisses?

Trent's kisses had always melted Reese's clothes right off, from the first time he'd pressed his lips against hers.

She sank down to the grass, sketching fast and furious as thoughts of Trent crashed over her like violent waves, then rolled back with soothing familiarity. Early on in their relationship, he had been able to take one look at her and know if she was sad, happy, confused, or longing to touch him. He'd lost that ability once they'd moved to New York City, but last night she'd felt him looking at her the way he used to. Really *looking*, as if he wanted to know everything she was thinking. Everything she was feeling.

Once upon a time, she'd known him that well, too. But she'd deliberately tried not to look that deeply into his eyes last night, had been trying to keep some distance between them. Which was why she hadn't seen the kiss coming, though she'd wanted it so badly she could taste him before their mouths even touched.

Once their lips touched, her mouth remembered the beauty and the magic of kissing Trent, and her heart had been right there with it, wrapping itself around him.

He'd surprised her and confused her with the kiss, but something told her he knew *that*, too. Just the way he'd noticed everything before they'd moved to New York. One sigh, one smile, one lift of her eyebrows, one crook of her finger toward the bedroom. There was nothing he hadn't noticed. Nothing he wouldn't do for her back then.

Her pencil swirled and skated over the paper, creating dark streaks and contours, mimicking the emotions that coursed through her.

Ten years ago, in the span of a few weeks, he'd made her his world—but then in the span of a few days in New York, he'd replaced their beautiful, sensual, loving world with work. He'd left at the crack of dawn each morning and returned long after she was asleep. Weekends weren't spent holding hands as they walked around the city or snuggled up together by the beautiful fireplace in their apartment the way she'd thought they'd be. Instead, they'd spent their days and their nights on separate planes.

She should have learned her lesson by now, should be able to look back at history and easily keep the walls around her heart thick and strong. But the truth was that last night, while she'd craved Trent's kisses, she'd craved so much more, too.

She'd wanted back into the depths of his heart. Because she'd never met a man who knew how to love so completely.

Only he didn't, did he? Or, if he *did* know how to love completely, was it simply that he just hadn't chosen to give his entire heart to her the way he'd promised?

The day they'd said their vows, she'd thought they were supposed to become one in a way that would last forever.

But forever had never come.

The sound of footfalls on pavement pulled Reese from her reverie. She squinted against the morning sun as Trent jogged along the sidewalk, closing the short distance between them. His muscles glistened from his run. One look was all it took to send her whole body aflame.

"Good morning, Reese." He set his hands on his thighs and drew in several deep breaths.

Her heart went a little crazy from being this close to him, when she could see so much delicious skin and hard muscle. She didn't dare try to stand after how wobbly her legs had been last night. Instead, she tried to play it cool and remained sitting.

"'Morning."

"I was wondering if you still enjoyed painting early in the day." He glanced at her drawing. "Do you mind if I take a peek?" Before she knew it, he was reaching for her hand and pulling her to her feet. "You look beautiful today."

"I do?" *Kiss me.*

No, no, no, the rational, protective side of her brain chimed in. *Don't do it.*

He moved closer. "You do. Even more beautiful than you used to be, Reese."

Why, oh why did he have to make her name sound like an invitation into his bed? Lust snaked through her insides, filling all of her empty places, just as it had when they'd first met.

"You look good, too," she said just above a whisper. Not only did her mouth have a mind of its own, but so did her hand. She couldn't help but reach out to touch him. The feel of his taut abdominal muscles beneath his T-shirt made her brain hiccup...and her entire body explode with heat.

He stepped closer again, and the toe of his sneaker moved between her feet. One hand held hers, and his free hand settled on her hip. "You're everywhere I turn," he said softly. "Even when you're not physically there, I sense you around me."

It was true; she felt it, too. She was falling into him, getting lost in his scent, his words, and those sexy eyes. His deep voice was reeling her in, and there was nothing she wanted more in that moment than to go up on her toes and claim his mouth again.

But after her mental trip down memory lane this morning, she couldn't forget what a huge mistake giving in to those urges with Trent the first time around had been. She couldn't make this mistake again, even if it—*he*—didn't feel like a mistake.

She forced herself to take a step back, as she had last night. And just like last night, she could see how much he wished she hadn't.

"Reese?" He began to reach for her again, and she clutched her sketch pad to her chest, even though she knew it wasn't nearly a big enough barrier between her heart and the man who still seemed to own it. "Don't you feel it? Just how good we are together? Just how good we could be again?"

"Yes, I feel it. *That* was never our problem."

He stepped in close again, bringing a wave of heat along with him, but Reese held up her hand to stop him. "No closer." She wasn't dumb enough to let herself touch him again. Not when she knew where even one more small touch would lead...

She thrust the sketch pad toward him to give herself space to think. "Here. You can look at my sketch now."

He took the pad but didn't step back and didn't look down at her drawings, either. "We should go out on a date."

"Trent." She rolled her eyes. Did he really think that would fix everything between them? "That's the same line you used on me ten years ago."

"It worked well then. I figured it might work well now."

"I can't think of one reason we should go out on a date." *Besides how much I've always loved you. And maybe those incredible abs. And your arms. I've always loved your arms. And the way you move your—*

"I can. We've never talked about things, Reese. About what happened. Why don't we go out on one date and talk? If we both hate it, we'll agree to put the past behind us and move on. But if we don't hate it..." He left that thought hanging between them, potent and way too seductive for her peace of mind.

Reese closed her eyes for a beat, and Trent's masculine scent wrapped around her.

"One date, Reese."

Someone needed to be rational here, so she opened her eyes and said, "Do you remember what our dates always led to?" She tried to suppress the surge of desire that came with the memories, but some things were pretty much impossible.

"How could I ever forget?" He stepped in closer again, bringing them thigh to thigh. "I'll behave myself."

I might not.

"Trent," she whispered, because if she didn't push something from her lungs, she'd give in to the craving to climb him like a dune and kiss that sexy smile right off his lips. Which was a *very* bad idea. No matter how good she knew it would be.

As if he realized he'd pushed her nearly to her breaking point, he took a step away and finally glanced at the sketch pad. "Reese...you drew this just now?"

For the first time since she'd started the sketch, she really looked at it and nearly had to reach for him to steady herself. The grassy knoll, bordered with wild, overgrown gardens, were only shades of gray on the sketch, but she could imagine vivid blooms of pink, yellow, blue, and white growing at varying heights, reaching for the sun from beneath the burgeoning greenery that was so plentiful around the island. She'd drawn the aged picket fence that lined a path between neighboring cottages and led down to the beach.

Reese ran her finger along the reflection of the lighthouse she'd drawn in the ripples of the water and followed it back to the strip of land forming a path to the lighthouse that seemed to sit alone in the middle of the bay.

When she lifted her eyes to Trent, she could see that he recognized the area as clearly as she did.

She'd drawn the very spot where they'd exchanged their vows.

It was far easier than she'd thought it would be to remember the good times with Trent and to be drawn in by him. Now that he'd moved back to the island, she knew she couldn't avoid him altogether even if she wanted to. And she wasn't sure she did. In fact, if she relied solely on her body and not her head, she'd definitely say she didn't want to avoid him.

The only way she could keep her hormones under any semblance of control around him was to open up the part of her mind she thought she'd sealed shut years ago, withdrawing one hurtful memory after another.

The way it had felt to wake up in their bed alone every day and going to bed alone too many nights while he was working late.

The overwhelming feeling every time she'd tried to venture out into the city—and the way Trent had been working too hard on growing his career to ever notice her discomfort.

How terrifying and heartbreaking the decision had been to walk out the door for good—and the painful, dark months that had followed.

The divorce papers that had sat on the table by her front door for weeks on end because she couldn't bear to admit the end of their relationship.

When her chest was aching so much she thought she might not be able to function, she lifted her eyes to his. In the space of a second, the hurt lifted its arms and dove out to sea as Trent rolled back in.

"We can't go out on a date."

"What if it isn't a date?" he said quickly. "What if it's just two old friends getting together to catch up? You used to be my best friend, and I've missed you. More than I can say. Please, just give me this one night to talk."

He'd always been a fantastic lawyer, smart but not slick, and with just a few simple sentences, he broke right through her walls. He'd talked about how they were each other's best friend, and she knew some divorced couples managed to be friendly with one another. Then again, those tended to be the couples that had been better friends than lovers anyway. Whereas she and Trent had always been equal portions of both.

But if she could learn to turn her body off and just be his platonic friend, wouldn't that make everything easier?

One time. No sex. Just an outing with a friend. We'll talk.

She felt like she was standing at the top of a slippery slope, trying desperately to gather the past around her like a shield. But when it came to Trent, even her strongest shields were way too weak.

If they were going to meet to talk, they definitely needed to go someplace public so they wouldn't be tempted to make the mistake of ripping each other's clothes off. Even if it was a *mistake* she was craving body and soul.

"I promised an aspiring artist who lives on the other side of the island that I'd go see her work at a flea market tonight. I guess you can come with me if you'd like."

The way his eyes lit up made her pulse go a little crazy, and she feared that even being in public might not help—but he was back for good, and she couldn't live her life in an emotional hurricane. If she and Trent were going to be living on the same island for the foreseeable future, then she needed to work toward a friendship—*without* benefits.

* * *

REESE COULDN'T SHAKE off her conversation with Trent. After all these years of trying to forget him, she'd given in after only a few brief conversations and one glorious, mind-blowing kiss. What would she do after spending an hour with him?

Because she knew he was right—they did *really* need to talk. She needed to forget the way he made her hot and bothered, look Trent in the eye, and hash out the past. All of it. But first she needed to get over to her parents' house and tell them that she and Trent were working on the mural project together. The island was small enough that her parents might bump into someone who saw them out together, and she didn't want them to get the wrong impression.

She drove to their house thinking about what impression she did want to give them. The real question was, what impression did *she* have? Where was this leading? She didn't have those answers yet. But she wanted her parents to hear about them working together from her first. She and Trent were simply working together on the mural and then going on *one* outing.

Definitely not a date. If they made it out the front door this time.

She parked in front of the cedar-sided Cape home she'd grown up in and then banged her head on the steering wheel. *What am I doing? What do I want?* With a sigh, she sat up straight again, and her eyes landed on the miniature lighthouse hanging from her rearview mirror.

Banging her head on the steering wheel wouldn't help this time. There was no denying that he'd never really been far from her thoughts.

She followed the driveway up to her parents' front door, hoping that her mixed emotions weren't evident all over her face.

She pushed open the front door and inhaled the wonderful aroma of freshly baked bread. Her mother had baked her whole life. *A warm and loving family starts with the love you pour into it.* And pour love she did. Judith Nicholson was a doting mother who always had a warm hug at the ready. She wore her white-blond hair cropped in a stylish pixie cut. When Reese was younger, her friends used to love to come over after school and for slumber parties, because her mother would treat them all as if they were her own daughters and kept the house stocked with homemade snacks. Reese hadn't realized until she was much older that her mother was dishing out life advice as she handed out cupcakes and doled out hugs.

"Mom? Dad?"

"In here, honey."

She followed her mother's voice into the kitchen and wasn't surprised to see her holding up flour-covered hands while her father tied an apron around her waist.

"Okay, love," her father said. "You're all set." He opened his arms to hug Reese. "How's my girl?"

"I'm good." She hugged her father and kissed her mother on the cheek. "The bread smells delicious."

"Have you eaten? The first two loaves are out of the oven. I can put some jam on a slice for you." Her mother reached for a fresh loaf.

"Oh, no thanks. I'm not hungry. I have to get over to the gallery, but I wanted to let you know that I got hired for the mural project over at the resort that I told you about."

Judith's eyes widened. She wiped her hands on a towel and said, "I'm so happy to hear that. You must be over the moon."

"I'm glad, but I'm a little nervous. You know how much the island means to me. I hope I can do it justice." She also knew how much of herself she poured into her artwork, and even after just one kiss, her inspiration was exploding. Would her mother see those raw emotions in her art and put two and two together now that Trent was back on the island?

"Oh, honey. You're so talented. Of course you'll do it justice," her mother said proudly.

"Does this mean you're working with the Rockwells? Or one of their staff?" her father asked.

David Nicholson was well liked and well respected by neighbors and friends, but to Reese he was the epitome of the perfect husband and father. He was retired now, but when he'd worked as an editor for Island Press, he'd eaten breakfast with Reese and her mother every morning before work, and he'd been home every evening in time for dinner. He'd never failed to ask both of them how their days were, and he cared—he really cared—about their answers. One of the hardest things for Reese about moving to New York had been leaving her parents behind. She'd be lying if she didn't admit that when she'd come back home, a piece of her had felt like she'd been tethered to them the whole time she'd been gone. She wasn't a needy, clingy woman, but she loved them too much to just grow up and move away, to visit only on holidays.

"Actually, I'll be working with Trent."

A look of interest passed between her parents before her mother said, "How do you feel about that?"

All I know is that I want to devour him and *yell at him every time I see him.* "I'm hoping it'll be fine. A little awkward at first, but..." She shrugged, wishing she had a better handle on her feelings about her ex-husband.

"I'm sure he'll do everything he can to make it a good experience for you," her mother said.

Including kissing me senseless, if I want him to.

Reese's parents had always encouraged her to follow her heart. They'd been supportive of her artistic efforts, and the summer she'd fallen in love with Trent, they'd been just as eager for her to find happiness. And when she'd come home six months after she'd married and moved away, with a shattered heart and broken dreams, they'd wrapped her in their loving arms and had never said a derogatory word about Trent.

They'd simply listened. For hours. Days. Weeks.

Years.

"You know we always thought Trent was a nice man," her father said, "but I know it must be overwhelming to not only have him back on the island, but also to work with him on the mural." He looked at her mother again before adding, "We're glad you stopped by. We've been wanting to make sure you're doing okay with it all, honey."

"I think it will just take a while to figure out how to navigate the new waters."

To this day they'd never made her feel like she'd made a bad decision falling for Trent, or that she should have known better than to get married so young. In her tender way, Reese's mother had shown her that she'd also hindered their ability to flourish in New York. She'd been so frightened about venturing out into the big, new city that she'd holed up in her apartment, unknowingly making Trent her entire world in a way that wasn't healthy for either of them, thereby adding more stress to an already difficult situation.

Her father put his arms around her again, and she gladly leaned in to his solid warmth. It had taken a long time for her to pick up the pieces of her life after their divorce. Once she had, despite underlying hopes that she'd written off as first-love leftovers, she'd never imagined that she and Trent would ever become close again. She'd certainly never imagined that he'd move back to the island.

And she'd never in a million years thought that she'd be so deeply at risk of falling in love with him a second time.

Chapter Eleven

ALL TRENT HAD thought about since this morning was Reese...and how badly he wanted her back.

But was it too late? Had he hurt her too deeply—and been too stubbornly stupid for too many years?

If he could do things all over again, he would erase the ten years between their divorce and today. No... If he could do things all over again, he'd erase all the ways he'd screwed up their marriage in the first place. He'd be wholly devoted to her instead of his career. And he'd never let one single second pass without her knowing just how much she meant to him.

But there was no time machine; there was only today. He prayed she'd at least consider giving him another chance.

Trent parked his car in front of Reese's house. She was close to her parents, and he hadn't been surprised to hear that she'd bought a two-bedroom house right around the corner from them. Trent tightened his grip on the gift he'd brought for her and paused before walking up the steps to her front porch, remembering the look on her parents' faces when he'd come after Reese to try to convince her to come back to New York with him. They'd treated him with respect and kindness, and the few times he'd seen them in town since then, they'd been friendly toward him, which surprised him, given that he'd swept their daughter off her feet, only to send her running back home, heartbroken, a few months later. If they'd swapped places, he didn't know if he'd be as kind. Looking back, he sure as hell didn't feel like he deserved their generosity.

Trent scrubbed his hand down his face. He'd known the second he'd met Reese that she was the only woman for him—but he'd allowed their connection to get severed by his need to succeed. How could he have been such a fool?

He *would* move heaven and earth for Reese, and he vowed to prove to her, and to her parents, that he was the best—*and the only*—man for her.

As he knocked on Reese's door, he silently reminded himself not to allow this first date to go the way their real first date had a decade ago, when they'd never even made it out the door before they were ripping off each other's clothes. They *would* make it to the flea market, even if he had to keep his hands in his pockets all evening to keep from touching her. The most important thing was that they talk tonight, really *talk,* especially about the hard stuff. Because it was killing him that he hadn't had a chance to tell her how deeply sorry he was.

When Reese opened the door, the evening breeze blew her blond hair off her shoulders. She'd changed into a peach sweater and a pair of jeans darker than the ones she'd worn earlier in the day. She looked stunning. Her lips curved up in a smile that thankfully reached her beautiful eyes, radiating straight to the center of Trent's chest.

"You're gorgeous, Reese." Even though he knew it was a dangerous proposition when he was intent on making sure they talked rather than ripped each other's clothes off, he couldn't stop himself from leaning down and kissing her cheek, lingering just long enough to drink in her sweet perfume and the feel of her warm cheek on his lips.

He could have sworn she nuzzled against him slightly before she said a husky, "Thank you."

Making himself take a step back from her,

rather than moving closer, which every cell in his body was urging him to do, he handed her the wrapped gift. "I saw this and thought of you."

"You didn't have to bring me anything."

He was surprised at the ease with which she pressed her hand to his chest the way she used to, before she seemed to realize what she was doing and pulled her hand back. *Old habits clearly die hard.* And hopefully true love never died at all.

"Are you nervous?"

She'd obviously felt his heart racing when she'd laid her hand on his chest. But he wouldn't have lied to her even if she hadn't already felt the proof of his nerves. "Yes, I'm nervous. I don't want to mess this up." Not when he'd screwed up so many things before and had ended up pushing away the person most important to him in the world.

They stood there for a long moment, gazing into each other's eyes, with an undercurrent of desire simmering between them and a world of memories tethering them together.

"I'm really glad you agreed to go out with me tonight."

"As friends," she reminded him, but her heart didn't sound completely behind it. She turned her focus to the gift and ran her hands along the flat top. "It feels substantial." Her delicate fingers trailed the edge of the wrapping paper. "The paper is beautiful."

He'd always loved watching Reese open gifts. Most people were so excited to see what was inside the wrapping that they tore it open—but while that was how Reese used to act toward *him*, when it came to actual gifts, she was all about savoring the moment. Unless, of course, she was *giving* the gift. Then she was like a kid trying to hold in a secret.

"I thought you might like it." He'd bought the gift wrap in New York a few years back, one of the many times he'd seen something and known Reese would love it. When he'd gone back to New York to pack his things and move to the island, he'd been surprised by how many items he'd bought over the years with her in mind.

She carefully lifted the tape and unfolded the edges of the wrapping paper, exposing the beautiful wooden box inside.

"Trent." Her wide eyes met his. "This is exquisite, but a Caran D'Ache wooden box set of aquarelle pencils? I can't accept this." She held the box out to him.

He gently pushed it closer to her. "You can, and you should. When I saw your drawing this morning, I could practically smell the flowers. They deserve to be as vibrant as you imagine them." He couldn't resist touching her again, and covered her hand with his.

"But..." She moved a little closer. "You shouldn't be buying me things."

"Why not?" His thumb brushed over her knuckles, and she squeezed his fingers as she'd done the other night in the parking lot.

"Because. I'm...You're..."

"*We're*, isn't that what you mean?" There was no denying the sparks between them. "Whether I buy you a gift or not doesn't diminish the strength of our connection."

He stepped closer, and she made a little whimpering sound.

"Trent," she whispered, before clearing her throat and adding in a stronger voice, "we have to go. I promised Tami I'd go look at her work."

It took every ounce of self-control to nod and move away from her rather than pull her into his arms. But when he couldn't shift more than an inch away, he realized she had hooked her finger into the pocket of his jeans, keeping him close.

The look in her eyes when she realized it, too, told him that she'd surprised herself with the move as much as she'd surprised him.

But despite his desire to press his body to hers and kiss her until neither of them could remember anything but how good they made each other feel, he was determined not to go too fast, or he'd be taking a chance of messing things up again with Reese.

He wrapped his hand around hers and unhooked her finger from his waistband, then kissed her palm. "Shall we?"

Her lips parted, as if he were asking her if she wanted to go into the bedroom—and the heat in her eyes told him she was considering it.

Sweet Lord, trying to keep his hands off of her so that they could talk was shaping up to be one of the hardest things he'd ever done in his life. "Leave, I mean. To see your friend."

"Yes." She shook her head as if she were clearing her thoughts. "We should leave before we end up replaying history." She walked into the cozy living room, where she grabbed her purse and a book off of a coffee table made from driftwood and glass. "Do you mind if we stop by Bay's Edge on the way? I promised to drop off a book for a friend."

"Sure," he answered, wondering who her friend was. He'd heard that she worked with the residents of the care facility and knew they all had to be just as much in love with her as he was.

Everything in her house told of the creative and interesting woman Reese was, from the Tibetan peace flags that hung over the fireplace to the double Papasan chair beside the soft couch and the passionate, emotional paintings she'd hung on the walls. He saw her in every one of them. He could so easily imagine how it would have been if they'd lived here together. Reese would have walked barefoot through the cottage in the mornings, sunk into the Papasan chair, then patted it and asked him to join her. And he would have appreciated every single second with her in his arms.

Could that fantasy ever become a reality?

Hands in pockets, he reminded himself as he followed her out and checked the lock behind them. "There are certain parts of history that are worth replaying," he said as he forgot his own reminder and draped an arm over her shoulder. When she stopped cold, he realized what he'd said and done.

"Everything feels so natural with you," he admitted as she turned to face him on her front step. "Sometimes I forget that it's been ten years."

"I do, too," she admitted. She was silent for a few moments, and he could see her weighing her thoughts before she finally admitted, "One minute I want to rip your clothes off, and the next I'm thinking about how long it's been and how much has gone unsaid."

He traced the edge of her jaw with his finger. "Reese."

"And then you touch me like that and say my name like we're in the bedroom and you're about to… *Ugh.*" She threw her hands up in the air. "This is so hard." She took one step away and spun around, eyes narrow with warning. "And don't make a sexy comment about *that* either."

Trent held his hands up in surrender even as he stepped closer and lowered his cheek to hers to whisper, "Just because something's hard and just because it makes both of us nervous doesn't mean it isn't worth it, Reese. Worth absolutely *everything.*"

Chapter Twelve

THIS WAS THE exact moment Reese had both feared and desperately wanted since the very second she'd bumped into Trent a few days ago.

Her heart thundered in her chest as she fisted her hand in his black button-down shirt—the one that set off his smoldering blue eyes. His shirt was unbuttoned at the top, which he *knew* drove her crazy. *Damn him.* She'd always loved to run her fingers through the smattering of hair on his chest. Trent was all man, and right here, right now, with his cheek pressed to hers and his warm breath whispering across her skin, she wanted him more than she ever had.

He drew back far enough to gaze into her eyes but remained close enough for her to see the starburst of gray surrounding his pupils, fusing with the blue that had gone nearly black with desire. She leaned in as he curled his fingers around the nape of her neck, and she couldn't stop herself from brushing her lips lightly against his.

It was almost like a taunt of the way their lips used to crash together in a collision of hot passion and greed. Feeling his body pressed to hers, their hearts dancing to a frantic rhythm, made her body react like the past ten years had never existed. In that instant Reese knew she was in serious trouble. And when he slid his hand to the curve of her back she heard herself moan.

She had no business burying her fingers in his hair, but she was holding on to only a shred of rational thought, and it was fraying fast. He groaned, a needy, guttural sound that sent her brain firing again. She pushed from his arms, and swallowed hard against the desire to forget right from wrong and kiss him, because this wasn't just some guy. This was *Trent*. But not the lawyer who gave up everything they had to climb his corporate ladder.

The mouth that had just brushed over hers, the hands that had caressed her, and the eyes that were staring back at her were those of the man she'd met a decade ago—and *that* was enough to scare her back to reality, because she knew he'd left that Trent behind ages ago.

"What was that?"

"Us," he instantly replied. "Inescapable, unbreakable us."

He was right. It was why she'd had to leave all those years ago—one touch from Trent could make her forget everything. She'd known it then, and she knew it now as she fought the urge to seal her lips over his and melt back into his arms. She took a step on shaky legs and reached for the car to steady herself while she tried to regain her resolve not to end up beneath his amazing body.

Reese was restless on the drive to Bay's Edge as she fought to make herself keep distance between them when she desperately wanted to be closer. Her body was still vibrating from their near kiss, and she had to silently remind herself again and again that this was a *talking* outing, not a *making-out* date.

Trent parked, then came around to open her door. He reached for her hand, and electricity shot up her arm and through her chest like fireworks. How was she supposed to navigate between her new, even more powerful feelings and the underlying worries of repeating the past?

She had to ask him, "How are we going to do this?"

"I don't know, Reese. But I'm hoping we can

figure it out together."

A car honked, which yanked her back to the parking lot they were standing in. "We should go in to see Tilly. She's one of my favorite people, and I know she'll love this book."

* * *

BETWEEN THE LUST running through his veins and the desire on Reese's face, Trent was sure they'd both spontaneously combust. But he could see how important her friend was to her, so he forced himself to put his hand on the small of her back and lead her through the parking lot.

"Hi, Kathleen," she said to the woman behind the reception desk. "Is it all right if I stop in and see Tilly? I brought her a book."

"Sure, Reese. Hello, Trent." Kathleen ran her eyes between the two of them, and her lips curved into a smile.

"Great to see you again, Kathleen. How's Tom?" Trent had played baseball with Kathleen's son when they were in high school.

"He's doing just fine. I wish he'd visit more often, but you know how that goes. Everyone's so busy these days. I heard that you and Quinn and Derek all moved back to run the resort. Is that right?"

"Yes, and it's good to be back. Please tell

Tom I said hello."

Trent instinctively reached for Reese's hand as they headed down a wide hallway. "How often do you teach here now?"

"Once a week, at least," she said as they came to the game room. "Don't hold my hand in here. It's hard for me to concentrate when you do."

"You do realize that makes it even more tempting."

She glared at him, but there was a hint of humor in her eyes. As he followed her into the game room, he fantasized about how fun it would be to watch her squirm with desire. But Trent knew he was getting ahead of himself. Just because she was still reeling from their almost kiss, just as he was, that did not give him permission to act like she was his, no matter how much he wished that she were.

"Reese!" A bald man waved from a table, where he was playing cards with two women and another man, who was sitting in a wheelchair.

A television played loudly on the left side of the room, across from a couch, where there were another two women sitting beside each other.

"Hi, Morris," Reese said as she walked toward him. "Hi, Norma," she said to a gray-haired woman who was watching them with inquisitive eyes. "Are you playing bridge?"

"Nope. Strip poker. Want to join us?" Morris winked at Trent.

Reese laughed. "Not tonight, but thanks for the invite."

Trent noticed that two women sitting at the next table were watching them with interest, too.

"Reese, don't you want to introduce us to your gentleman friend?" Norma asked.

"Of course." Reese held Trent's gaze for a beat too long, and he knew she was trying to figure out how to introduce him. "This is Trent Rockwell." Not her ex-husband and not her almost-date for the night, either. Just his name. "Trent, this is Morris and Norma Rickenbacker."

Trent held out a hand to shake Morris's. "Nice to meet you both." He took Norma's hand between both of his and held it for a moment. "Does your granddaughter Katie own the florist shop in town?"

"Yes, she does," Norma said. "You were in school together, weren't you?"

After he said that he had been, the two women from across the room called out, "Reese?"

"Hi, ladies. How are you tonight?"

"We're fine, but aren't you going to introduce us, too? I'm Martha," one of the women said to him.

"Hi, Martha." Trent went to greet her as Reese asked where Tilly was.

"And I'm Carin," the darker-haired woman said. "Are you two on a date?"

Before answering, Trent turned to see if Reese wanted to chime in, but she was crouched between Norma and Morris, talking with the couple.

"I sure hope so," he finally answered. He answered several more questions about himself and then Martha interrupted.

"Reese is really sweet."

"Yes, she is," Trent agreed.

"And pretty, don't you think?" Carin added.

"Gorgeous." Clearly, these women were intent on a little matchmaking, which he was all for.

"Don't forget smart." Morris tapped his finger on his forehead. "Our Reese is a very bright woman."

Trent turned to agree just as Reese rose to her feet and looked toward the entrance to the room.

"Tilly!" Reese went to greet a tall black woman who was pushing a walker into the room.

Tilly's eyes lit up when she saw Reese. Reese embraced her, and Tilly closed her eyes while returning the hug. It was obvious how much both of them treasured their friendship.

"I didn't expect to see you tonight, Reese," Tilly said, eyeing Trent with questions in her eyes.

"I promised to bring you this book." Reese walked with her over to an armchair by the television, and Tilly lowered herself into the chair.

"It looks like you brought more than a book. Who is this handsome man?" Tilly coughed and pulled a tissue from the sleeve of her thick sweater.

"Are you getting a cold?" Reese's eyes filled with concern.

"It's nothing." Tilly stuffed the tissue back into her sleeve. "Just a little cold." Tilly had a very friendly face, and Trent could tell by the way she squeezed Reese's hand that she didn't want Reese to worry about her. "Hello there. I'm Tilly."

"I'm Trent. It's nice to meet you."

"Very nice to meet you, too. It was kind of you to come by with Reese."

"They're on a date—at least he hopes they are," Carin called from across the room. "Aren't they cute together?"

Reese's eyes widened as Carin added, "He's very nice, too. He's a Rockwell, and he's just moved back to the island to help run the resort."

"Carin used to work in human resources," Tilly explained to them. "She can get information out of a stone." She coughed again, and Reese crouched beside her chair.

"Would you like me to ask someone to get you cough medicine? Or would you like a glass of water?"

Tilly's eyes warmed again. "Thank you, sweetheart, but I'll be fine. It's just a little cold. Go have fun tonight and thank you for the book." She pressed her hand to the cover. Reese gave her another hug, and Tilly held her tightly again before pushing her back and saying, "Don't you worry. I'm as tough as they come. A little cold isn't enough to break me."

When Trent leaned down to embrace Tilly, she whispered, "She's a wonderful girl."

He whispered back, "Yes, she is."

Trent turned to find Carin and Martha standing with open arms, waiting for their hugs, too. By the time they left, Trent had hugged Morris and Norma, too, and Reese was shaking her head.

"Do you have to be so darn likable?" she said with an exasperated tone as they climbed back into the car. "Those poor women will be dreaming about you all night long."

Trent fought the urge to lean across the console and take her in an intoxicating kiss as he said, "It's not them I want to dream about me."

Only you.

Chapter Thirteen

CROAKERS PARK WAS bustling with children giggling and running about, while friends sat chatting on benches and families walked through the flea market. Several tented booths created a horseshoe-shaped border around the grassy lawn where the children were playing.

"Do you remember the last time we went to a flea market together?" Trent asked after they'd gotten out of the car.

Of course she remembered. She'd never forgotten one second that they'd spent together. It was crazy that the sparks between them hadn't faded one bit—if anything, they felt stronger after being apart for so long. But she couldn't let herself forget how quickly he'd changed in New York. She shouldn't be pulled right back into his arms without some sort of assurance that he'd really changed.

Unfortunately, *knowing* she shouldn't and *fighting her attraction* to him were a world apart.

"We went behind the boulders," she finally answered.

He reached out to tuck a lock of hair behind her ear. "You were so sexy, Reese."

"We almost got caught so many times." She flushed with the memory of that afternoon. They'd been looking at arts and crafts, and every time Trent touched her, she wanted him more, needed him more. And then finally— *finally*—when neither could hold back another second, they'd stolen off to a secluded area of the park and made love behind a screen of boulders.

Now he gazed into her eyes and said, "I never could get close enough to you. In the months we were together, all I wanted was to love you more, to become part of you."

She tore her eyes away, her throat thick with emotion. Painful emotion now, rather than the attraction that had been bubbling back up between them. "If that's true, then you quickly lost your way." And she still didn't understand why he had let her go without even fighting for her all those years ago.

Her voice brought him back into focus. "I

did lose my way. I didn't know how to handle our relationship back then, but I've changed, Reese. And I promise I'm going to prove it to you."

She wanted to believe him, but she'd given him unconditional love and trust before, and he'd been reckless with it. How could she trust him now?

She watched a young couple walk through the market carrying a bouquet of fresh flowers and holding hands. Why did it look so easy for everyone else? Then again, it had felt so easy for them at first, too, before they'd gone to New York.

Was it this island? Could their love survive only in this fairy-tale environment?

But even as the questions went around and around inside her head, she knew better than to try to figure out the last ten years in the next ten minutes. She needed to get their outing back on track, but now that talking had evened the score with almost making out, she wasn't sure *what* she wanted anymore. Talking about the past was heartrending. Whereas almost making out was incredibly drugging and delicious.

"Maybe we shouldn't make any promises today," she said softly. "Maybe we could just browse and enjoy the day, okay?"

For a moment, she thought he might push

his case again, but then his lips curved up into a smile and he said, "I already am enjoying the day, Reese. More than I've enjoyed anything in a very long time."

There was nothing more beautiful than Trent Rockwell's smile. And even though they'd been skirting the edge of some really difficult memories so far today, her heart suddenly felt like it was flying.

* * *

THE SUMMER TRENT had met Reese and everything had seemed so new and exciting, they'd often visited flea markets, galleries, and old bookstores. He'd just come out from under several grueling years of law school, and while he knew that just about anything would feel like a reprieve, what he felt when he was with Reese was miles beyond anything he'd ever experienced.

Now, just getting to hold her hand as they walked from one booth to the next, rocked him to the core. This was what he wanted—another chance at a life with Reese.

But would she ever want that, too?

Sometimes, when she forgot the past, she smiled up at him so easily. Other times, however, he could see the clear hesitation hovering in her eyes. She was here with him today, but that didn't mean she'd forgiven him for hurting her. Or that she ever would forgive him enough to give him a second chance at loving her the way she deserved to be loved.

He was so incredibly lucky that she'd agreed to this date, and he wanted to understand everything she was feeling so that he could make sure he never made the same mistakes again.

But he knew Reese well enough to understand that she had to be totally, one hundred percent ready. Until she felt she could handle it—all of it—it didn't matter how much he pushed. He'd only push her away if he wasn't careful. His mother, Abby, had always said, *Reese really thinks things through. It's one of the things I love best about her—that I always know she'll give every option careful consideration.* Trent loved that, too, and now all he could hope was that she'd carefully consider being with him again, rather than outright rejecting him for his past mistakes.

He'd wait as long as it took for her to make up her mind. He felt as if he'd lived a lifetime in the last ten years, and now he knew what would fulfill him and what he'd been holding out for all these years.

Reese.

Just then she made a happy little sound and tugged him toward a booth full of books. It was just what she used to do when they would go to a flea market together, and yet again he prayed that this outing meant she was going to give him a chance at reconciliation. Because he honestly wasn't sure how he could ever move past her again.

Again? Who was he kidding? He'd never moved past her in the first place. Wasn't that why he'd found something wrong with every woman he'd dated since their divorce? Wasn't that why the idea of moving back to the island had been slowly simmering for all these years? Wasn't that why he'd bought the wrapping paper and why almost every other thing he'd ever purchased had been with her at the forefront of his mind, from linens—*Ooh, let's get the super-high thread count. I love the softness!*—to the shirts he wore—*I love you in black and navy.*

Reese picked up one of the books to show to him. "Are you still looking for this one?"

He was an avid collector, and it meant a great deal to Trent that after all these years, Reese still remembered his treasured list of books. In the first weeks they'd dated, he'd told her about the books he wanted to read. The books weren't the old classics, but they had been suggested to him over the years by friends with similar interests, professors, his family. They ranged in topics from philosophy to nonfiction recounts of war stories. Reese had suggested that he start a list, much like her inspiration notebook. She'd jot down things she wanted to paint. When she was in search of inspiration, she'd flip through the list and find a note she'd scribbled at an earlier time, and it would spark a painting. Before they'd married, she'd bought Trent a special leather-bound notebook for his list, which had become one of his treasured possessions.

"I am. And I can't believe you remember the list so well still."

"I remember everything, Trent. Not just the bad, but the good, too."

He couldn't help but press his lips to hers. For a second she went still, but he didn't want to pull away, and when a soft, surrendering sigh escaped her lungs and filled his, he knew he didn't need to.

Their mouths moved in perfect harmony, and right there beside a table in the flea market, with people milling about and their bodies creating enough heat to ignite the book in Reese's hand, he felt as if their hearts were reaching for each other, coming back together, bridging the years with silent hopes for a future.

Or was that just wishful thinking?

Her soft curves melted against him, and as they drew apart, she sighed. It was a dreamy, wanting sound that sent him reeling with desire.

"I can't forget about Tami," she whispered.

It took a minute for his lust-drenched brain to remember who Tami was.

"I should go see her before it gets too late," Reese said as she set down the book. "If you want to stay to look through the rest of these books, I could come get you when I'm done."

"I want to be with you, Reese. More than anything else in the world." He slid his arm around her waist and held her close as they went in search of the eager, budding artist.

* * *

TAMI PRESTON WAS eighteen years old and full of youthful dreams and fangirl enthusiasm. She gushed over meeting Reese and kept smiling at her mother with an I-can't-believe-she's-here look in her wide eyes. Reese was happy to let Tami know just how great her artwork was, while also sharing a few thoughts on ways to bring more depth to her paintings and sketches.

It warmed her heart to see Trent paying for one of Tami's paintings. He was so thoughtful. But then, fast on its heels, came that same question she'd been circling again and again since he'd come back into her life: *Why did he let ten years pass before seeking me out?* She still found everything about him alluring, from his wit and charm to his willingness to give her space when she needed it. But why, oh why, had he waited so long?

Ten years ago, she'd felt selfish asking for more of him when she knew he was working so hard to make a name for himself in his new profession. But she'd grown up with parents who put their relationship above all else, and that's what she'd thought she'd found with Trent in those early weeks of their whirlwind romance. What's more, she'd seen that same commitment in his parents' relationship, and she'd believed Trent when he'd assured her that nothing would ever come between them.

Now, as he came to her side and placed a hand on her lower back, her heart was aching for a second chance, but the questions still lingered. Would he ever really put her ahead of work? Would he resent her if he did? And could she be more understanding about his hours and the demands of being an attorney, especially now that he'd taken on so many responsibilities at the resort as well?

At the same time, she had to ask herself— did she really want to be his *entire* world? Because she loved the sharp-witted, practical, and methodical side of Trent, which earned him accolades in the legal world, as she'd seen documented over the years in articles in the *Wall Street Journal* and the *New York Times*. She had always been so proud of him and of all of his accomplishments.

So, no, she didn't want to change that part of him. At least not completely.

But she *did* want to know that his heart skipped a beat whenever he thought of her, the way hers always skipped when she thought of him. She wanted their love to be strong enough to withstand a few late nights, but also be important enough to him that he would want to come home to her in the evenings...and that when he left their bed each morning he would feel a pang of longing to stay.

Oh God. In the space of one outing, she'd already mentally inserted herself back into his life.

"Thank you so much for coming all the way here to see my work. You can't imagine how much it means to me." Tami embraced Reese.

"It was my pleasure. You're really talented. Keep painting, and you have my e-mail address and phone number. Contact me anytime. I'm always happy to share thoughts with another artist."

Tami's eyes widened. "I can't believe you just called me an *artist*. I'm hardly that good."

"Nonsense," Reese said with a smile. "Your work is excellent, and the great thing about art is that everyone's talent is different. The minute you created your first painting or sketch and said to yourself that this was what you wanted to do, you became an artist!" She hugged Tami again, then wrapped her arm around Trent's waist. "Have a great show."

It had taken no thought to wrap her arm around Trent and snuggle against his warm, familiar body like she belonged there. Right now she felt like she *did* belong there. Being with Trent felt the best kind of right, even if it should feel wrong based on the problems they'd never been able to resolve.

She knew they needed to deal with it, but did it have to be right this second, when her heart was full and her body ached for the closeness they'd shared? Right now all she wanted was for this feeling of goodness and wholeness to continue. She wanted to be with the only man who had ever made her feel truly alive.

She tried to distract herself from her burgeoning desires by telling Tami's mother, "Your daughter is very talented, and I'm sure with your encouragement she'll go far."

As they walked away, Trent said, "You just made her day." He kissed Reese's temple as his hand slid to her hip. A moment later his gentle touch felt even more intimate as his thumb stroked it. When his fingers slipped beneath the edge of her sweater and brushed against her skin, heat blazed through her.

Oh God, she didn't just want to dip her toes into the goodness of them—she wanted to jump in with both feet and submerge herself. To tangle together and drown in the desire swelling between them.

"You didn't have to buy one of her pieces, but I'm so glad you did."

"It's for you to have, Reese." His voice was low and as thick with restraint as her body felt. "One day she's going to come visit you, and when she sees this painting among your things, it will mean the world to her."

The sun was just beginning to set as she turned to face him, giving the chilly evening a romantic glow. "I love that you thought of that. That you even recognize how special something like that could be in the first place." She couldn't resist touching his chest, laying her palm over his beating heart the same way she had earlier that day.

Oh, how she'd missed touching him like this. Missed being able to look up into his blue eyes and see his smile. Missed lying safe and warm in the circle of his arms.

"I felt your joy every time someone admired one of your paintings. Even before we were married, when a tourist would stop to watch you paint or sketch on the beach, you would light up. How could I not understand something that was such a big part of my wife's life?"

Hearing Trent say *my wife* made her heart skip a beat, but it was the way he was looking at her, as if he still felt their deep connection just as strongly as she did, that had her breath hitching in her throat.

He drew her closer, and she went willingly into his arms as he told her, "I hurt you deeply, and I'm so very sorry. But I never stopped caring about you, and I want to make it up to you. I want to fix everything that I broke. Give me a chance, Reese. Let me show you how I've changed. Let me earn your trust again. Let me prove to you that I'm worthy of your love."

So long. She'd waited so long to hear him say that.

"Please, sweetheart. I never meant to hurt you. I was young and stupid, and not fighting for you ten years ago was the biggest mistake I've ever made."

His eyes were filled with so much sincerity, his voice laden with so much remorse, that suddenly she could barely think. Her fingers curled in his shirt as she closed her eyes and let her body take over. And boy did it ever take over.

There was nothing tender about their kiss as their mouths came together in a possessive, needful kiss. His mouth was hot and hungry, and her hands were greedy as they roved over his shoulders to the muscles on his back. She wanted to press her nails into his skin and mark him as her own.

God, how she'd missed him. But they weren't in the past anymore. All that mattered was right here. Right now. And oh how she *needed* him. How she *wanted* him. She sank deeper into him, into the kiss, against his hard, virile frame, desperately trying to get closer.

"Car." She barely got the word out before he took her in another demanding kiss. She'd always loved knowing the effect she had on him, and tonight was no different. Feeling the hard proof of how much he wanted her, too, pulled a moan from her lungs, and she wanted *more*. More of his emotions, more of his strength, more of everything he had to give her. She hadn't felt these animalistic urges since the last time she'd been with Trent. She'd almost forgotten his power to transport her to another dimension. To a place where only they existed.

That thought brought her mind spiraling back to the moment—to the fact that they were groping and kissing in the park—and not even behind a wall of boulders this time.

She drew back in a panic, her eyes searching the area. Luckily, they were far enough from the booths that no one was giving them a second glance.

"Come on." He took her hand and they half ran to the car, stopping every few feet to kiss some more.

Trent placed the painting on the roof of the car and pressed his body to hers. Her back hit the cold metal door, making the titillating friction between them even stronger as he slicked his tongue out against hers, claiming her in another passionate kiss.

She was *this close* to ripping off his shirt when she heard the door unlock. He helped her in, and instead of leaning down to kiss her again, he searched her eyes. Her heart swelled even bigger, knowing that he wouldn't just take unless she wanted him to. And unless she was ready to give herself to him, too.

"I need you, Trent." She'd been waiting ten years for this moment and didn't want to wait another second longer. She pushed him toward the driver's side door. "Hurry."

Chapter Fourteen

REESE LOST TRACK of the roads as the sun faded and the headlights of the oncoming cars came on. She lost track of everything but Trent, who had reached for her hand and was squeezing it tightly, like a lifeline. Which seemed fitting, considering that whenever they were together he—*they*—blocked out the rest of the world without even trying.

She'd expected him to take her home, or to his suite at the resort, but when he pulled over on a narrow dirt road and cut the engine, her pulse quickened. *This* was who they had always been at their best. Spontaneous. Ravenous for each other. Neither one of them overthinking. Just wanting. Needing.

All of each other.

She scrambled over the console and

straddled his hips, sealing her lips over his. Trent held her face, keeping her exactly where he wanted her. She loved the way he deepened the kiss, making her dizzy as he wound his fingers in her hair and angled her head, urging her mouth open wider as he kissed her more forcefully. Reese tore at his shirt, needing to see him, to feel his skin against hers. Their mouths parted just long enough for him to pull her sweater off and then tug his own over his head and toss it on the passenger seat.

He claimed her in another kiss that had her moaning with need as he unhooked her bra and tossed it aside. He groaned as he brushed his thumbs over the taut peaks, kissing her again, taking her higher, and higher still, as he fondled and teased her with his hands. And when he lowered his mouth to one peak and licked out over it, she gasped at the pleasure of having his hands *and* his mouth on her again. She felt feverish. Delirious.

And yet she couldn't get enough. There was hardly any room to move in the cramped car, but he still managed to slide off her jeans and panties between kisses. One sweet kiss on the sensitive skin at her inner thigh. And then another on her kneecap. And then one at her ankle, before he kissed his way back up her naked skin. She'd never felt so adored, never relished her sensuality the way she did as he finally found her with his mouth. The warm slick of his tongue over her had her crying out and arching against him.

She hadn't forgotten how good it was to be with him, but even in her memories it hadn't been this good. Maybe, she thought with the few brain cells she had left, ten years of anticipation had heightened every nerve, every fiber of her being, readying her for his touch in the most incredible way.

So close. She was already so close. But the first time she went over the edge of bliss, she wanted Trent with her. Wanted to be able to feel his heart beating against hers and see his eyes go dark with pleasure.

Her fingers were already threaded through his hair, and now she tugged at him. "Please," she begged. "I need you. Here. With me." Thankfully, he didn't need her to explain any further before he climbed back up her naked body and reclined the seat.

God, how she loved the weight of him, the way he gazed down at her like he wanted to climb beneath her skin. His hard length pressed against her belly, and she gripped his biceps as his mouth claimed hers again.

"Condom?" he asked hastily.

"I'm still on birth control. And it's been ages since I've been with anyone," she confessed.

"Me, too. And other than with you, I've

always used protection."

She didn't have to think about it, didn't need them to go into any more separate history. "Love me, Trent. That's all I want. Just for you to love me."

He gazed into her eyes, the air around them pulsing with need, their hearts beating frantically with anticipation. The edges of his beautiful mouth curved up as he whispered, "I always have, Dandelion."

Her world stilled. She never imagined hearing him say that he loved her again...and she never dreamed he'd ever again use the nickname he'd given her the very first time they'd made love.

Dandelion.

Emotion and desire coalesced, and her desperate need to be close to him overwhelmed her ability to fully process the meaning of his confession.

He lowered his lips to hers and whispered, "You're so beautiful. So soft. So perfect," at the same blissful moment that he gripped her hips and sank into her.

"Trent." He filled her so completely, and when their bodies began to move, there was no caution, no hesitation.

His scent was intoxication. His power, his passion, sent waves of ecstasy through her. She took him as aggressively as he took her, meeting each of his powerful thrusts with a lift of her hips. She clutched his biceps, his shoulders, his muscular back, touching everywhere and anywhere she could reach.

I've missed you so much, she thought. *I dreamed of you so many nights, wishing you were with me.*

As thrust after thrust took her higher, closer to the edge, her head tipped back and his mouth found her neck. *Oh yes.* He remembered exactly what she liked. He nibbled and sucked, driving her out of her mind. And when he slid a hand between them, teasing and taunting, she instantly shattered around him.

Still shuddering from her incredibly intense climax, she wrapped her legs around his waist, feeling the thrill of his arousal in the tightening of his muscles. He circled her body with his arms, bringing her so close against his chest, as if he couldn't bear to have air between them. And then he was taking her right back to the edge again, each thrust slower now, stroking over her sensitive nerves.

She dug her nails into his skin. "More...Harder...Please..."

"Beautiful. You're so damn beautiful, Reese." He clutched her tight and reared up, thrusting harder. "I've waited so long to be with you again."

"Too long," she managed in a breathless

voice, holding his arms for dear life as another climax tore through her.

He buried his face in her neck and breathed her name seconds before surrendering to his own release. She wrapped her arms around his back, loving the feel of his throbbing heat inside her.

"Reese." Nothing had ever sounded sweeter than her name, spoken in the deep voice that she'd never been able to forget, no matter how many lonely nights she'd spent without him.

Only now, though his slow, sensuous kisses told her he hadn't been lying when he'd said he'd always loved her, reality was already rushing back in. The reality of having slept with Trent on yet *another* first date, even though she'd vowed up and down not to do just that. She never slept with a guy on their first date!

But this wasn't just any guy. This was Trent. The man she'd once adored.

Love me, Trent. Her own words from just minutes ago hit her like a brick. *That's all I want. Just for you to love me.*

Oh no! Not only had she said it in the heat of the moment, but she'd meant it—*wanted him, needed him*—from the very tip of her head to the soles of her feet.

She sighed as she realized that she was more confused than ever.

As if he could read her mind, he slowly

raised his body from hers, took her hand to help her up, and silently gave her her clothes to put back on. After they were both dressed again, they sat on the hood of the car beneath the stars, and she wondered if he'd needed the chance to cool off as much as she had.

"I should have asked if you were sure," he said softly.

"You know how much I wanted you," she assured him. "More than I wanted to breathe."

"And now?" He touched her chin, bringing her eyes to his.

From the tightening of his jaw and the furrowing of his brow, she knew he could see her uncertainty about where to go from here. Her heart raced again as she tried to figure out what to say, how to explain that the desperation to be in his arms again was colliding head-on with the fear of repeating their past. Her skin became clammy as she tried to fight the terrifying fear of racing forward at breakneck speed, the way they had the first time. She wanted him—God, how she wanted him—but the knowledge that what they'd done before hadn't worked and the realization that she was practically powerless to resist the white-hot desire between them coiled into a knot and drove her to her feet.

"And now...I want to kiss you and run from you at the same time."

Though hurt flickered in his eyes at her honest answer, he didn't lash out. Instead, he slid from the hood of the car and reached for her hand, gathering her in his arms and holding her close. But with every stroke of his hand down her back, more and more unanswered questions simmered up from deep inside her—and finally bubbled over.

"Why?" she needed to know. "Why did you wait ten years?"

He hesitated for only a second or two, but it was more than enough time for anger and hurt to wind together and spew from Reese's mouth.

"*Ten years*, Trent." She pushed away from him and paced. "Do you have any idea how many nights I prayed you'd make time for me?" She spun around and faced him again. "Any idea how many years I longed to be with you?" Tears of anger welled in her eyes, and she pushed at his chest. "Talk to me, damn it. I deserve to know why."

"I can't answer you any better than to say that I was an idiot. I don't know the whys of it all. I only know that I screwed up. But I never, *ever*, stopped loving you."

She turned away again, trying to walk off the dark emotions that swamped her, but it was impossible, and when she looked at him again, she *needed* him to hear her—and to know that how he'd treated her was not okay. "Damn right you screwed up. Ten years, Trent. *Ten years!*"

"I tried, Reese. I came after you when you first left me. I really thought we could make it work."

"You didn't try!" Her limbs shook. "You rationalized."

"You're right. That's exactly what I did." He ran a hand through his hair, working his jaw in frustration. "But at the time I had no idea just how badly I was screwing up. You have to know that. You know me. You're the only person who has ever *really* known me."

He reached for her again, but she turned out of his grasp.

"I thought I knew you when we were here on the island, but that guy I met and fell in love with was a world away from the man I ended up with in New York."

"Reese, you were everything to me. You still are." His voice was filled with so much sorrow. "Everything about us was so right, so real, and so easy, that I knew it was true love. But what I didn't know, and never slowed down enough to realize until it was too late, was that the move had thrust us both into a completely different world. You left everything you knew and everyone you loved for us. For me."

She clenched her eyes shut, remembering the anguish of leaving her parents and friends. "I did give up everything to be with you, and I was sad about it. But then I realized..." She stopped to catch her breath and wipe her angry tears away. "I realized I had you, and that was all that mattered. But then it turned out I didn't actually have you at all. I also realized after it was all over that I was relying too much on you." Realizing the apologies needed to go both ways, she said, "And you need to know how sorry I am that I didn't do a better job of standing on my own two feet."

"No. I was the one who abandoned you, and I was too busy to see what I was doing. You didn't do anything wrong, sweetheart."

"I did," she said. "We both did. And then we lost each other."

Just as she closed her eyes to try to gain control of her emotions, he stepped in closer and touched her hands with the utmost gentleness. "May I?"

She nodded, needing his comfort and wanting his love, despite the anger that had just erupted like a volcano. He gathered her against him as he said, "I was young and stupid and so in love with you that I believed our relationship could withstand anything. And it can, sweetheart. I truly believe that. But we need to both be in it together. Always a team. No matter what."

She fisted her hands in his shirt as he held her close and bared his soul, taking full responsibility for something that wasn't solely his fault. When he gazed deeply into her eyes, she felt her heart crack open. Forcing herself from the comfort of his arms was harder than almost anything she'd ever had to do, but she held her chin up high, pulled her shoulders back, and looked into his eyes with what she hoped was a self-assured gaze.

"I wish I could tell you that I could be a part of that team again. I wish I could be as sure about our past as you are—"

"The only thing I'm sure about," he interrupted, "is that I want you in my life. And that I'll do anything, be anything, change anything, to be with you again."

Ten years ago, five years ago, maybe even three years ago, she'd have softened at those words and taken them at face value. But she hadn't realized until this very moment how much all those years had strengthened her.

"I'm not a naive nineteen-year-old anymore. I know promises can be broken, and I have a whole life here that I love." All the anger had left her voice by now, but any tentative hope for what might come was tamped down by the unknown that hovered around them like a cloud. "Being with you is wonderful in *so* many ways, but it's also scary, and risky, and..." She crossed her arms, bracing to be strong— just as she had ten years ago. "I need time to process everything. I need time to think."

"I'm not a stupid kid anymore, Reese. I *will* prove that to you. I *will* win you back. Our love is too strong for this to be anything but true love. I screwed up royally—maybe we both did—but I'm not going to let our past ruin what could be the best part of the rest of our lives. I love you, and I don't expect you to tell me that back tonight. But I hope you'll continue to open yourself up to the possibility of us. I promised to always love you, and I'll do whatever it takes to be with you. And when I do, I'm praying that the only 'Dear Trent' note you'll want to write in the future will be to tell me how much you love me. Just as much as I love you."

Chapter Fifteen

STANDING ON THE dewy grass beside the resort the next morning, Reese pulled her hair back and secured it with an elastic band, thinking about Trent. Last night he hadn't tried to hide from his faults, or gloss over them. He'd simply been the same open, honest, and loving man she'd fallen in love with. The one she'd thought she'd lost forever ten years ago...

But today Trent wasn't the only one she was thinking about. Not when she knew she had to take a good, hard look at herself, too. She'd meant it when she'd told him she wished she'd been better able to stand on her own two feet during their marriage. And even though he'd told her she didn't have anything to apologize for, she knew that she did.

When they'd lived in New York City, Trent

had never been able to take a full lunch hour, but he'd asked her more than once if she could come to his office to share a brown-bag lunch on a nearby park bench. At the time, those fifteen minutes didn't seem like they could make or break their relationship. But now she could see that even a quarter of an hour would have been enough to at least share a few kisses...and to remember how important they were to each other. It wasn't that she hadn't had the time—the truth was that she'd been scared. The subway had seemed daunting and unsafe, no matter how many times Trent assured her it wasn't. And the cabs drove so fast and crazy that she was always sure they'd crash.

A decade ago, he'd been way too busy building his career, and she'd been afraid of her own shadow. Ten years older and wiser, Reese was no longer that scared nineteen-year-old. Not even close. And hadn't Trent told her the same thing about himself? That he'd grown beyond the twenty-six-year-old she'd been married to?

Seabirds flew overhead, and Reese watched them swoop down toward the beach. With a long inhalation, she tried to push away her endlessly swirling thoughts about love and forgiveness for a while and turned her attention to the wall that would become her canvas. Being with Trent last night had caused a surge of inspiration that had driven her out of bed before the sun had even risen—the same kind of eruption of creativity she'd experienced when they'd first been together.

This morning, instead of seeing blank white walls before her, she saw flowers swaying in a breeze as it swept across the sandy beach and up the hill, like silent music that only the blooms could hear. She imagined verdant leaves and petals bursting with colors so vibrant and real that she could practically smell their sweet fragrances. She dragged her fingers along the rough surface, tracing the area where the picket fence would be painted. She imagined the grooves of the gray, aged wood, the dots of the nail heads, and the sprinkling of sand that she'd paint, showing how the Cape beaches touched everything around them.

The same way that Trent touched every part of her when he was near.

It had been easier to repress her feelings and deny them completely when he was living in New York all these years. But now, knowing he was staying in the resort—and that he was never more than a few minutes away—made it impossible to keep pretending that her feelings for him weren't hovering just under her skin, vying for release.

She hadn't planned to make love with him

last night. She'd planned to take it slow, to let her feelings simmer as she explored whether or not they were capable of a more mature love.

But even as she thought it, she couldn't keep from rolling her eyes. It was yet another truth she had to face this morning—she couldn't have put the brakes on last night if her life had depended on it, simply because she had no self-control when it came to Trent. Being in his arms again, being that close to the man she'd always loved, hearing her name roll off his tongue—it was sensation overload.

The very best kind of sensation...

She lifted the wooden box of pencils he'd given her and slid her palm over the sleek finish. He knew her so well. To think that he'd bought it because he'd recognized the image she'd sketched made it even more special. She opened the lid, and her breath caught in her throat at the sight of her favorite photograph of the two of them.

She hadn't seen the photograph since returning home. She'd left it beside the note telling Trent she'd left him, hoping it would be enough to spur him into wanting to make things right between them. Her heart ached with the memory.

Ten years ago it hadn't been enough. What did it mean that he'd given it back to her now?

She lifted the photograph with a shaky

hand and remembered the lovely afternoon at his parents' house when his mother had taken the photo.

They'd been unaware that Abby had taken the picture. Then again, when Trent and Reese were together, their love and connection had always overshadowed anything and everything. It didn't matter where they were or how much they loved the people they were with. Their love was boundless.

Or at least it had been for a little while.

The picture's edges were frayed, and her image was slightly faded, as if Trent had rubbed a thumb over it many, many times. In the photo, Trent was sitting on the grass, and Reese was sitting on his lap, facing him. He had one arm beneath her knees, holding her leg in place like he didn't want to take a chance of her running off. They were both smiling so broadly that her heart squeezed even now, as she remembered the feel of their foreheads touching. If she concentrated hard enough, she could still hear his voice when he whispered, *I can't wait to marry you, Dandelion.*

Goose bumps shivered up her limbs with the memory. *Dandelion.* When he'd called her that last night, it had left her breathless. How could one word, one voice, one man, feel like *everything*?

She set the photo in the top of the box and

tried to stop thinking about how unbelievably good, how perfectly *right,* it had felt to make love with him again. She could still feel the press of his thighs against hers, his big hands clutching her hips, and the heated look in his eyes...

She'd never needed words with Trent, because his eyes never lied. The day they'd gotten married, she'd known how much he loved her. Their first morning in New York City, when he'd forgotten to kiss her goodbye, she'd seen just how preoccupied he was with his new life and career. And then, just one week ago, she'd known the moment she'd looked into his eyes outside of Shelley's that he still loved her...and that he wanted them to go back to the way they used to be.

But was love enough? And even if it was, how could they possibly go back to the way they used to be when at least she was a totally different person now?

Reese picked up the sketch pad and, fortunately, despite her endlessly swirling thoughts and questions, it didn't take long for her to become absorbed in defining the elements in her sketch. Short, continuous strokes gave way to M-strokes, changing direction constantly to create grass in motion, as if the wind were blowing. Her hands moved without thought, creating jagged lines for bushes and shorter, more refined strokes for the roof of the cottage behind the gardens.

The flowers represented new life, and the stable cottages anchored each side of the drawing, giving way to the fluid movements of the bay, which was watched over by the lighthouse in the distance. The Rockwells wanted the mural to represent the island and the community, and this would be an ideal representation, the perfect blend of warmth and promise.

In her mind, she couldn't help but insert herself and Trent into the picture, hand in hand as they recited their vows. *I promise to always love you. Forever.*

Forever meant taking all that love and desire that brought a couple together and working it like clay. Re-forming it as their lives evolved, changing shape, sometimes softening, other times remaining slightly rigid, but in the end bound together as one solid unit.

They'd both learned the hard way that forever took more than words. It took effort and follow through, and that's exactly where they'd fallen apart. But now, every time she saw him, every time she heard his voice or felt his touch, every time she thought of him, it pushed the painful memories of their separation a little further away...and gave her hope.

Hope that somehow managed to feel fragile

and beautiful, frightening and thrilling, all at the same time.

* * *

TRENT SET THE bag of groceries he'd spirited away from the resort kitchen on the counter of his suite, and as he washed his hands, he reflected on the fact that after spending a decade trying to push thoughts of Reese away so that he wouldn't have to face all the hurt he'd caused, she'd been there with him the whole time. Always on his mind and in his heart.

Work had been a way to self-medicate the ache of losing her. Working even more hours after she left had given him little time alone in the apartment they'd once shared. But he'd still missed her every minute of every day, no matter how hard he'd worked to tell himself that a practical guy like him should have known better than to let his heart get the best of him.

As he tossed banana slices, pineapple chunks, a handful of blueberries, and a bunch of fresh baby spinach into the blender, he thought about the things he and Reese had said to each other last night. She'd been right to feel angry about how badly he'd blown it. But even though the pain of losing her had left him feeling raw and shredded to pieces, he'd never been angry with her. He'd been hurt. And he'd felt guilty. Because Reese had left everything she'd known and loved behind, and he'd let her down.

Trent scooped toasted wheat germ and sprinkled it into the blender, then measured the coconut water and honey and added them to the mix, as well. This was Reese's favorite smoothie, Passion and Glory. After he finished blending the ingredients, Trent poured it into a large cup, then left his suite and went in search of her. Knowing Reese, she was already working on the mural. He'd always loved how inspired she was and how much her art fulfilled her.

Reese turned as he came around the corner. Thankfully, the instant their eyes met, her lips curved up in a sweet smile. She was radiant in her knit cap, blond tendrils framing her beautiful face. She had the most beautiful legs, long and lean, beneath her jeans.

"You're beautiful," Trent said as he came to her side. Instinct—and the same desperate need he always felt when she was near—brought his lips to her cheek.

Despite the emotional upheaval they'd both experienced last night, she didn't stiffen against his touch, which was a huge relief. But he could tell she was nervous by the way she was nibbling on her lower lip. Hell, his heart was going a mile a minute.

"You don't look so bad yourself," she replied as she took in his running shorts and T-shirt. "Are you just coming back from your run?"

"No. I haven't gone yet." He handed her the cup. "I made you a Passion and Glory smoothie. I even added the toasted wheat germ you love."

"You remembered how to make it after all these years?"

He smiled, knowing his admission would make him seem like he'd been pining over her for a decade, which until the last few days, he hadn't realized was true. "Actually, I usually make them on the weekends for myself. They were a hard habit to break." *Just like you.*

"Thank you." She took a sip and closed her eyes. "Mm. That is delicious. I haven't had one since... In a long time."

"Because it reminded you of us?"

When she nodded, Trent hated knowing she'd gone without something she loved because of him. He stepped in closer. "I'm so sorry about last night. Not that we made love— you know I love being close to you, and I wouldn't give back those moments with you in my arms for anything—but I know it was too soon."

"It wasn't," she said quickly, surprising him with both her words and the warmth of her hand over his. "I wanted you just as much as you wanted me. And I refuse to regret what happened last night. It's just that this is all a lot to take in. But..."

She paused to try to gather her thoughts, and his heart hammered even faster as he waited for her to finish. Only, she didn't finish it with words. Instead, she put down the cup, lifted her hands to his face, and gave him a kiss that was sweet and seductive all at once.

"Thank you for the smoothie, Trent. Have a good day working at the resort."

He couldn't quite figure out how to form words as he stepped away, walking backward so that he could hold the image of her in his mind for as long as possible. He blew her a kiss and jogged away with a big grin.

Despite the incredible kiss she'd just given him, he knew the road ahead likely wouldn't be completely smooth. But nothing in life that mattered was easy. He'd never failed at a damn thing besides his marriage—the one and only thing that mattered.

What he'd felt when he was making love with Reese last night—and what he saw in her eyes every time they were together—was pure, unadulterated love, whether she was fully ready to accept it or not.

He believed in them, and hopefully, in time, she would, too.

And until then, he prayed there would be

lots and lots more kisses, just like the one she'd given him today.

* * *

REESE COULDN'T STOP smiling as she drove to her gallery. Once inside, she went directly to her workspace and, without second-guessing herself, tacked the picture of her and Trent to her easel. For the next few hours, while she wasn't able to concentrate on any one thing for too long, every time she saw the picture, joy bubbled up inside of her.

"What is with you today?" Jocelyn asked as Reese organized a new display of paintings for a second time. "It's like you're on speed."

I'm on a new drug called Trent. Reese stopped in her tracks with the thought and bit her lower lip to keep the words from escaping. Especially since Trent wasn't actually new, was he? More like she was back on an old drug that was suddenly more addictive than ever.

"I just..." *Need to stop thinking about how good it felt to be with him last night—and how much I loved kissing him again this morning.*

"I haven't seen you like this since—" Jocelyn's eyes grew huge. "Oh my God, you slept with him! Did you at least make it out of your apartment this time?"

"Of course we did." She purposefully left off

the *just barely* part of the sentence.

"Well," Jocelyn said in her own defense, "considering we're talking about the man you had sex with in the bathroom of the movie theater, in the car by the pond, behind the bushes in the park—"

"Boulders! They were boulders, not bushes!" Why had she ever shared those details with her friend? *Because I was bursting with excitement. Only now I'm older. More mature. I've lasted*—she glanced at the clock—*a few hours without gushing like a schoolgirl.*

"Whatever." Jocelyn brushed her clarifications aside. "Just tell me one thing. Am I allowed to be excited for you, or do you want me to tell you to slow down?"

"Honestly," Reese said as she forced herself to sit like a normal person in a chair even though her insides were still bouncing all around, "I don't know what I want or how you can help. I only know that the minute we kissed, it was like all those years never happened. We're still so in sync with each other. We're still so..."

"Mushy. Sappy." Jocelyn smiled. "And, obviously, still deeply in love with each other." When Reese's eyes went wide at that statement, her friend said, "I knew it the second I saw the picture on your easel. He's back in your heart, isn't he?"

"You look as conflicted as I am about it," Reese said. "Your eyebrows are all pinched together and your jaw is tight. *You're* the one who's supposed to have the clear head in this."

"You're my best friend in the whole world, and you know I want you to be totally happy. If Trent makes you happy, that's wonderful, but..." Jocelyn paused before saying, "This is very familiar. What if after six months he's right back to working a hundred hours a week and I have to mop up your tears again?"

"He says he's changed, that he didn't know how to handle our relationship before. Neither of us did, Joce. I screwed up just as badly by being so damn scared of everything in the city." She met Jocelyn's concerned gaze. "All I know is that when I'm with him, I feel alive again, and when we kiss..." Her insides went gooey again, and her knees went weak just thinking about Trent's mouth on hers. "When we kiss, everything feels right again. But..."

"Then you remember how hurt you were."

"And I get scared," Reese said with a small nod, thankful that her best friend understood her so well. Because she'd never needed her more than she did right now.

"Tell me what you want me to do," Jocelyn said. "How can I help?"

"Just promise me that you'll be honest with me. If you think I'm acting crazy, if you think

I'm getting too wrapped up in him, promise me you'll say something to me."

"Do you *really* want me to be honest? Or is this one of those honest-in-a-BFF-way things, where I'm supposed to support whatever you want and keep my worries to myself?"

"Pure honesty," Reese made herself say, "even if it hurts."

Jocelyn look undecided for a moment, before she finally sighed and said, "Okay, then here it is. The pure, honest truth. Are you ready for it?"

Reese gulped. "I'd be lying if I said yes, but I want you to lay it on me anyway."

"I never thought you were over Trent. I know we tried to get you there, but I have never seen you happier than when you two were good together. He's here now, not in New York. His life is different. Your life is different. You're not a naive nineteen-year-old anymore. You're a grown woman with your own gallery, *and* your artwork is shown in some of the most prestigious galleries in New York and Boston. There's hope and promise in all of that. But...And there are two big 'buts' coming." She gentled her voice and expression to soften the blow. "The flip side of his making you so happy is that losing that happiness nearly destroyed you, and I can't stand the thought of you being hurt like that again. But maybe that's the risk you have to take to find out if your love for each other is as true now as you once thought it was."

Reese covered her face with her hands and groaned. "What am I going to do?"

"Paint. You've been running around here like you can't get your mind wrapped around any one thing, and the only way you have ever been able to center your mind is to paint. Go. I can handle the gallery. Your answers will come through your art. They always do."

Chapter Sixteen

FINDING THE DEED should have taken Trent an hour, not several days. Fortunately, the kiss Reese had given him had him soaring so high that even the frustrating search for the deed couldn't dull his mood.

The elevator doors opened on Chandler's floor, and Trent's chest tightened. Grandparents were supposed to be doting and loving toward their grandchildren. Or at least warm and friendly. Trent often wondered if perhaps Chandler had once been that way, before his wife died. But all Trent could remember was the way his grandfather had treated Grandma Caroline, like she was all the way at the bottom of his priority list.

As he stepped from the elevator, a memory whipped through him so suddenly that he had to press his palm to the wall to steady himself. *I'm last on your priority list—not just second to your job, but seventh or eighth, after your workday, parties, office events, and whatever else might lead to your success.* Reese had said this to him ten years ago after he'd chased her back to the island to ask her why she'd left him with nothing but a note saying she couldn't be married to him anymore. *I don't even recognize you anymore, Trent. What happened to the man I fell in love with? Where did he go?* Trent's father had encouraged Trent and his siblings to strike out on their own, away from the island, away from Chandler, to ensure they could live their lives out from under Chandler's oppressive thumb. But had Trent taken Griffin's push too far? Had he tried to prove himself despite *all* costs—even when he'd been losing the love of his life?

The sound of his grandfather's wheelchair turning into the hallway pulled him from his thoughts, but he didn't have the wherewithal to push himself upright. Not when his mind was still drenched in *What the hell did I do?*

"Trent?" Chandler grumbled as Didi pushed his wheelchair closer.

Trent forced his shoulders back, his stomach knotting. "Grandfather." He lifted his eyes to Didi but was unable to force a smile. "Didi."

"It's nice to see you, Trent." Didi's warm tone softened his ache a little. She deserved a kinder greeting than a grumble that reminded Trent of the very person he didn't want to be.

"You too, Didi." He finally managed a smile.

Turning back to his grandfather, he said, "I've looked for the transfer documentation in the archives and in the office files. I'd like to avoid a trip to the courthouse, if possible, and I'm wondering if you have any idea where else Robert Faison might have put the files."

"Faison." A deep vee formed between Chandler's brows. "You didn't find the deed with the rest of our corporate documents?"

"No, and I've been through them all. The deed was never formally transferred to you. You must be receiving tax bills in your father's name. I mean no disrespect, but didn't you notice? Didn't the accounting staff notice?"

"The tax bills always came in his name," Chandler said as his frown deepened. "I never worried about it."

"I had hoped that we might have the original documentation, but since we don't, I'll get to work putting together new transfer documents. Do you know if your father had intended to transfer the property prior to his death?"

"Of course he did. He signed all of the paperwork. Robert Faison had it, and I assumed they'd been filed. When he died so suddenly—" Chandler stopped his uncharacteristic dithering. "Do whatever needs to be done. I need that deed."

"Yes, of course."

"Didi." Chandler motioned for her to push the button for the elevator.

Trent rode down the elevator with them, and when it opened, he pressed his hand to the door, holding it for Didi to push his grandfather's wheelchair into the hall.

"Thank you, Trent," Didi said as she settled a hand on Chandler's shoulder. "We're going down to the beach for a walk. Would you like to join us?"

Though Chandler looked surprised at her invitation, he didn't counter it. And for a moment Trent was tempted to go with them. If only because he couldn't imagine what a walk on the beach in the middle of the afternoon with his grandfather could possibly be like. Maybe Chandler really *was* changing his ways, just as Quinn had suggested a few weeks back when he'd overheard Chandler and Didi talking about commitment to family.

"Thanks for the invitation, but I've still got to take care of a few things in my office." And the rest of his day would be all about Reese.

But as soon as he got back to his office and began gathering the documentation he'd need to prepare a new transfer of the deed, he couldn't stop thinking about Reese—or how seeing himself in Chandler turned his stomach.

He'd apologized to her again and again these past days, but he knew those apologies weren't good enough. He needed to do something more to make up for his past mistakes. The documents could wait—it was time to take a ride over to her gallery.

Just as he was about to head out, his office door swung open and Sierra walked in, looking pretty in a long wine-colored skirt. She didn't even waste time on a greeting before saying, "How're things working out with Reese and the mural?"

"She's got a great sketch of it already."

"That's good." Her gaze softened as she clarified, "But I was asking about *you*. Are you okay with working together?"

Trent knew how much Sierra loved the idea of being in love, and she'd been heartbroken when he and Reese had broken up. Hell, they all had been. "I'm more than okay with it, Sierra. I want her back. More than anything."

"And Reese? What does she want?"

"More time."

Sierra came around the desk and embraced him. "Love like you two shared doesn't just go away. I'm sure she'll come around. Who could possibly resist my loving, smart, handsome oldest brother?"

* * *

FIFTEEN MINUTES LATER Trent stood on Old Mill Row, staring up at the sign above Reese's gallery, wondering how he could have missed seeing the significance of it all these years. He studied the yellow dandelions on the left side of the sign, then followed their metamorphosis as they moved across the painting. The yellow flowers made a textured and graceful transition to parachutes of fluff, the delicate hairs separating and floating away toward the upper-right side of the sign. Below, the word *Dandelion* was elegantly tucked among the grass.

The endearment had come to him the first time they'd made love. There was something magical and ethereal, beautiful and soft, about dandelion fluff as it was swept away in a whisper of wind. Its beauty was almost indescribable, and there was something so magical and full of hope within its beauty as it traveled in the wind that it made everyone smile.

Just like his Reese.

How could he have spent a decade visiting the island and never put two and two together?

He'd been so bogged down by the pain of her *Dear Trent* letter that he'd never seen the sign hanging above her gallery for what it was—her love letter to him, just waiting for him to return and figure it out.

Renewed hope filled his chest.

Inside the gallery, Jocelyn was busy with a customer, and when he didn't see Reese, he took a moment to really look at Reese's paintings for the first time in far too long. Her passion came through in the sexy, dark curves of the images, and he saw her playful side in the lighter paintings. Though most of her artwork was abstract, Trent had always felt that through her art he'd been given a glimpse into her soul. When Reese was happy, she used flowing, delicate strokes, rather than the contrasting, muted, or dramatic flairs that showed her darker moods. But the paintings he loved best were the ones where light and dark overlapped and she painted angular shapes with smooth, fine lines, then filled them with thick, bold colors—or when she created edgy strokes and softened them with pale, earthy hues.

At last he came to Reese's easel, and his eyes landed on the photograph of the two of them that he'd given her in the box of paints. His heart tugged at the sight.

"She put it there this morning. But she's not

here now."

Jocelyn's voice startled him, and he turned to see Reese's best friend standing behind him with her shoulders and chin set in a strong manner and a serious look in her eyes. Trent knew how close Jocelyn and Reese were and that they'd always shared everything with each other. By the way she was scrutinizing him, he guessed she knew he and Reese had made love last night.

"I'm not going to hurt her again, Jocelyn. Hurting Reese any more than I already have is the very last thing I want to do."

"Look, I can see that you're still in love with her," Jocelyn said flat-out, "but you've been gone a long time, Trent. She's not a kid anymore. She has a life here on the island. A good life, with friends and her gallery. She's happy. And it took her a really long time to get there. She's incredibly strong, but she's also—"

"Sensitive." Trent turned to look over a few of Reese's darker paintings before looking back at Jocelyn. "I know how complex and wonderful Reese is, and I know you want to protect her. I do, too." He held her gaze. "You're right. I'm still in love with her. More in love than ever before. I know I screwed up, and I have a hell of a lot to make up for. But I swear to you, this time I'm going to be the man she needs me to be. And I'm going to make her happier than she ever knew she could be."

As he spoke, Jocelyn searched his eyes, but he wasn't worried about what she'd see. The love he had in his heart for Reese would overshadow all else.

Jocelyn finally smiled at him, as if he'd just passed a test. A really big one. "She's at home, in her studio."

"Thank you. Not just for telling me where she is, but for always being there for her. Especially when I wasn't."

Chapter Seventeen

MUSIC PLAYED SOFTLY in Reese's backyard studio. It was a small studio, no bigger than a shed, but it was the perfect size to paint in, with plenty of windows to let in as much natural light as possible. The combination of the studio and the close proximity to her parents' house were the two things that had sold her on the cozy cottage, and since moving in a few years earlier, she'd planted lovely gardens and decorated both the cottage and the studio in her own unique and colorful style.

She wore a pair of her painting overalls and was already covered with streaks of paint from pouring all of her emotions into the old canvas she'd pulled out of the back of the closet in her studio. She'd started the painting when she and

Trent had first started dating, and then she'd gotten so caught up in their relationship that she'd set it aside. She'd tried to find her muse after moving back to the island, but while it came easily for other paintings, this one hadn't spoken to her. It had remained unfinished for all this time, a raw mess of emotions shoved into the back of her closet.

But when she'd come into her studio this afternoon, she'd been immediately drawn to the painting. And now it was finally coming together, bursting with passion and color.

Reese rarely picked favorites among her work because each piece was so different that it was nearly impossible to choose. But the painting she was currently working on spoke to her far louder than all the rest. She felt as if it were rooted so deeply in her heart that she could finish it with her eyes closed.

She held the paintbrush in one hand and took a step back to study it. Lipstick red rounded out two chins, contoured with wide strokes of black, which faded into pink and fluorescent-green bows of two mouths. Aqua blue, pink, and more black streaked over contours of misshapen cheeks and over the ridge of two equally misshapen noses. Four eyes gazed out at her, a mix of blues and greens and peppered with amber. Two bodies twisted like tornado funnels, swirling together, drawing strength and sharing heartache as they created energy that soared up toward the sky in bright starbursts and jagged lines.

To a stranger it might look like two faces had been put into a bottle, shaken up, and splattered onto a canvas, with two bodies that had also been stretched and twisted and bound together, then coiled beneath the whirlwind of emotions on the faces. But to Reese the images weren't tangled at all. They were as real and as raw as the explosive emotions inside of her. And just as Jocelyn had said, the more she painted, the better she felt.

"Reese?"

She spun around, shocked to find Trent standing just inside the door to her studio. All of her emotions had risen to the surface over the course of the afternoon, and now she felt as if her skin were on fire as he stepped forward, giving her an easy yet sensual smile that made her insides melt.

"I didn't mean to startle you. I knocked, but you were lost in your work." His eyes slid over her like a caress before he asked, "Can I see what you're working on?"

"It's not finished," she said, but she stepped aside to let him look at the canvas.

He stared at the painting for a long time without saying a word, and her heart leaped to her throat, knowing that he'd see her emotions all over the painting. By the way he was assessing it, and glancing back at her with darkening eyes, she knew she was right.

She stepped in front of the painting, feeling raw and exposed as she said, "There's a lot I still need to do to it."

"I think it's perfect." His voice was deep and soothing, as if he understood just how vulnerable she was feeling. "I missed watching you paint, Reese. I always thought it was so incredible to watch you get completely swept up in your work."

Just the way she was getting swept up in him right now. Twice today he'd surprised her with unexpected visits. This morning she'd kissed him. And now? Well, she wasn't good enough at lying to herself to think they were going to get by with just a kiss this afternoon.

"Tell me about this one."

He was pointing at a painting that reminded her of a storm coming in through the clouds. Carefully stepping over her tarp, which was splattered with paint, she moved around open paint cans and set her paintbrush with the other drenched brushes, before she replied.

"It's called *Struggle*."

It was such an angst-filled word, but she could find no better way to describe the deep purple, yellow, orange, greens, and every shade of blue she could create that streaked violently across the canvas. There was no landscape, no houses in the distance, just the raging, disjointed storm, coming together from all angles. Only when the driving clouds collided did the colors soften, finally giving way to graceful flourishes as they edged off the canvas.

"I should have guessed," he said softly as he turned to face her. He used to be able to guess the names for her paintings, as if he could see right into her heart just by looking at them. "You were incredibly talented when we first met, Reese, and you're even more so now. I was so pleased when I started finding your artwork in New York galleries."

"You saw my work in New York?" It truly hadn't occurred to her that he might have seen her paintings during his years living in the city. He'd worked so many hours when they were together that she couldn't imagine him taking off time to visit a gallery.

"I had a business meeting with the owner of one of the galleries, and once I saw your work there, I went looking for more."

"Why?"

He reached for her hand. "Because your art is a piece of you, Reese. I bought every piece I could get my hands on, until I had no place else to keep them."

"You bought them?"

"I told you that I never stopped loving you,

and I meant it. After you left, your paintings were the only way I could be close to you."

He gathered her into his arms, but even though that was exactly where she wanted to be, she pulled back, saying, "I'm covered in paint."

But he pulled her in close again. "It's *your* paint, Reese. And I love knowing something of yours is now a part of something that's mine."

That was something the old Trent would have said, but New York Trent would have been worried about his clothing and one of his colleagues seeing a stain on his fancy suit. She took pleasure in the marked difference.

"I'm so happy you made it, Reese. Despite what happened between us, your dreams of showing your work in galleries came true."

"It almost didn't happen," she admitted.

He slid his warm hands up her arms and asked, "Why not?"

"Oh, Trent." She tried to take a step away, but he held her gently. "It's so hard to talk about that time of our lives."

"Reese, we made mistakes, but I know we can learn from them so that we don't make the same ones a second time. Please talk to me."

Could they really learn from their mistakes? Because she sure felt like she was falling right back into his arms just as quickly as before, and she was just as powerless to resist.

"I went by your gallery again," he said softly when she didn't respond. "You named it after us, didn't you?"

"It's been called Dandelion since I opened the doors. You just now noticed?"

"Even thinking about you hurt, so I did everything I could to bury my head in the sand. We spent a lot of time avoiding each other, remember?"

"All too well," she admitted.

Because she'd done exactly the same thing—buried her head deep in the sand so that she wouldn't have to look around and see signs of Trent everywhere on the island. The first place they'd kissed. The first place they'd made love. The first place they'd said *I love you.* But now, as she gazed into his loving eyes, she was struck by the sincerity in them. Struck, too, by the realization that it was time to finally lift her head all the way out of the sand and face the man standing before her.

"You're right. We've gone way too long without talking about what happened."

All of the chairs in her studio were covered with supplies, so they sat on the floor among the paint fumes and wet brushes. Trent immediately tugged her in close, pulling her legs over his lap, the way he always used to. Despite the difficult conversation they were about to have—or maybe because of it—she needed the closeness. And she could tell that he did, too.

But even as she wiggled in closer while her heart went crazy—and the look in his eyes told her that he wanted her just as much as she wanted him just then—she knew they really did need to talk. Because sex without love had never been her thing. Not ten years ago. And not now.

"Trent..." There was so much she needed to say to him that all the words got tangled up inside her head. "I don't know where to start," she admitted in a soft voice.

"I think maybe I do," he said, his words gentle, soothing her the same way his hand stroking over her back worked to calm her jumping nerves. "Yesterday you asked me why I waited ten years to come back for you. Today I think I may have finally figured out the reason. At least part of it."

"Tell me, Trent. I need so badly to understand."

"I never really loved New York City. Not the way everyone thought I did." She was stunned by his confession, but she made herself stay quiet to let him continue speaking. "As the eldest Rockwell, I felt so much pressure to succeed, and I was afraid to let my family, and myself, down by coming back to the island. I knew my father didn't want me to end up working under Chandler's thumb the way he had his whole life. So even though New York never really fit—especially not without you—I stayed because I felt like I had something to prove to everyone." He shook his head. "And now I wish I had come back years ago. Come back to you and the life we should have had here together."

Reese was struck dumb as she tried to fit what he'd said into the reality she'd believed for ten years. She'd thought he craved the busy, corporate environment and the challenge of getting to the top of the industry ladder. But could she have been as blind to his true emotions as he'd been to hers back then?

"But after I left you that note," she said slowly, "when you did come back to talk with me that final time, you told me you had to work those crazy round-the-clock hours to gain footing. And I knew there was no point in trying to argue with you, not when you had such laser focus on success."

"I was twenty-six, Reese. Full of invincibility and driven to succeed, and too blinded by the belief that I needed to make sure the Rockwell name meant as much in New York as it did here on the island that I refused to consider any other options." He ran a hand through his hair in obvious frustration. "Ten years later I now know that while other lawyers were living and breathing the business, I wasn't working round-the-clock because I loved the law above all else. I was simply trying to prove to everyone that I was worthy of the Rockwell name. Worthy of my position in our family. I was trying to show Chandler that I didn't need his name to succeed. And I wanted my father to feel that guiding us to leave the island and get out from under his father's thumb was a good thing."

"It *was* a good thing. You are so well respected in your field, Trent. Regardless of your reasons for working so hard, I won't let you try to tell me otherwise. And I definitely don't want to take that away from you."

"You're beautiful when you're adamant."

"Stop... Your touch is kryptonite to my mental abilities. It's so easy for me to forget everything we went through and end up in your arms again, but..." She stopped and looked into his eyes. "I want to make sure being together is more than just physical. That it's emotional, too. And honest. As honest as we can possibly be with each other."

Which was why she suddenly knew she needed to be completely honest, and finally admit the truth to him about why she'd fallen apart in New York. "Ten years ago, New York City terrified me. Right from the start, I was all but paralyzed by the noise and the chaos and the traffic."

"Sweetheart." He brushed a lock of hair back from her face, his touch as tender and loving as it had ever been. "Why didn't you tell me how you were feeling?"

"You were so busy at work, and you were so supportive of my painting. I didn't want you to know how weak I was. Didn't want you to think I couldn't handle our new life." She nibbled on her lower lip, feeling terribly vulnerable again.

"You were nineteen, and you'd lived on the island your whole life, where practically everyone knows one another. Being overwhelmed doesn't make you weak. Hell, I was overwhelmed by New York and all the pressure that came along with the competitive law firms."

"You were?" She wondered if he was saying that to lessen her own insecurities. "You never told me."

"What kind of a husband would I have been if I'd laid my worries on you? At least that's what I thought back then, when I was young and stupid. So damn stupid not to have seen what you were going through, too."

"If I hadn't hidden my true feelings from you..." She inhaled a shaky breath, wondering if they would have been able to save their marriage if they had been honest and open with each other back then.

"You're not hiding them now," he said. "And neither am I. I'd say that's a good first step for a future together, wouldn't you?"

"It is," she agreed, but she knew they weren't quite done revisiting the past yet. "The day before I left New York, I got sick of feeling so overwhelmed, not just by the city, but by the thought of talking with gallery owners, too. So I bit the bullet and went to an important gallery I'd just read about, intent on seeking out the owner."

"You obviously made a great impression on him or her."

"I wish I could say that I did. But it was all accidental. When I got there, there were so many ritzy, important-looking people, that I chickened out. I didn't talk to anyone, barely had the guts to leave my card at the front desk. By the time I ran out of there, I *knew* I didn't belong in New York. I got lucky that the receptionist was trying to make a name for herself in the art world and liked the painting I put on my card enough to reach out."

"You keep telling me how scared you were, but you made it happen anyway, Reese. And I'm proud of you. So damn proud."

His continued—and boundless—faith in her touched her so deeply that her next words spilled from her lips, coming straight from her heart. "I'm sorry I left the very next day. I'm sorry I left you with nothing but that note when I should have been brave enough to say goodbye face-to-face. It must have been horrible to come home and find my letter."

Trent pulled her in closer and slid his hand to the nape of her neck before saying, "Do you know that feeling when you're watching a horror movie and your skin feels like it's on fire, and you're holding your breath, waiting for the ax to fall?"

She nodded.

"I felt like the person that ax falls onto."

"I'm sorry," she whispered. "I'm so tremendously sorry. All these years, I had somehow convinced myself that you came home and found the note, then sort of shrugged it off and buried yourself in more work."

"Shrugged it off? Did I make you feel like you meant that little to me?" Hearing that made him feel like his heart was being hollowed out.

"I don't know that I *thought* that, but I always wondered what you felt when you found the note. Thank you for being so honest with me."

"I will always be honest with you. Even if the truth is hard for both of us to hear. Which is why I need to know, what did it feel like to write the note?"

"It felt like I was holding the ax and I was

beneath it at the same time. I remember shaking like a leaf. I think I wrote it five times before finally deciding I was really leaving."

He tugged her in close again. "I'm sorry I put you—us—in that situation, Reese. I adore you, and I'll never do it again."

"And I'm so sorry that I couldn't figure out how to make our marriage work," she said softly.

He didn't argue with her, but simply said, "I forgive you, Reese." He took her hand in his before asking, "Do you think you can forgive me?"

"Yes."

And with that one word, it was as if a huge weight had been lifted from her shoulders. She gazed into his eyes, feeling infinitely better than she had in years. "Do you know how many times I imagined having this talk with you?"

"I know I've imagined it at least a million times." He turned her palm over in his hand and stroked over it with his fingertips, making thrill bumps rise all across her skin. "Maybe we needed that time apart to grow and mature and to really figure out what we wanted in a relationship and in our careers and our lives."

She nodded, thinking that maybe he was right about that. "Lately I've been wondering if I put too much pressure on us to fit into the perfect marriage mold—home by six, dinner on the table. I realize now that's not how things work for everyone."

"Sort of like the way you keep trying to get us to slow down now?"

"Slow has never been our forte, has it?" she admitted, before adding, "Unfortunately, I'm not sure we're very good at marriage either."

"Maybe we weren't very good at marriage because we weren't ready for it." She appreciated that he hadn't pulled away at her painful statement, but gathered her closer, instead. "People grow, and they change. I've changed, Reese, and I'll do whatever it takes to prove to you that I know how to love you the way you deserve to be loved."

Her pulse quickened and she was filled with hope. She pressed a finger over his lips. "I don't want any more promises tonight. And even though I know I'm going to need us to slow down again in the morning, right now I don't want to have to worry about putting on the brakes. Tonight I just want to let the wind carry us both, wherever we need to go."

He sealed his lips over hers, and when he rolled her onto her back, right onto the palette of paint, she didn't care about getting paint on either of their clothes...Nor was she going to worry about taking it slow when, in the wake of their totally honest talk, fast felt exactly right.

"God, you feel good, Reese. Like I've finally

found the missing piece of me."

Paint smeared all over them as they kissed, desperate for more. She tugged at his shirt, fumbling to undo the buttons, but when paint made it slippery, she couldn't wait and gripped both sides of his collar to tear it open, sending the buttons flying across the room.

He lifted her up and unhooked her overalls, then pulled her shirt over her head. They tumbled into the paint again as they kissed and groped and slid around in it. She wiggled out of her overalls while Trent stripped bare. When he came down over her again, all of his glorious muscles were perched above her.

And then he lowered his mouth to hers and kissed her dizzy. Her head and body were both reeling as he kissed his way down her body, slowing to kiss the swell of her breasts, teasing each taut peak until she was on the verge of release. She pushed at his shoulders, needing his mouth on her, wanting him to love her in all the ways he always had.

His hands traveled over her ribs, down the curve of her waist to her hips. The strength of his hands and the softness of his lips made her ache for more. He spread his big hands over her thighs, and finally—*God, finally*—brought his mouth to her center. His hot mouth, the scrape of his teeth, made her body shudder, her veins fill with heat. Her sighs felt heavy, growing shorter, harsher, more desirous with every slick of his tongue. Anticipation mounted, until she felt as if she might burst.

"Trent—" She rocked her hips, frantically twisting the tarp below them.

Somewhere in the distance she registered the sound of a paint can tumbling over, but she was too focused on chasing the orgasm that was just out of reach to process it. When he slid his fingers over her inner thighs, around her sex, but didn't touch her where she needed it, she nearly lost her mind until she looked down and realized his hands were covered in paint.

Seconds later, when he brought his mouth to her again, she lost all control. Her hips bucked against his mouth, and he held her down, keeping her at the peak of the most intense orgasm she'd ever experienced.

She grasped at the tarp, panting as her fingers slid in the paint. "Please, Trent. Take me *now*."

He moved up her body, lacing their paint-soaked fingers and pinning them beside her head as he pushed into her, filling her completely. His lips crashed over hers in a mind-numbing kiss, obliterating any chance she had at rational thought. But a moment later he slowed his efforts, torturously so.

"Faster," she pleaded against his lips.

"Yes"—he kissed her deeply—"we were

always good at *fast*."

He released her hands, and she grasped at his back and shoulders, feeling the tight pull of his muscles slide beneath the slick paint on her hands as he clutched her hips and buried himself deeper, time and time again. He angled her hips the way they both loved, bringing them as close together as two people could possibly get.

And when he gazed deeply into her eyes and said, "I truly love you," she tucked his words away to revel in later, as he took her up, up, up, and then they both fell blissfully over the edge.

Chapter Eighteen

TRENT HADN'T COME to Reese's studio to make love to her until his heart felt so full that he thought it might explode. And after they'd washed the colorful paint from their skin and made love again beneath the warm spray, he thought for sure she'd rethink things and tell him that they *were* moving too fast.

He readied himself for the blow as he pulled on his slacks. Now that they'd become even closer and he'd just loved her body and soul, she'd fully reclaimed the part of his heart that he'd locked away for so many years. The part that had never stopped loving her. Not for one single second. Reese stepped gracefully into a clean pair of panties and grabbed a T-shirt from a drawer, the sweet curves of her hips disappearing beneath the hem that dipped over her thighs. When she turned to face him, he realized she was wearing his favorite old T-shirt, which she must have taken with her when she'd left New York.

His heart had already grown impossibly fuller by the time she reached for his hand and surprised him by saying, "Stay with me."

God, there was nothing he wanted more. But he didn't want to push her too fast and end up losing her again, so he made himself ask, "You're sure?" If she said she only wanted him to stay a few minutes and then she'd need her space, he'd take it. A few minutes, a few seconds. Any amount of time with Reese was more than he thought she'd ever give him again.

But instead of saying any of that, she gave him the sweetest smile he'd ever seen as she led him to her bed, then climbed beneath the covers, motioning for him to join her. When he kicked his pants back off and crawled in beside her, she snuggled against him in what was once her favorite sleeping spot and draped her arm over his chest.

He wrapped her in his arms, full of intense gratitude.

"I thought I needed to slow us down," she said as she rested her chin on his chest and turned a soft, loving gaze toward him. "But I don't think that's what I really want."

"Tell me what you *do* want." And he would move heaven and earth to give it to her.

She ran her fingertips down over his bare chest like she used to when she wanted him to stay put and talk to her. She needn't worry. He wasn't going anywhere.

"I don't think we're capable of slowing down our need for each other, and I can live with that." She dropped her eyes for a beat, then met his gaze again. "I love that part of us, Trent. I love it so much I probably should seek treatment to stop from always wanting you. Trent-Lovers Anonymous," she teased.

"That would be Trent-*Lover* Anonymous, and if it's up to me, I'd rather you stay as far away from that treatment as possible." He kissed her forehead, and she smiled, but then her eyes turned serious.

"We know how to love each other. We just need to figure out the rest of *us*. Step by step. Piece by piece. I know that fast, crazy love is who we are, but I also know that we need to work on the things we aren't so good at. Because if we just up and move back in with each other the way I'm so tempted to do..." She paused and shook her head. "I'm afraid if we don't lay a good foundation this time everything could just blow up again the way it once did."

"Agreed." He scanned the room. "Do you

have a pad of paper and a pen?"

"What? Why?"

"So we can make a list and—"

She laughed and rolled her eyes at the same time. "I know that's how you figure things out, but you and I are not one of your legal proceedings. We're people, with hearts and souls, needs and wants. We can't build a strong foundation for our relationship with a neat and tidy list. Of course I know you'll make lists in your head during your morning runs, and I'll figure some of it out through my art. But *us*? We need to communicate with words and actions and feelings."

He propped himself up on his elbow so they were facing each other. "Okay."

"Okay." She blew out a relieved sigh, but then she frowned.

"What's wrong?" Was he already screwing this up?

"I was just wondering, do you think we should take a break from sex until we figure everything else out?"

"There's nothing I want more than for this to work again, for *us* to be together again, forever this time. But our physical connection has always been an important part of our love. If you want to go without, I will, but..." He ran his hand up her thigh and pressed his hips to hers. "It'll be torture."

"*Of course* I don't want to do that!" She bit her lip, and he was hard-pressed not to kiss the now-damp flesh. "I just want to be able to think straight."

He kissed her before saying, "Okay. Think straight."

She playfully pushed him away and he laughed. "You're impossible, and I love it, but..." She managed a serious tone. "I want you to know that I'm going to work on telling you how I feel right when I feel it, instead of bottling it up for so long that it eats me up inside."

"And I want you to know that I'm not going to put work—or anything else—ahead of you."

"What else do you need from me?" she asked him.

"You're perfect just the way you are."

"That's sweet and romantic, but I want *real*. We're good in bed together. We know that. You make my heart and my mind spin like crazy. But we obviously stink at communicating outside the bedroom. I could have supported your career better. I could have attended more of the social functions with you in New York City instead of begging off because of my own discomfort. I could have met you for lunch and taken the scary subway. And I *will* do that this time. Well, there's no subway here, but if we return to the city..."

He couldn't resist kissing her again. She

was really giving them another chance, and he felt like he was the luckiest man on the planet.

"I missed you on those evenings. But I wanted you to be happy, and I knew you were never happy at those functions." He remembered sitting with his colleagues over dinner, each with their wife or significant other, while he was alone. He'd known then things weren't ideal, but he'd been so wrapped up in getting through each day and proving himself that he'd never slowed down enough to figure out what to do about it. And then it was too late.

"I wish you would have told me then that you missed me, that you needed me there no matter what. If you had, maybe I would have pushed myself harder. I don't know for sure what might have happened had things been different. All I know is that we've got a second chance at a future. And I want us to give it everything we have this time, without letting all of our fears and pride catch us in their grip."

Trent felt like all of his dreams just might come true after all. At least, if he didn't completely screw things up again. Which meant he needed to have the courage to actually communicate with her by asking, "Are you sure you want this? Are you sure you want me? I am one hundred percent *in* this relationship, but if any part of you isn't, I need you to tell me."

"See?" She was beaming at him as if he'd just said the most wonderful thing in the world. "We're already communicating so much better. We're bridging the gap that we thought our physical love would fill ten years ago." She pressed her lips to his, then said, "Yes, I want this. Yes, I want *you.* I have never stopped loving you. I'm just scared that as things come up, I'll clam up and you won't notice. Or that I'll stop supporting your work and you'll forget that our relationship needs attention." She reached for his hand and threaded her fingers through his. "It's hard for me to admit this to you, but I'm scared, Trent. Scared to open myself up to you again and end up even more hurt than before."

"I know, sweetheart." He pulled her in close. "I'm scared, too."

"You're never scared."

"That's not true. I just never used to let anyone know I was scared. But I've never been more afraid of anything than I am of losing the only woman I've ever loved for a *second* time. I'm scared that coming back to the island sends the wrong message to my grandfather or that I've somehow let down my father. I'm scared that even after all these changes, and the ones I'm going to make in the future, I'll still mess things up with us. I've had ten years to try to figure out what makes my life complete, and what I know for sure is that you're the only person, the only thing in this crazy world that makes me feel whole. And the only thing that can truly make me happy is loving you the way you deserve to be loved, every second of every day for the rest of my life."

"Oh, Trent..."

He lowered his lips to hers with a tender kiss, one she returned just as sweetly, before asking, "When do you think we should tell our families that we're trying to make things work again?"

"Actually, I'm going to have breakfast with my parents tomorrow morning, because I don't want them to hear about us from someone else before they hear it from me. If everything does end up working out between us, I'll want you to come with me. But for now I think I should talk to them myself first."

He tried not to clench up at the way she'd said, *If everything does end up working out between us.* She'd been nothing but honest about needing to build a new foundation beneath them, step by step, one piece at a time. And she was right...even if all he wanted was to get down on one knee right this very second and ask her to be his again forever.

Still, he wanted her to know, "If you end up deciding you'd like me to be there, my day is pretty open. Just call or text, and I'll swing by to say hello to them."

"You have no plans? No resort business to make yourself crazy over? No legal work to bury yourself in?" Disbelief was evident in her tone. "Even I've got tons to take care of between the mural and my gallery."

"Tomorrow's Sunday, and since I've been back on the island, I usually meet up with whatever family members are free to have lunch. I've also been going over to Shelley's café to help out with getting it ready for her grand opening in two weeks. I'd like to tell my family we're dating again, if it's okay with you."

Thankfully, she didn't pause before saying, "Of course it's okay with me. And if you need me," she added with a smile, "just let me know."

"I always need you, Reese," he told her as he curled his body around hers the way he always used to. *"Always."*

Chapter Nineteen

REESE FELT TRENT'S arms tighten around her waist the following morning and smiled. It felt so right to share a bed with Trent again, and their talk last night had done wonders for her nerves. She even felt a little guilty having so much on her plate today when Trent's day was wide open. Wasn't that a shocking change?

She rolled over in his arms, and he kissed her forehead. "Good morning, beautiful. Are you freaking out, or are we okay this morning?"

His hair was tousled from going to bed with it wet from their shower, and he had a light peppering of scruff along his jaw, but it wasn't just his looks that continually tugged at her heart. It was all of him, and the fact that the first thing he wondered about was her state of mind made her even happier.

"I'm so happy you stayed." But she also knew she needed to be completely honest and admit, "And I'm also freaking out a little."

"Only a little?"

She gave him a small smile. "Okay, I might be freaking out a lot, actually. But I'm starting to realize that doesn't mean I have to run from what I'm feeling. It just means there's a lot on the line with us...and I don't want anything to go wrong."

"It won't, Reese. Because we *are* going to build that great foundation that we need this time."

He sounded so confident, but after their talk last night, she now knew that freaking out didn't necessarily just go one way. She hadn't been the only one scared in New York City; Trent had been scared, too. Not only had she never told him how terrified she was, but she had never thought to ask him if he felt the same way.

"What about you?" she asked him now. "Any second thoughts?"

"Only that I love waking up with you...and that I love you even more this morning than I did last night." He slipped his warm hands onto her waist beneath the hem of her T-shirt. "What time are you meeting your parents?"

"I don't need to leave until eight, so we have a little time." She eased her body over his.

"Maybe if we make love now we won't tear each other's clothes off in some inappropriate place later."

"Inappropriate? Your studio is hardly inappropriate."

"The car?" she reminded him, then silenced him with a kiss as she straddled his hips.

She could still hardly believe that Trent was here with her. Not just in her bed, but back in her life again. Every moment with him was so exciting, and at the same time, there was a lazy sensuality to every kiss, every caress, every whisper of need as they loved each other with the morning sun washing over them.

She gasped with pleasure as he sat up, then wrapped her legs around his waist to bring them even closer together. She buried her face in the crook of his neck and he groaned out her name as they moved together. Two lovers rediscovering the joys of waking up in each other's arms and greeting the day with the sweetest pleasure imaginable.

Sweeter than anything else she'd ever known...

* * *

AN HOUR AND a half later, nerves sizzled in Reese's stomach as she walked through her parents' front door. It had been more than a little nerve-racking to honestly communicate with Trent, but their talk last night and this morning had started to lift at least part of the heavy weight she'd been carrying on her shoulders. Now it was time to be just as up-front with her parents, too.

The house smelled like coffee, sausage, and eggs. It was a comforting, familiar smell that, with the exception of when she'd lived in New York, she'd enjoyed every Sunday of her life.

"Mom? Dad?" She followed the delicious aroma into the kitchen, where she found her mother working on a crossword puzzle.

"Hi." She kissed her cheek.

"Hi, sweetie. Let me get you some coffee." Her mother pushed to her feet.

"I've got it, Mom. Where's Dad?" she asked as she filled her mother's mug and her own.

"He was just called into the volunteer fire department for a last-second drill. They got the fire simulation machine in for the morning and wanted to run the whole crew through it again. You know how much he loves working with the fire crew, but he's really sorry to miss having breakfast with you." Her mother took the cup of coffee from Reese, then said, "Sarah called, and she sent a few new pictures of baby Oliver." Her mother reached for her tablet and swiped through the photos to show Reese, and she was glad for the extra few minutes to gather her thoughts.

"He's just gorgeous, isn't he?"

Reese looked at the pictures of her darling little nephew, her heart tugging as she remembered the sweet baby smell of his skin and how lovely it had been to hold him in her arms. "He's gotten so much bigger since I came back," she said, in awe of his gorgeously pudgy little cheeks.

She'd returned from her sister Sarah's house last week filled with resolve to finally move forward with her life. Reese was twenty-nine years old, and after spending a few weeks caring for little Oliver, she felt the tug of motherhood in the wings.

She wanted the children she hoped to have one day to enjoy the same loving family life that she always had. And now that Trent had moved back to the island, and after all the strides they'd started to make with each other, she suddenly wondered if they might have another shot at forever after all.

Which brought her right back to the news she needed to share with her mother.

She put the tablet on the table. "Mom? I have something I'd like to talk to you about."

When her mother immediately focused her full attention on Reese, just the way she always had when Reese needed to talk, the words she'd been planning to say tangled up on her tongue.

"I... Um..." This was harder than she'd imagined. Because for all that she felt so happy and hopeful whenever she was with Trent, as soon as she left his arms, her worries kept wanting to come flooding back.

"What is it, honey?" her mother asked. "You look a little flushed."

That would be the butterflies in my stomach. Telling her mother about Trent made it *real.* Maybe she should wait until they had proven to each other that they could make it work this time. But she didn't like the idea of hiding anything from her parents. Not when they'd always supported her no matter what and trusted her to make good decisions. She needed to show them the same trust. Besides, hiding her feelings hadn't worked with Trent all those years ago, had it? Clearly, it was a habit she needed to break.

"Trent and I are...well, we're sort of dating again." When her mother didn't respond right away and Reese couldn't quite read her expression, she asked, "Do you think I'm crazy for seeing him again?"

"I've always liked Trent, and there was no doubt about how much he adored you." Her mother pressed her lips together, as if she were weighing the rest of her answer. "But the important thing, Reese, is how *you* feel. When you came back from visiting Sarah, you were ready to move on and think about starting a family and finding a man who would be your forever love. Is Trent your forever love?"

"Once upon a time, I was certain he was. And then when everything fell apart, I tried to convince myself he wasn't. But now?" She shook her head. "Is it crazy if I hope he *does* end up being my forever love?"

"If you ask me, crazy would be letting love slip through your fingers a second time." Her mother put her hand over Reese's. "You never stopped loving him, did you?"

"*Never*," Reese whispered. "I feel so much for him that at times it's hard to remember why we broke up. But I'm scared. I don't want to get hurt again. And I don't want to hurt him."

"Of course you're scared, and he probably is, too. Honestly, I'd be surprised if you both weren't. Risking everything for love is always brave. But risking everything for love a second time? If you ask me, that's the bravest thing of all."

"Thank you, Mom." She put her arms around her mom and hugged her close. "For always understanding. For not ever judging. And for listening and being here whenever I've needed you. Even though Trent and I are still trying to work things out and nothing is totally certain yet about our future, I didn't want you and Dad to find out that we were dating again from someone else first. Especially since I can't seem to be able to stop myself from kissing him, even if we're in public."

"I feel just the same way about your father," her mother said, "even after all these years. But while lust is easy, lasting love—the kind that carries you through illness and hard times and pulls you through to the other side even stronger than you were before—*that* takes work."

Reese could hardly believe her conservative mother had used the word *lust*.

"Now, honey. Don't look at me like I just dropped the F-bomb. I'm a woman. I know all about lust."

"I'm not sure I want to talk about this with you." Reese was only half teasing. "I like thinking about you as my proper mother who doesn't think about *that*."

"Well, that would make me rather boring, wouldn't it?" Her mother smiled.

"Not that I don't appreciate you being willing to share your thoughts on...*that*...but there is something else I wanted to ask you about. You and Dad have a perfect marriage. You're always together, and he's always put our family ahead of work and everything else in his life. How did you get to that point?"

"We do have a rather ideal marriage, but it's still a give-and-take. Trust me, we've had our moments. It wasn't always easy for your father to put us first. He missed out on a few promotions, but family was always important to him. To both of us." She paused before admitting, "I might have enjoyed a little more zest and spontaneity. A few unscheduled dinners and impromptu date nights. Marriages should have a little wiggle room, not be so structured. Enjoy the moments as they come."

"Wiggle room," Reese repeated, chewing on the thought.

"For my generation, dinner on the table and reading the newspaper together was what we were brought up with. But your generation is different. More lively. Dinners out are more commonplace. So is getting together with friends, going on outings and changing your destination midway. Those are all wonderful things. I can count on one hand the number of times we've done that. We've lived our lives on trolley car tracks and it's mostly been wonderful. But for you? I think you should allow wiggle room. And not just on the day-to-day things. Because no matter how much you want to get things perfect this second time around, you're probably not always going to get things exactly right. A little wiggle room to make mistakes and then fix them would probably help take the pressure off of both of you."

"Thank you, Mom. For everything."

As Reese left and headed for the resort where she was planning to work on the mural for a few hours today, she found herself continuing to think about what her mother had said. Everything Reese and Trent had done together as a couple was spontaneous—except when it came to their marriage. Had she expected too much, too regimented of a life together, with set expectations of when he'd arrive home from work and how their life would play out? And wasn't her mother right that now she was so scared of things going wrong again that she was expecting perfection out of both her and Trent?

Wiggle room. Definitely something worth considering.

Chapter Twenty

TRENT SAT AT a table at the Hideaway with Derek, who had just spent the last ten minutes griping about trying to run his masonry and building business in Boston from the island. When his brother pushed his sleeves up, Trent noticed a bandage by his elbow.

"What did you do this time?" Derek was an adrenaline junkie. The bigger the risk, the more gratifying the thrill. Cuts and bruises came with the territory.

"I had a run-in with a rock when I was hang gliding. But it was nothing. Only seven stitches."

"Did you have Didi stitch it up?" Trent cocked a brow. "She's a hell of a lot better with a needle than the doctor at the local clinic," Derek replied, before saying, "So...you and Reese? You're a thing again?"

Trent had been planning to tell his brother—and the rest of his family—today. But he had a guess who had already planted the seed in his brother's head.

"I take it Sierra mentioned our conversation?" The one where he'd told his sister he wanted Reese back more than he wanted anything else in the entire world.

"Who else?"

Trent laughed, knowing that the only reason his sister had talked to Derek about Trent and Reese was because she was full of hope that the two of them could make things work the second time around. In fact, Sierra was fairly *bursting* with that hope.

She'd so loved having Reese as a sister-in-law. Clearly, she was ready for them to be sisters again. One day, when his sister finally fell in love, he sure hoped it went smoother for her than it had for him or Quinn. And the guy she fell for better treat her like a princess, or Trent and his brothers would tear the guy apart with their bare hands.

"Yes, we're a couple again." And if he didn't screw anything up this time around, he prayed things would stay that way. He'd been thinking about Reese all day, and the hours couldn't pass quickly enough until he'd see her again at dinner and find out how her talk with her parents had gone. She'd sent him a text message with no words, just a heart. He'd texted back, but he hadn't heard from her again, so he knew she had to be immersed in painting.

"I'm really happy for you, Trent. You two were always good together. Plus," he added with a grin, "it's better you heading to the altar than me."

"The altar?"

"Sierra and Shelley are so excited about you and Reese that they're practically planning your wedding."

Sierra and Shelley aren't the only ones, Trent thought, even though he knew he shouldn't be letting himself race ahead that fast. Reese was right—they needed to work on building a really strong foundation first.

"Right now," he admitted to his brother, "we're just taking it one day at a time and trying to get things right this time around. But if I have it my way, we'll definitely be moving in the wedding bells direction."

Derek shook his head. "What is it with you and Quinn? Is being married really that great?"

It could have been. If only I hadn't blown it.

But Trent simply eyed Derek's bandage. A few weeks ago he'd gotten a cut on his shoulder and he'd had Didi stitch it up for him, and before that it was his forearm, which Didi had also stitched up. Now Trent couldn't resist saying, "I'm sure Didi is as good with a needle as you say she is. But is that the real reason you're constantly knocking on her door?"

Derek scoffed. "I told you before, I don't have a death wish. Which means Didi's off-limits."

Trent's phone rang. He pulled it from his pocket, hoping it was Reese, and was both disappointed and annoyed when his grandfather's number appeared on his screen.

"Speak of the devil." He mouthed *Chandler* to Derek, then answered the phone. "Hello."

"Hello, Trent. I'm sorry to bother you on the weekend, but your grandfather has asked that you meet him in his office as soon as possible." Chandler's secretary, Darla, sounded very apologetic.

Respect for his elders was so ingrained in Trent that he felt pressure to accept his grandfather's summons, regardless of the fact that he and his brother weren't done with lunch yet. "Okay. I'm over at Sierra's restaurant. I'll be there in ten minutes."

"Chandler beckons..." Trent pushed away from the table.

"So what? He's out of the business, Trent. It's in our hands now. He doesn't own you. You don't have to jump up and run over there."

"No, but he is our grandfather," Trent reminded him.

"I'm pretty sure that means more to you

than it does to him."

Trent didn't want to get into an argument with his brother, so he ignored that comment as he threw a handful of bills on the table. "Will I see you at Shelley's later to finish up those shelves?"

Derek looked out the window at the blue sky. "It's a good day to go windsurfing. But I'll head over afterward."

"Try not to get any more injuries," Trent teased as he headed for the door. "Or maybe you should, since at least then you'd have an excuse to go see Didi again." He hightailed it out of there before Derek could throw his beer mug at him.

At least there was one bright spot to being pulled away from lunch and called to the resort—the brightest, most beautiful woman in the world, who was looking cute as hell with colorful streaks of paint on her arms and clothing as she worked on the mural.

Trent always loved watching Reese paint and seeing just how intimate a process it was for her. Last night when he'd come into her studio, she'd been assessing her work, deep in thought. But now, as her lean arms dragged the paintbrush over the wall with long, smooth arcs over her head, then faster, shorter strokes, before transitioning into longer, slower strokes again, it was as if she wasn't even thinking. She called it being in *the zone*. Which was exactly how he felt whenever they were together. Like nothing else existed in the world but her...and every move was meant to be.

Trent admired her for a few minutes, debating going inside without interrupting her, but he couldn't stay away.

He walked down the sidewalk toward her, but Reese must have been concentrating too deeply to notice. She didn't turn to greet him, or give any indication that she sensed him near. That didn't surprise him, but what *did* surprise him was that it stung a little—and that made him realize what she must have felt like while they were in New York, when he could barely see past his work.

He took a step closer, afraid to startle her for fear of ruining her beautiful painting. "Hi, gorgeous," he said softly.

She glanced over her shoulder—her paintbrush still moving—and smiled. "Hi! I didn't expect to see you this afternoon."

"Chandler asked me to drop by his office." He leaned forward and kissed her. "I don't want to interrupt. I just wanted to give you another kiss, and also to find out how your parents reacted when you told them we're together again." He brushed a lock of hair away from her face. "I hope it went okay."

"It went great. My dad wasn't able to be

there, but my mom had some really interesting stuff to say. Some of it ended up being about lust, which was..." She made a face, and he laughed. "But she also had so many amazing insights about making love last."

"I'd love to hear what she had to say." Her parents had a great marriage, just like his did. It was too bad neither he nor Reese had asked their parents for advice the first time around. Perhaps that was part of what came with being older and wiser. And having less pride...

"I'm still processing it all, but one thing she said that really resonated was how we shouldn't put pressure on each other to be totally perfect or to live on a rigid schedule. That there has to be room to make changes and adapt to each other's moods and desires and to allow for mistakes and then recover from them. The past few hours, I've been thinking about how right she is. Real life might not always be perfect, but that doesn't mean it can't be *amazing*."

The last thing he wanted was to screw things up with her again, but had part of his problem been that he set the bar so high for himself that true happiness always felt just out of reach? "Everything your mom said sounds right on the money. It makes me think we should have talked more with our parents before, asked for their advice."

"At least we're asking them to share their wisdom now." She went onto her tippy-toes and gave him a kiss. "I'm so glad you stopped by."

"I am, too. I didn't want to throw you off your groove, though."

"It's exactly the opposite, Trent. Every moment with you is helping me get *into* my groove. I'm knee-deep in the mural and *loving* every second of it. I really need to thank your family for giving me this project."

"You'll have a chance at Shelley's grand opening, if you'll come with me."

"Do you think they'll be ready to see you and me together again?"

"Sierra and Shelley sure are," he told her with a grin, though he left off the *wedding bells* part for now. "And Derek told me at lunch that he's really happy for us and thought we were always great together. But the question isn't whether they're ready."

She trapped her lower lip in her teeth and nodded. "I know it isn't about them. It's about us. I'm scared," she said softly, "but I don't want to hide what I feel. Not from our families, not from myself, and especially not from you."

"We both have our eyes open this time around, and I made you a promise that I'm never going to break." He kissed her again, lingering at her lips long enough that people walking past them couldn't help but stop and stare. *And wish they had a love like ours.* "I should get upstairs before Chandler calls again. Are we still on for dinner?"

"Yes," she said, dipping the brush into the can again. "Meet me at my place?"

"Six?"

"Perfect."

* * *

AS TRENT WALKED inside the resort, he worked to prepare himself for the transition from bright and sunny Reese to his dark and stormy grandfather. He exited the elevators on his grandfather's floor, cleared his throat, and pulled his shoulders back, slipping into professional mode. As a lawyer, he'd had to do this mental shift at least a thousand times. But it was a much harder transition after seeing Reese, with thoughts of her smile fresh on his mind...and her kiss still tingling on his lips.

Chandler's assistant, Darla, was relatively new, having been hired after she'd moved to the island from North Carolina following a nasty divorce. She was in her late twenties, with a two-year-old son, and from what Trent had heard, she was living with her aunt and uncle, having lost both of her parents a few years earlier.

She looked slightly uneasy as he approached. "Sorry about this, Trent. I know you try to take the weekends off, but he didn't want to wait until Monday."

"No problem, Darla." But as the words left his lips, he realized that it actually *was* a problem. What if he'd been with Reese when the phone call had come? Would he have raced off to meet Chandler? Heck, he should be out there with her right now, keeping her company while she painted, enjoying watching her work on something she was so passionate about.

"Trent." Chandler's deep voice greeted him. "Have a seat." Wearing a white shirt and striped tie, with his frail shoulders pulled up high beneath his ears, Chandler was dressed as he was every day of the week.

Trent wondered if there was ever a time of day when he let his guard down, and it made him sad to think that his grandfather was always this uptight, or miserable.

"Good afternoon, Grandfather." He smiled at Didi as he sat down, wondering how she managed to stay sane, keeping up with Chandler's gruff demeanor without ever looking tired or disgruntled, especially when her workweek wasn't just Monday through Friday. Chandler was clearly more than a full-time proposition. Only someone as strong as Didi could put up with him.

"It's nice to see you, Didi," he said to her. But as Trent sat before his grandfather on Sunday afternoon, he wondered again what the hell *he* was doing there. Just because he'd agreed to take over running the resort with his brothers and father didn't mean he'd agreed to give his grandfather his entire life.

"Is the paperwork for the deed transfer complete?" Chandler's eyes never wavered from Trent's. His tone was cold, businesslike.

Wouldn't it be nice, just once, to hear his grandfather ask how he was doing or how he liked running the resort? But that wasn't Chandler's style. Chandler was all business all the time, and it made for tiresome conversations.

"I'm waiting on finalization of one document. I'll make an appointment with the notary and bring it up for signature Tuesday morning before filing it with the county."

Chandler nodded. "Very well," he said in a dismissive tone.

"Is that all you needed?" Trent couldn't keep the disbelief from his voice at his grandfather's gall, calling him in to the resort on a weekend for one question that could have easily been handled over the phone.

When Chandler nodded, Trent nearly opened his mouth to say that they could have accomplished that in a phone call or e-mail rather than a face-to-face meeting. But he'd always gone out of his way to be cool-headed and even-tempered with his grandfather, so instead of laying into him, he turned and headed for the door.

"Is it true that you and that Nicholson girl are seeing each other again?"

Chandler's question stopped Trent in his tracks. He clenched his jaw and reminded himself that Chandler wasn't specifically being rude to Reese. He was rude in general.

"Her name is Reese, and yes, we are seeing each other again."

But Trent was no longer interested in fighting the urge to lay into his grandfather. Work was one thing, but he was *way the hell* off base if he was going to insult the woman Trent loved.

But before Trent could say another word, Chandler grumbled, "'Bout damn time," leaving Trent too stunned to reply at all before Didi wheeled his grandfather away.

* * *

BY THE TIME the sun began its slow descent from the sky, casting a grayish hue over the resort, the right side of the mural was beginning to take shape. Deep brown mulch edged a grassy knoll surrounding billowing gardens, which gave way to the aged walls and peaked roof of a bay-side cottage. Reese stood on a ladder painting an umbrella of leaves in shades of green and yellow in the rear of the garden. A few more hours and the trees would be done. She'd been so consumed with the mural that every stroke of the brush felt like it was coming straight from her heart as she poured her love of the island, and in turn, her love for Trent, into her work.

She painted the yellow flowers at the base of the mural, remembering the afternoon of her wedding when Trent had picked the same flower for her. They'd dreamed of one day having a cottage of their own and a gaggle of children who would play in the yard and skip along the beach. She dipped her brush in the paint and moved to deeper shades of green, remembering how Trent had planned to teach their children to sail and play ball, and she had planned to carry on her mother's Sunday-morning breakfast tradition. She'd wanted to teach their children to appreciate art while Trent instilled a joy of reading. But they hadn't stayed together long enough to have a cottage or a family.

Her heart squeezed as she stepped from the ladder and rounded out a flower bed, adding touches of the sun's glare to the leaves. She could practically feel Trent with her now, sharing her memories as she crouched at the base of the mural.

"Reese...this is incredible."

She turned at the sound of Trent's voice, thinking it was in her head, and started at the sight of him. Would she ever get used to how handsome he was or the way hearing his voice made her spirits soar? He'd changed clothes since she'd seen him earlier, and in a pair of linen pants and a white cotton shirt, he had the carefree appeal of the island-loving guy she'd fallen in love with. Tucked in his right arm was a bag from the Hideaway. His smile widened as he looked over the mural.

"I was a little worried that it was too much, with all the different colors and textures. It's not too overwhelming?"

He stepped closer and kissed her. "No. It's passionate and beautiful, and it looks so real we'll have to keep people from walking into the wall thinking it's a garden."

"You're sweet." Both his compliments and his lips.

"I'm honest." He kissed her again, lingering a little longer this time. "I brought dinner. I thought we could have a picnic on the beach."

"A picnic on the beach sounds wonderful, but I'm still totally in the zone right now." She waved to her paints, spread along the ground at her feet. "I just need a little more time to work tonight."

"Of course. Whatever you need. I'll leave this here in case you get hungry, and I'll head over to Shelley's to get a jump on the work I need to do." Trent left the bag on the grass and kissed her before heading for the parking lot.

She immediately turned back to the mural, adding a few extra touches to the flower bed. Even taking that sixty-second break gave her a fresh perspective when she assessed the mural and she suddenly saw a dozen things she wanted to add and a half-dozen other small changes she wanted to make.

She'd just launched into the next phase of the mural, when a breeze swept over the hill from the bay and made her shiver. At last she noticed the darkening of the sky as daylight fell away and evening crept in.

That was when it suddenly hit her: *What did I do?*

She scrambled along the ground, packing up her supplies and tossing her wet paintbrushes into an empty paint can. She'd clean them after she apologized. Trent had made an effort to be romantic and spend time with her, and she'd chosen to stay and work?

How could she have been so stupid and so rude? Especially after complaining about him brushing her off for work all those years ago.

She tried not to speed up the road toward

the old mill, but the idea of hurting Trent the way she'd been hurt burned like acid in her belly.

Five minutes later, Reese threw the car into park and raced up the hill toward Shelley's Café. She pushed through the bushes, stumbling as she ran across the front lawn and burst through the front door.

"Trent!"

He dropped his tools, his brows furrowed as he opened his arms, and she ran into them.

"What's wrong?"

"I'm sorry! I should have stopped painting. I didn't mean to blow you off."

"Reese, what are you talking about? You found your groove. I completely understand."

She pulled back enough to search his eyes and knew he really *did* understand. "You don't think I was a jerk? Because I think it was pretty jerky not to gush over an impromptu picnic dinner with the man I love."

"Of course you weren't a jer—" He paused. "Wait. Say that again."

"I think I was a—"

He pulled her in closer. "No. The last part."

Reese thought back to what she'd said. She hadn't realized that she'd said *the man I love* aloud, but she could see in Trent's eyes that he loved hearing it. Was it too fast? Was she too trusting?

But when she gazed into Trent's eyes, she knew she'd spoken the truth.

"I love you, Trent." It felt freeing—and scary—not just to admit it to herself, but to say it aloud.

"I love you, too, Dandelion. So much." He kissed her softly.

"But—"

He pressed his finger to her lips. "I know we have a ways to go before we're back on solid footing. I know we have lots more steps to take together. But tonight, just knowing we still love each other...it means everything to me, Reese."

Reese twined her arms around his neck. "You're so unfair. Everything you say makes me fall a little harder."

"I don't see the problem." He kissed the tip of her nose. "But I know how important communication is in our relationship, so let me answer your earlier question. You weren't being a jerk. But if you ever are, I won't hesitate to tell you. And I want you to tell me, too." He lifted her into his arms and guided her legs around his waist. "But not in a note. Face-to-face communication from here on out."

She brushed her lips over his. "Face-to-face. Always. And thank you for giving me wiggle room to screw up and then get it right again." Even if Trent didn't feel like she'd messed up as badly as she thought she had, she felt a lot better knowing she'd taken responsibility for the way she'd slighted his offer—and even more secure in their relationship, knowing that they could talk things through. In owning the bad and the good, they were building an even stronger foundation.

"Wiggle room. I like the sound of that...especially the wiggle part," he said before sealing his lips over hers.

It felt so good, so right, to be in his arms again. She melted against him as he deepened the kiss, and she gathered the back of his shirt in her hands, pulling it up so she could feel his skin. A moan escaped his lungs as he cupped her rear.

"Shelley might—" she managed before kissing him again.

"—walk in," Trent agreed, taking her in another toe-curling kiss.

"Good thing my gallery is right across the street, isn't it?"

She laughed with surprise as he lifted her up into his arms. "I can walk."

He silenced her protests with a kiss. And the truth was that it was incredibly romantic to be carried out beneath the stars...and then over the threshold of her gallery.

"Trent," she said softly once they were inside. "This reminds me of..."

Her heart got caught in her throat, and she

couldn't finish. But she could see from looking into his eyes that he was remembering the same thing. "You're even more beautiful now than you were on our wedding night."

"So are you."

For a long moment, they simply held on to each other as memories slowly transformed into a love that was new and fresh and wonderful.

And then she smiled at him and said, "I have a couch in the back room."

His answering grin was so full of sensuality that it made her heart pound with renewed heat. He moved quickly through her gallery, and the next thing she knew, she was naked and lying beneath him, his fingers threaded through hers, his wonderfully heavy body pressing hers into the leather cushions.

"I love you," she said again.

There wasn't just intense heat in his eyes as he moved into her, but there was emotion, too. So much emotion that she felt his love in every thrust of his body into hers. In every brush of his lips over her skin. In the tightening of his fingers over hers.

And, most of all, in the beating of his heart against hers as they found pleasure unlike any other in each other's arms.

Chapter Twenty-One

BY NOON THE next day, Trent still couldn't stop wishing he was back in Reese's bed, holding her in his arms. Last night, they'd made love in her gallery and then gone back to the mural to pick up and clean her painting supplies, she'd invited him back to her house again. They'd tumbled into bed as hungry for each other as ever, and when they'd woken up this morning, Reese was so inspired to paint that after seducing him yet *again*, she'd leapt out of bed and taken off to chase her muse.

He slid the vase of heliotrope he'd picked for Reese while he was out running closer on his desk and inhaled the scent of the flowers, anxious to give the pretty purple blooms to her. Heliotrope symbolized eternal love, and when he and Reese were first dating, they used to

243

pick them at their favorite overlook and make promises to each other. Silly promises, like *I promise never to shrink your favorite shirts*, or, *I promise to make sure you never run out of azul-blue paint.*

All he'd wanted was to be with Reese again. But what he hadn't realized was that it would be a hundred times better the second time around, simply because they were finally starting to communicate. If only Trent had realized that they weren't communicating ten years ago. Now he saw it all so clearly, and it made him want that clarity in all aspects of their relationship, which included talking with Reese's parents as soon as possible. They needed to know that he not only had never stopped loving their daughter, but also that he was going to keep loving Reese every second of every day for the rest of his life.

He picked up the paperwork for the deed transfer and headed up to Chandler's office for their meeting, thinking about how he was feeling more and more like the man he wanted to be. A man he and Reese could both be proud of.

Chandler's thin lips curved into a smile as Trent entered his office. He smiled so rarely that Trent was taken by surprise.

The smile tugged at a memory he'd long ago forgotten, from back when Chandler still lived in the home he and Caroline, Trent's grandmother, had shared. Chandler had been watching Trent and Caroline playing a board game beneath an umbrella at a table on the deck. And as his grandfather gazed at his grandmother, his eyes had warmed, and he'd smiled in the same way he was now. Trent couldn't have been older than eight or nine, but he still remembered being struck by that undeniable look of love on his grandfather's face.

As he stood across the desk from Chandler now, he found himself wondering how thick—or thin—the sheet of ice his grandfather wore like armor really was.

"Trent, did you bring me the paperwork?"

"Yes, as well as the extra copies you asked for." Trent handed him the documents and smiled at his grandfather's nurse. "How are you today, Didi?"

"I'm well, thank you." Her long blond hair cascaded over her shoulders. She wore a tan dress that stopped just above her knees and was belted around her slim waist. She looked regal standing beside Chandler as she put a hand on his shoulder. She did that often—checking in with his grandfather without saying a word—and Trent noticed that his grandfather's eyes momentarily softened as he looked up at her before returning to the documents and narrowing once again.

"Your message said not to bring the notary to your office. Is there an issue you'd like to discuss?" Trent asked.

"No. No issue. I'll see to it that the proper documentation is filed." Chandler set the paperwork on the desk and met Trent's gaze. "Thank you for putting this documentation together, Trent. I appreciate your efforts."

Trent was knocked off-balance for the second time in five minutes. Chandler hadn't thanked Trent once since he and his siblings had taken over the resort. In fact, in two months' time, he'd received nothing more than snarls and commands from his grandfather.

"You're welcome," Trent finally managed as Chandler gripped the arms of his wheelchair and shifted his attention back down to the paperwork on his desk.

When Chandler slipped right back into his tight-lipped persona and didn't lift his eyes again as Trent took a step toward the door, he wondered if he'd imagined the entire exchange. For a brief moment, he could have sworn they'd really connected.

Damn it, he thought as he stopped and turned back to face his grandfather, they were going to connect this afternoon whether Chandler wanted to or not. He'd told Reese that he wanted his family to know they were back together—and suddenly, the person he most needed to know was his grandfather.

"I'd like to thank you, too, Grandfather."

"For what?" His grandfather looked as surprised as Trent knew he'd looked just seconds ago, when Chandler had thanked him.

"I may not have ever moved back to the island if it weren't for you. Thank you for opening that door. You managed to help me see what was really important," Trent continued, "and to get my priorities straight. I should have never let Reese go. I should have fought for her with everything I had. I wish I'd been able to see it sooner, but thankfully, it's not too late, because she and I are together again now. And I'm going to get it right this time, no matter what it takes."

As he bent to hug his grandfather, Trent noticed Didi's eyes were damp. And then, for the first time in as many years as he could remember, Chandler's frail arms encircled him in an answering hug.

"I'm proud of you, Trent," Chandler said.

Trent froze, blinking his damp eyes.

"Go on," Chandler grumbled a moment later, though the glassy sheen of his own eyes gave him away. "I have work to do."

As Trent left Chandler's office, he gave silent thanks that it had turned out his grandfather didn't have a heart of stone after all. It truly gave Trent more hope than anything else ever would.

Still reeling, Trent stopped by his office to pick up the flowers for Reese. A few minutes later, he found her working on the mural. She was talking with a woman and a little dark-haired boy who couldn't have been older than three or four, with big blue eyes and a mop of dark hair. The little boy tried to touch the wet paint, and Reese crouched beside him and smiled.

"I'm sorry, sweetie. We can't touch the wet paint, but you can touch this part." She touched the part of the mural that had already dried.

The cute little boy pressed his fingers to the dry paint.

Reese handed him a clean, dry paintbrush. "Would you like to paint?"

He grinned and nodded enthusiastically, sending his dark bangs flopping on his forehead. Reese guided him to a blank part of the wall, where he enthusiastically began painting. She glanced up at Trent, and when their eyes held for a moment, he couldn't keep his brain from running away with him, already imagining the kids they'd have together. A little girl and boy who had her big smile, amazing talent, and deeply loving heart.

When the woman and child walked away a few minutes later, Reese suddenly noticed the vase of flowers he was holding. She immediately pressed her nose to the pretty purple petals and inhaled. "Mm. I love that smell, like vanilla and almonds mixed with cherry pie."

He smiled at her description of the scent. He never would have come up with that combination himself, but she was exactly right.

"Where did you find heliotrope?" she asked as she breathed them in again.

"Right there." He pointed to the right side of the mural, and down in the corner she'd painted a patch of heliotrope; the purple was bright and beautiful against the backdrop of pink and yellow flowers and long blades of bright green grass.

The overlook had always been their special place—where they'd first met and where they'd made so many promises to each other.

Promises that he hoped would last forever.

* * *

REESE COULDN'T BELIEVE Trent had thought to pick the very flowers they'd used like wishing stars. Then again, before they'd moved to New York, he'd been so romantic and thoughtful that she shouldn't have been surprised. He took one of the flowers and tucked the stem behind her ear. "There's my island girl."

"I promise never to give up a chance for a picnic with you again."

"And I promise never to put my career ahead of you."

Her eyes were soft with emotion as she said, "I promise to always hang my wet towels up."

Loving the way she could go from serious to playful, he chimed in with, "And I promise to always put the cap on the toothpaste tube."

They leaned in to kiss again, but before her lips touched his, a female voice said, "Get a room, lovebirds."

They both turned at the sound of Sierra's voice. His sister was smiling, obviously pleased to have found Reese and Trent kissing.

"Trent brought me flowers. Aren't they pretty?" Reese didn't know why she was nervous. She loved Sierra like a sister. Trent slid a hand to her lower back, and the gentle touch helped ease her nerves. "I was just thanking him."

"It's okay, Reese. You can kiss my brother *all you want*," Sierra assured her. "I'm so glad you're dating again. I hated when you two were broken up. It wasn't fun being between a lifelong friend and my brother."

Reese was riding her own roller coaster of emotions, thinking back to the few guys she'd dated over the years and how she'd told Sierra and their other friends that she'd never felt connected to any of them. She remembered just how careful Sierra had always been not to bring up Trent, even when he was in town visiting. She had protected Reese as much as she'd protected her brother, and for that Reese would always be thankful. She wouldn't have wanted to hear about Trent's private life while they were apart.

Trent turned an apologetic gaze to his sister. "Sierra, I never realized how awkward that might have been. I'm sorry."

"We got through it," Sierra assured him. "But don't do it again."

Got through it.

Suddenly, Reese realized that's exactly what she'd been doing. *Getting through it.* Oh, how she'd missed waking up with a smile beside the man she loved and feeling her stomach flutter every single time she saw him. She'd been nervous about asking him back to her house again last night, but honestly, even if their future wasn't yet completely certain, how could she regret the chance to spend an entire night in his arms?

"I'm sorry, too, Sierra." Reese slipped her arm around Trent's waist, glad that they weren't communicating better just with each other, but with their families, as well. "The divorce was both our faults. I really appreciate that you stood by me and didn't end our friendship when Trent and I split up."

Sierra made a face. "Like that was ever an option. You and the girls got me through all those times when my brothers were hovering around me like guards. I love you and our friendship." She hugged Reese, then hugged Trent, too. "And I love you and your bat-shit-crazy protective nature." She grinned at both of them. "But I love you both even more now that you're giving each other a second chance."

Trent set the flowers down beside Reese's supplies, then said, "I've got to go take care of something right now. Can I see you later?"

The strictly rational part of Reese's brain was telling her to put the brakes on their super-speed romance, but every other part of her wanted him with her again tonight...and tomorrow morning, too. Especially when warmth flooded her as she remembered how wonderful it was falling asleep with him spooning her and then waking up in his arms again.

"If you'd like to come over to my house again tonight," she ended up saying, "that'd be great."

He pulled her into his arms and whispered, "I'd love to."

Reese watched him walk toward the

parking lot with a goofy smile on her face. Only when Sierra said, "It really is great to see you two together again," did she realize Trent's sister was still standing there.

"Oh, sorry," Reese said with an apologetic smile. "I kind of got distracted for a second."

"No apologies necessary," Sierra said with a wave of her hand. "And the mural is gorgeous, by the way. It's full of so much heart, and you're really capturing the beauty of the island. Of course, for island girls like us, that would probably be hard not to do, right?"

"It sure would," Reese agreed.

She'd been doing a lot of thinking about what her mother had told her. If Trent needed to go to the city to take care of his practice, could she handle it this time? She'd traveled to the city a few times over the years to meet with gallery owners, and she'd learned to not only manage her fears, but to actually enjoy the noise and the chaos. It wasn't where she'd want to settle full-time, but the nonstop excitement of the city might be a nice contrast from the slow-paced island life every now and then.

Maybe it wasn't just their marriage that had needed more wiggle room, but Reese needing to give *herself* permission to be herself, even if that woman wasn't always the same exact person from day to day. Sometimes she would want peace and quiet. Sometimes she would want noisy excitement.

And she was starting to see that, most of all, she wanted Trent.

"My mom and I are getting the final head count together for Shelley's grand opening," Sierra said. "You're coming, aren't you?"

"I wouldn't miss it for the world. And, Sierra, I want to thank you and your family for awarding me this project. It's been such a thrill."

Sierra pressed her lips together, like she was trying to keep from saying something, then blurted out, "Were you nervous when you found out Trent was managing the project?"

"Nervous doesn't even being to touch the emotions I experienced," Reese admitted. "But I'm so glad he was. We've been given a second chance, and even though I don't know for sure what will happen in the long run, I do know we're both trying a lot harder this time to make it work."

"Well, that's a heck of a lot better than what you've both been doing for the past ten years," Sierra said in her no-nonsense way. "And I know it's probably scary for you to think about the long run a second time around, but *I* have one hundred percent faith that you two can make it work. Because if you could see the way you two look at each other..." She sighed. "Now if we could only find a wonderful man for me before my brothers find him first and scare him away. Maybe you should keep Trent too busy with all those kisses for him to hover over me like a protective warrior chief."

Reese laughed and said, "Consider it done."

Because there was nothing she'd rather do than keep Trent busy with sweet and sexy island kisses...

Chapter Twenty-Two

"I'M STILL IN love with your daughter."

Reese's parents, Judith and David, were sitting close together on the couch beneath a big picture window that overlooked their backyard. As soon as they'd sat down, they'd reached for each other's hands at the same time, and Trent appreciated seeing Reese's parents comfort each other and present a united front. They were incredible role models for a marriage done right. If only he'd learned more from them ten years ago.

He remembered how easily they'd welcomed him into their lives when he and Reese had first met. Her parents had been as warm and loving as his own family had been toward Reese. Sitting here with them now, all these years later, in the house that still smelled as if the walls themselves were freshly baked from sugar and spice, he hoped they'd see that his intentions toward Reese were spoken from his heart.

As Trent waited for them to respond, he realized he'd never been so nervous in all his life. He knew how important Reese's parents were to her, and the truth was that their approval meant a great deal not just to Reese, but to Trent, too.

"We've actually been expecting something like this for a very long time, Trent," David finally said.

Behind his wire frames, his brown eyes were full of concern, but thankfully, he wasn't automatically shutting Trent down. Instead, he was kind enough to say, "Judith and I would like to hear what you have to say."

Trent had always liked and respected David. He was a smart, stable man who put family first, a loving, supportive father to Reese, and was well liked by everyone around town.

"I know ten years is a long time, and I wish I'd been able to see things clearly far earlier than this." Trent shook his head. "No, what I really wish is that I'd never hurt Reese in the first place. That I'd done everything right instead of doing it all wrong. But I swear to you, I'm going to get it right this time. Coming back together with Reese isn't a whirlwind decision for me, even though I'm sure it appears that way. For ten years I debated coming back to the island, but I wasn't ready. But I do know that Reese belongs here. She's the most loving, passionate woman and you two, this island, her friends, her gallery… Without all those things in her life, she's not whole. And I truly believe that I'm part of what makes her whole, too. Just the way I know she's the other half of me."

Trent hadn't fully planned what he was going to say, but as it turned out, he didn't need to. When it came to his love for Reese, there was no holding back.

Of course, that didn't mean her parents were going to suddenly embrace him with open arms just because he wanted them to. David pushed his glasses up the bridge of his nose, taking much longer to answer than Trent was comfortable with, before finally saying, "Trent, you're a good man. Well respected, a hard worker, and you come from a great family."

"Thank you." Trent waited anxiously for the *but*.

"Everyone is allowed to make mistakes, but where my little girl is concerned, one mistake is enough. I know you probably both made mistakes in your first marriage, and that's your business. But I'm still her father, and it doesn't matter how old or independent she is, I'll always worry about her. It took her years to get over her broken heart, so if you're going to pursue her again, you'd better be damned good and ready to be the man you promised to be."

* * *

REESE DECIDED TO quickly stop by her parents' house to thank her mother for her advice and to see if she could finally talk with her father, as well. She was surprised to see Trent's car parked out front. As she stepped through the kitchen door and heard him talking, she swallowed the greeting she'd been ready to call out.

"Reese is a caring, talented, intelligent woman with a big heart and a strong will." Every word Trent spoke was filled with love. "I promise you that I will treat her as the love of my life, because that's who she is."

Ohmygod. Reese held her breath. Her pulse quickened with the realization that Trent was speaking with her parents about *them.* Was this the *something* he'd said he needed to go take care of?

"I know I didn't do a good job of being the husband she needed me to be before, and I know how upset both of you were when we divorced. It is something I'll regret for the rest of my life. All I want to do now is spend the rest of my life loving, protecting, and cherishing her.

If she'll have me. Which I know is still a big *if.* I will respect her needs and I'll pay attention to all the unspoken things I missed the first time." He paused, and Reese fought to hold back tears.

"Trent," her mother said, "of course we were upset when you divorced. You two were so young before, and you were both changing your lives dramatically. We can also see that you truly are in love with Reese, even after ten years apart. But we'd be lying to you if we said it's easy for us to see her taking this leap again when there are no guarantees that things between the two of you will work out better this time."

Tears were slipping down Reese's cheeks as her father began to speak again.

"We trust Reese," her father finally continued. "And despite the mistakes you've made, we feel that you're a good man." A relieved breath whooshed out of Reese, and she had to sink back against the wall as she heard her father tell Trent, "But you're not kids anymore. Reese is ready for a real life, a real family, with a man who will be there for her when she needs him. Whether there's office work to be done or not. We trust you, Trent, and we trust our daughter," her father continued. His words brought fresh tears to Reese's eyes. "If Reese does end up feeling that you're the love of her life, we won't stand in the way of you two being together again. But if you do anything to hurt her again—"

"I won't, David. And I can assure you that my love for Reese will always drive me to be the man she deserves. But I know it's not words that will prove that to you. I need to make up for all the wrong I did before with my actions and behavior and to give Reese the wonderful life she deserves. The life together that we both deserve."

* * *

BUTTERFLIES HAD BEEN nesting in Reese's stomach ever since she'd snuck back out of her parents' house, and not just from hearing Trent say all those wonderful, loving things. Her parents had been so careful not to influence her with their opinions about her divorce. Even when she was living with them right after she'd left New York, when the smallest memories would make her cry, her mother would hold her and say things like, *Don't worry, honey. This will all work out.* Her mother had given her comfort and support without condemnation, and never once said a bad word about Trent or blamed her for their failed marriage.

Now, however, she finally knew exactly how they felt. Their caution where she was concerned didn't surprise her. After all, she herself was trying to be as cautious as she could be, given the gravitational pull between her and Trent. But what, she was dying to know, did Trent think about his discussion with her parents? The two of them were now in her kitchen cooking dinner. She loved her cozy home, and she loved it so much more with Trent in it. The eat-in kitchen wasn't very big, so they were working side by side at the L-shaped counter in front of a large picture window overlooking Reese's gardens. She glanced at the vase of heliotrope on the sill, feeling a little giddy at what it represented. Trent was slicing carrots and cucumbers, and every few minutes he'd lean in for a kiss. When she'd first seen the home, she'd remembered how she and Trent had dreamed of having a home overlooking the bay. Something small, like this one.

Reese watched Trent as he opened the oven and pulled out the warm buns, placing them in a basket, a smile on his lips and a sexy look in his eyes. God, she loved him. Right down to her toes. It was a scary love because it was so big—bigger than ever—and they'd failed once already. But she had a feeling that this time it was worth fighting for—no matter how long it might take for her to be sure.

As she watched him move through her

kitchen, she realized that she'd been trying to make their breakup black-and-white. To find concrete answers and put blame into perfect little niches. But love didn't work that way, and it wasn't fair to even try to manage that. Had he worked too much ten years ago? Sure. But wasn't that what young, ambitious attorneys did? And hadn't it been unfair of her not to give the city all she had and figure out a way to get over her discomfort and try harder to make a life in New York? Every way she turned it in her mind, she kept circling back to how lack of communication had magnified those issues— quickly turning the fissures between her and Trent into valleys that neither one of them knew how to cross.

Trent hadn't yet mentioned seeing her parents, but she hoped he would bring it up soon, because she didn't want there to be any walls between them, or any secrets anymore. That was when it suddenly hit her—didn't that have to go both ways? Which meant that she shouldn't be keeping from him that she'd overheard their conversation.

He set the basket on the table and wrapped his arms around her waist from behind. "How did your painting go today?"

She closed her eyes as she inhaled. How could his scent make her body crave him so desperately time and time again? "It was great.

I got much more done than I'd thought I would."

"Mm. That's good." He nibbled on her neck, making her whole body warm. "Almost as good as you taste."

Reese set the knife down and turned in his arms. It would be so easy to just let their evening take a purely sensual path. But falling into bed with each other rather than talking hadn't worked the first time around, had it?

So instead of giving in to the urge to simply thread her hands into his dark hair and kiss him, she said, "I went by my parents' house tonight to thank my mom for giving me so much to think about. But you got there before me...and I overheard your conversation with them."

"I was just about to tell you about our talk, but it looks like you beat me to it," he teased.

Her heart warmed, knowing that he'd planned to share it with her. "Everything you said to them tonight, Trent, it meant so much to me. And I know it meant a ton to my parents, too, even if they weren't exactly giving you their blessing quite yet."

"Your parents have always been so good to me. And they're right to be cautious. No parent should have to watch their child be in pain. I'm just glad they didn't kick me out on my ass and tell me to keep away from you or else. I'm luckier than I deserve."

"Only a truly brave man would go face the parents of his ex-wife to let them know he was sorry for hurting her and that he wants a second chance. You deserve every ounce of luck...and you deserve this, too."

Standing on tiptoe, she touched her lips to his, and as he tightened his hold around her waist, she could feel his heart beating against hers. She traced the bow of his lower lip with her tongue, and she loved the sigh that escaped his lips with the slow tease.

He'd always known just how to turn her on, like he was born with that knowledge, and she loved the chance to rehone her own seduction skills. When she felt the smile on his lips as he kissed her, and in the growing roughness of his touch, as if he couldn't hold back, it sent her desires soaring. She slid her hands beneath his shirt and up his back, feeling his muscles go tight.

"I love when you kiss me. When you touch me," he said against her mouth.

She pressed her lips to his neck and dragged her tongue just above the collar of his shirt. "I love the way you taste."

She slid down his body, lifting his shirt so she could press soft kisses to his stomach. Oh, how she loved the feel of his firm stomach, the heat of his skin against her mouth. She pressed his hips back against the counter and worked the button and zipper on his jeans, then slid her hand inside them, stroking him through his cotton briefs. His head tipped back with a hiss as she hooked her fingers into the waistband of his jeans and pulled everything down to his ankles, freeing his erection.

"Reese," he whispered as he tangled his hands in her hair, his voice thick with desire.

She slid her hands along his hips as she placed soft openmouthed kisses along his inner thighs. Feeling the heat of his skin on her lips and the flexing of his muscles beneath her tongue made her heat up all over. Teasing Trent had always been a thrill—when she could control herself enough to slow down, that is.

She slid her hands up to his hips and slicked her tongue along his hard length. He sucked in air between gritted teeth. She loved seeing, hearing, and feeling her effect on him. She wrapped her fingers around his shaft and swirled her tongue over the tip, teasing and taunting and earning another needy groan from Trent. When she couldn't resist him another second, she took him in her mouth, stroking him with her hand as her tongue worked its magic.

"Reese, I've got to have you," he pleaded, lifting her to him and stripping off her shirt.

He sealed his lips over hers as they both

kicked off their jeans.

"We never" —she kissed him again—"make it to the bedroom."

"That's" —he kissed her harder—"our love."

He swept one arm over the table and sent everything sailing across the room as he slowed just enough to gently lower her onto the table. He claimed her with a breathtakingly soft kiss as he pressed in deep, filling her with sharp pleasures that radiated through her core and exploded in her chest. His strength was overwhelming from the waist down as he drove into her, but his hands were gentle and loving, gliding over her breasts, sending more waves of pleasure through her entire body. His mouth— *his hot, glorious mouth*—caressed and promised, discovered and demanded, making her dizzy with need. And then his lips were on her breasts and his tongue was circling her sensitive, taut peaks as he kept up the strong thrusts.

Shivers ran down her spine as her climax built, and when he moved one hand between them and raked his teeth over a nipple, the orgasm tore through her. Her hips bucked off the table as she cried out, "Trent, oh God—"

He captured the rest of her words in his mouth, kissing her savagely and sending more currents of pleasure pulsing through her.

Gazing into her eyes, he said, "I love you so much, Reese. I can't get close enough to you. I want to become a part of you. Forever."

Reese wrapped her arms around his neck and pulled him to her, reveling in the magnitude of his *forever* and the feel of his hot, strong body against hers. *You always have been,* she thought as her heart danced to a frantic beat.

And the way Trent gazed at her just then— as if he had read her mind—made her feel even crazier, and she pawed and groped him, kissing and nibbling at his skin. He knew exactly how to touch her in all the places that made her crave more as their hips came together time and time again.

He buried his face against her neck, and the warmth of his breath coalesced with the scintillating sensations of his scruff against her tender skin, his hands, and the way he filled her so completely. She slammed her eyes closed as another climax gripped her and clawed at his back as his entire body flexed tight and they both tumbled over the edge together.

* * *

TRENT WANTED TO stay right there wrapped around Reese forever, but since the table wasn't the most comfortable place in the world for either of them to lie on, he gathered her in his arms.

"Let me run you a bath."

"For two?" she asked as he carried her toward the bedroom.

"For two," he confirmed with a smile that promised far more than just a simple bath together.

She glanced down at their flushed chests and laughed as she said, "We're always *naked*."

"I think that has something to do with being in love."

"Or being unable to keep our hands off of each other." She laughed again. "But I'll take the first option, too."

They were heading through the bedroom toward the bathroom when he noticed a package wrapped with a blue ribbon on the center of the bed. He stopped and asked, "Were you expecting a gift from someone...in your bedroom?"

She shook her head, then motioned for him to put her on the bed and pulled him down beside her. Her hair was tousled from making love, her skin was still flushed, her neck and cheeks were pink from his whiskers, and she was gloriously naked. The fact that she didn't try to cover up her body told him she was opening up to him and starting to really trust him, as well. The nervous edge she'd been harboring also seemed to have dissipated, and his heart soared.

"After I came back to the island," she said softly as she picked up the package and the note beside it, "I couldn't help but do some of the things we used to do, like go to flea markets and look for your favorite things." She lifted one shoulder and dropped her eyes, looking adorably shy as she said, "I think it was my way of still being close to you, and over the years I picked up a few things for you."

She handed him the note. "I thought about sending these to you more than once but then I worried that you already had them or whether you'd even want something like this from me." She gave his hand a little squeeze and added, "I'm glad I didn't. It's so much better to be able to give this to you in person." She gave him her own wicked little grin as she added, "Especially while we're naked."

Trent read the note. *Dear Trent, look at me.*

Confused, he lifted his eyes to Reese, who was grinning. "We said no more 'Dear Trent' notes. Only face-to-face communication." She leaned closer and kissed him, before saying, "Dear Trent, I never stopped thinking about you. You were with me at every flea market, every craft show, and every walk on the beach over the past"—she lowered her voice to a whisper—"ten years. I've missed us. Love,

Reese."

Trent folded her in his arms, soaking in the love behind every word of the most beautiful note in the world. And as the words settled into place inside his mind—and his heart—he realized this new face-to-face note was finally replacing the memories of the one she'd given him the day she'd left New York ten years ago.

He tipped her chin up with his fingers and pressed a kiss to her lips. "Thank you, Reese. I love you, too." He couldn't have asked for anything more.

"Don't you want to open your gift?" She handed him the gift, which he seemed to have forgotten about.

"I can't imagine what could mean more to me than the note you've just given me."

She was like a kid on Christmas day; her eyes lit up with anticipation. "Open it and see!"

He untied the ribbon, and the wrapping fell away, revealing a stack of books. He stared down at the hardcover copy of *Treasure Island* by Robert Louis Stevenson, and his throat thickened.

"It's a *real* first edition," she told him as she opened the book to the title page and pointed to the publication date. "See? 1883. And the copyright page was left blank. I even looked for the errors on pages two and seven you told me about." She flipped through the pages again.

"'Dead Man's Chest' isn't capitalized."

"I can't believe you found this, sweetheart. I've looked everywhere for it but could never find it." Everywhere but a Rockwell Island flea market. "This must have cost thousands of dollars. You shouldn't have done this."

"Don't worry. I bartered for it with my art the summer after we separated."

The summer *after* they'd separated? A sharp pang speared his chest. How could he have been such a fool to wait so long to return to the island—and to Reese?

"I can't believe you bartered your work for me, after everything we went through." He pulled her in close again and buried his face in her hair. "What did I ever do to deserve you?"

"You loved me."

And then, with that beautiful answer making his heart feel as if it might have grown too big for his chest, she bounced on the mattress, buzzing with excitement as she pressed her hand to the next book on the pile. "There are more!"

She handed him a first edition of the *The Call of the Wild* and a copy of *Where the Wild Things Are*. "I remember when you took me to the tree house that you and your brothers and sister built, and you said that you hoped one day to bring your kids there and read them these stories. You said you loved the outdoors and that the island was the perfect place for kids to live out their dreams of living in the wilderness and becoming king or queen of it all."

He smiled with the memory. "My brothers and I used to spend nights in that tree house." Their mother had found the giant tree that grew almost parallel to the ground, with branches reaching out like a giant hand, and she and their father had given them all the tools, and the guidance, they'd needed in order to build what would become the Rockwell children's Inspiration Point.

"You said that you and Derek used to take off at night to be 'one with nature' and that Quinn and Ethan thought you guys were nuts for venturing out in the middle of the night."

"That was so long ago. I'm surprised you remembered, and so glad that you did."

"How could I forget? You were so passionate about it."

"I was. It's strange. In my twenties, I thought the only way to have a great life was to move off the island. I was so sure of it, when really, all I ever needed was right here." He set the books on the mattress and pulled her in close again. "Those were such fun times. I'm really glad I'm back. Finding a cool tree in the woods in the middle of a concrete jungle would have been impossible, and I *do* want my kids to love the wilderness and everything nature has to offer."

He looked at her for a long moment, desperately wanting to say, *our kids*, but afraid that might be too much too fast and would scare her off just when she was beginning to really let him in. As he pulled her close again, he thought about how Reese wasn't the naive girl she'd been all those years ago. She'd grown up, matured, figured out what she wanted and what she needed in her life, and all of those changes resonated in her confidence and her success. But her love was still just as intense, and as real, as it always had been.

Just as intense, and as real, as his love was for her.

Chapter Twenty-Three

EVERY MORNING TRENT awoke with Reese in his arms felt even better than the one before. And every night when they made love, then talked late into the night, sharing their hopes and dreams, was pure magic.

And yet before they made any official plans to move in together, Reese kept saying she needed more time. *Just to be sure.*

He was disappointed. Actually, it was far more than just disappointment. The thought of living without her again was brutal—something he didn't want to even contemplate. He'd missed her so much over the years that he couldn't get enough of her now. But he knew that just because he was ready to change everything in his life for her didn't mean he should expect her to feel exactly the same way.

Especially so soon. Come Monday morning, Trent was lamenting being apart from her all day after the incredible weekend they'd just spent together exploring the other side of the island, when a story in the newspaper caught his eye.

"Maribelle Penner has a show today in Boston. Isn't she one of your favorite artists?"

Her eyes bloomed wide. "Yes. I can't believe you remembered. What time is her show?"

Trent scanned the article. "Nine to six." He did a quick mental run-through of his to-do list for the resort and his legal practice and decided none of it was critical. Definitely not as important as Reese. "We should go. We can take the ferry and catch a cab to the exhibit."

"I was hoping to finish the lighthouse on the mural today. And what about your work?"

"The lighthouse? My work? Is this the same woman who wanted more time together?"

"You're right," she said slowly. "This is one of the things we were missing. But are you sure? I doubt your grandfather will appreciate you taking off on a Monday to go look at art with me."

He wrapped his arms around her waist. "First of all, spending time with you is far more important than anything else I have to take care of. And second, it turns out that Chandler is glad that we're back together."

"He is? Why didn't you tell me?"

"I went to see your parents right after I spoke with my grandfather. I know it's no excuse, but after the conversation I had with them, Chandler completely slipped my mind."

"Wiggle room," she said softly. "It's obviously not a huge deal that you didn't tell me right away. I just don't want us to fall back into our old habits of keeping things from each other. Especially such shocking things like Chandler actually saying he's happy we're back together. Now," she said, smiling to let him know he was already forgiven, "tell me his exact words."

"It's 'about damn time' that you and I are together again," he said in a funny approximation of his grandfather's gruff voice. "I think he's going soft in his old age."

"Wow." Her eyes were full of emotion as she said, "I always knew there was more to him than it seemed."

"You always did have a soft spot for him for some inexplicable reason," he said with a wry grin, "but I never thought I'd see it myself."

"Well, even if he is going soft"—she rocked her hips against his and smiled that naughty little smile he'd always adored—"you're definitely not. You know what?"

He could hardly think straight enough to reply. "What?"

"Now that I've thought more about it, I should blow off painting and you should blow off work so we can head to Boston. But first..." She reached for the buttons on his shirt. "We should deal with this lust thing we always run into when we're out and about."

* * *

THE FERRY RIDE was romantic and chilly, giving Reese the perfect excuse to snuggle closer to Trent. It had been tempting to stay in bed all day with him, but she knew this trip to Boston was an important one for both of them. Trent needed to show her that he could be spontaneous, and she needed to show him that big cities didn't scare her anymore.

They could have gone inside, but Reese loved the feel of the brisk air against her face, and she didn't want to miss a second of the scenery. As the island fell away in the distance, the Boston skyline came into view, reminding her of when they'd moved to New York. Back then, she'd experienced a conflicting rush of emotions from the fear of leaving everything she knew and loved behind while also being excited to see what the future held. This time, however, as Trent tightened his grip around her shoulder and kissed her temple, there was only excitement. Because it was starting to feel as if her life was just beginning.

Reese had traveled off the island plenty of times to go to the Cape, or to visit friends or her sister in Oregon, but she only went to the bigger cities like New York or Boston when she absolutely had to meet with gallery owners, for quick one- or two-day trips. Fortunately, any feelings that might have tried to filter in about being an island bumpkin who didn't fit in with the "cool kids" quickly dissipated as she looked around the city and realized it was a beautiful, perfect blue-sky day. Children were holding their parents' hands. Lovers were kissing on street corners. And the hustle and bustle suddenly seemed less chaotic and more full of fun and possibility. Even the air around them felt different from the air on the island, as if the energy of the crowd bound together and electrified it. After paying the cab fare, Trent draped a protective arm over Reese and his eyes darted along the busy sidewalk. She suddenly realized that *he* didn't seem entirely comfortable on the crowded streets.

How had she never noticed this before? She'd always assumed he was like a chameleon, able to fit seamlessly into any environment. But now that she thought about it, he sure seemed more like his old self and much happier on the island than he'd been when they'd lived in New York.

"You okay?" Trent asked.

"Yes. I'm great." She smiled at him. "Are you?"

He smiled back. "I'm with you, so how could today be any better?"

But she had a feeling he wasn't telling her everything. Not because he wanted to hurt her by holding things back, but simply because they didn't have much practice yet with being really good communicators. Which was why instead of letting it go, she asked, "Do you miss the hustle and bustle of the city?"

Trent shook his head. "Not even a little."

"Really? You're not just saying that?"

He frowned, as if he'd just realized he should have been more forthright when she'd asked if he was okay. "Let's go find a quieter spot so that I can explain." He led her several steps away from the gallery and the throngs of people trying to get inside.

"I came back to the island because my grandfather mandated the takeover, but the decision to change my life and accept his offer wasn't one I made lightly. Because of my practice, the idea of moving was complicated. Although, honestly, I had been thinking about it for years, and once I came back and entertained the idea on a more serious level, the *right* decision became crystal clear. I wanted to be back on the island because I love it there. I'm still the guy I was when you met me, the guy who loved to take walks and throw rocks into the bay, run on the beach, and read on the deck. I also realized I wanted to be part of running the resort, which I know is far from what I felt when I was building my practice. I'm a Rockwell, and I'm proud of that. I want to be part of my family's legacy."

He tucked her hair behind her ear, so focused on her that she could tell he was oblivious to the people walking by and the line forming outside the gallery. As he gazed into her eyes, the din of the streets fell away for her, too.

"And then there was you, Reese."

"But you just said you came back for all those reasons you just listed. Not for me."

"Those were the reasons I was willing to admit to myself. But the most important reason of all was *you*. Only it wasn't until I watched Quinn and Shelley fall in love—and when I spent enough time on the island again to see my parents together and remember what true love really looks like—that I fully realized what I'd so stupidly thrown away."

"Just like how until we bumped into each other last week," she told him, "I didn't want to admit to myself that I was still in love with you."

"I'm done with lying to myself, Reese. I

want you. I want to live with you and I want to raise our family on the island, not in the city."

"But your practice is in New York. Won't you eventually have to go back?"

"That's another thing I wanted to discuss with you." He glanced around them, looking as if he actually had forgotten they were standing in the middle of a busy sidewalk in downtown Boston. "Do you want to find someplace more private? Or would you rather wait to talk about this more until after we see the exhibit?"

"We've already waited long enough, Trent." They could be onstage at this point, and it would still come down to just the two of them. "And I need you to know I'm not that scared nineteen-year-old girl anymore. I visit New York and Boston a few times each year for my artwork. If you need to go back, I can handle it now."

"Sweetheart, I *know* you can handle anything. You're an amazing, capable woman. You've built your own business; you have your work in major galleries. Of course I know you can handle the city, but you won't need to. Because I'm planning to sell my practice."

Shock sent her mind reeling. "Sell your practice?"

"Yes. I've already set the wheels in motion."

"But you worked so long and so hard to build it up. How can you just let it go?"

"Letting go of it now doesn't make the work I put in mean less. I'll always be proud of the career I built in New York, but it's time for me to work on building other parts of my life. Most important of all, our life together."

"But I thought you loved practicing law. I'd hate for you to give up something you're passionate about because you think it's what I need you to do."

"I'm handling all of the legal aspects of the resort and helping the resort to grow, so it's not like I'll lose that part of myself. And the truth is, it's what *I* need me to do. Selling the practice will allow more time for me to be there for you as a boyfriend and, hopefully, as a husband and a father to our children someday soon."

He was saying the things she'd wanted desperately to hear all those years ago. But it was all coming so fast—just like everything had come between them—that her heart, and her mind, couldn't stop spinning.

"I know you were brought up to always put family first, Trent. So when you began working ninety hours a week, I wondered how you could have changed so fast, and now…" She took a deep breath to try to calm her racing heart. "Now I feel like you've changed, just as quickly, back to the man I fell in love with before. I love the changes, but I hate that the speed at which they're happening is leaving me doubting even the slightest bit."

"Of course I wish you didn't have any doubts," Trent told her, "but I understand why you do."

"Things have been wonderful," she said, "and I wish I could throw myself back into our relationship without any hesitation, but..."

When her words fell away, he tipped her chin up to look into her eyes. "We promised to always tell the truth. No matter what. Whatever you need to say to me, I can take it."

"I still need more time to be one hundred percent sure, Trent. More time to look fear in the eye and vanquish it. More time to make absolutely sure that I'm still moving forward instead of backward. I know you're ready for more, and I—"

"You don't need to apologize for anything. I wasn't asking you to share your feelings to push you anywhere you don't want to go. I just didn't want to make the mistake of assuming I knew what you were thinking like I used to and then getting it all wrong. Thank you for telling me everything you're feeling, Reese."

"You know what?" She smiled at him, and he felt like the sun had finally come out. "Now that we're getting the hang of it, I think we might actually be pretty good at this communicating stuff. Heck, even *Chandler* sounds like he's getting better at sharing his feelings."

"I can't believe I'm giving credit to my grandfather," Trent said with a wry smile, "but really, his summoning us to the island gave me the push I needed to see things more clearly. There's no one in my life I want to impress but you, Reese. You're everything to me. You always were. I just lost my way for a while."

"We both lost our way, but all that matters is that this time we're helping each other find our way back, one step at a time." She took his hand in hers and pressed it to her heart. "Together."

Chapter Twenty-Four

WHILE REESE MARVELED at everything in the gallery, from the elegant marble floors and grand sculpture exhibit in the entrance to every piece of art inside—Trent marveled at how joy came so naturally to her. No matter how many times he saw her smile, the next smile still tugged at his heart. And as they walked through the gallery hand in hand, Trent realized that for the first time in years, he felt *free*. He hadn't realized how repressing his true feelings all these years had made everything seem heavier and more difficult. But after telling Reese how he really felt, and what he truly hoped for, he finally felt alive again.

"I didn't realize we've been here so long," Reese said after looking down at her watch. "Are you bored?"

"Never, as long as I'm with you. And there are few things better than watching you be surrounded by art that you love so much."

"I really do," she said, her eyes lighting up as she pointed at the painting they were standing in front of. "You can see the artist's Mediterranean roots in the vivid colors and the depth and textures of her work. It's like she's taken the richness and vibrancy of the sun and layered it onto every painting."

"They are unique, that's for sure, but no more beautiful than yours."

"You're my biggest fan," she said as she went up on her toes and kissed him.

"What's your favorite piece?"

Her eyes sparked with heat as she told him, "*You.*"

Just as he swept her into his arms so that he could kiss her breathless in the middle of the crowded gallery, his cell phone rang with Chandler's ringtone. *Not today.*

"Your grandfather?"

Obviously, even though they were working on verbal communication, Reese could still read most of his expressions like a book. "The one and only." He pressed his lips to hers for far-too-brief a moment. "Excuse me for a second." He stepped to the side and quietly answered the call.

"Trent? Hi. This is Darla. I'm sorry to

bother you. I know you took today off, but Chandler would like to see you."

"What's the issue?"

"I'm not sure, exactly. But he mentioned that he was unable to find the file on one of the LLCs."

Trent thought about the gap he and his grandfather had just begun to bridge and how hopeful it made him for a closer relationship with him. Then he shifted his gaze to Reese, who was alternately admiring the paintings again...and looking back at him with a concerned expression on her face.

Normally, Trent would jump on the next ferry back to the island, but he wasn't trying to build a *normal* life with Reese. He was working to build an *extraordinary* life with her.

Chandler Rockwell had always been controlling, and it was high time Trent took a stand and regained some of his own control. His decision was swift and made without guilt: Unless there was a dire emergency, he was done playing his grandfather's game at the expense of losing time with Reese.

"Please call my assistant and ask her for whatever he needs. If she can't find it, let Chandler know I'll be in tomorrow and I'll handle whatever he needs then."

When he ended the call, Reese immediately asked, "Is everything okay?"

He draped an arm over her shoulder and pulled her close. "Everything is perfect."

* * *

BY THE TIME they returned to the island after eating a romantic dinner at a cozy Italian restaurant, it was after ten o'clock.

"Thank you for such an amazing afternoon," Reese said as they cuddled on her couch.

"Thank *you* for spending the day with me in Boston." He pulled her in closer. "And I really love being here with you, too. Your home is everything you always said you wanted. Cozy, safe, and warm in a way that makes me want to hold you here on this couch forever."

"If it weren't for you," she said as she smiled up at him, "I might never have thought to buy it. I was so young when we met. I didn't know anything about life, and you taught me so many important things, even when I didn't know you were doing it."

"What do you mean?"

"We've talked about the painful mistakes we made, but there was so much good between us, too, Trent. I think it's time we start talking about those things, too."

"I agree, sweetheart. Especially," he teased, "if it means I actually managed to do something right back then."

"You always talked about planning for the future and making sure the kids we wanted would have a loving home that they could return to when they were older. I remember thinking, *I'm only nineteen and just out of my parents' house. How can I plan where my kids will grow up?* I never really thought past tomorrow, and even then they were just thoughts of how much I loved you and wanted to be with you. And then for a long time after our divorce, I was just circling around and around where we went wrong...while also secretly hoping, and waiting, for everything to magically go back to the way it was. But then, when I saw this house, I knew it was a platform for me to finally spring forward. It had all the things both of us always wanted, and the truth is, I thought about you a lot as I bought it. At the same time, though, I was also thinking about what I wanted for my own future. One without you." She was silent for a moment as she said, "But now here we are. Just like I always secretly wished for."

"I had just as many secret hopes and wishes, Reese. And now they're all coming true."

"I still can hardly believe you blew off Chandler so that we could stay in Boston."

"No one was dying. Nothing was on fire.

We've got a lot of years to make up for, and I don't want to miss a second with you."

She gave him a soft kiss before saying, "Well, I'm sure he's going to take back what he said about being happy that we're back together now. Because if he called, I'm sure he thought what he needed was important."

"*You're* important, Reese. You matter most. Everything else in my life, the resort, my practice, it'll all work itself out. But I am not going to make any more mistakes with you. From now on I want you to always know I'll be there for you. No matter what else is going on, you, and the family I hope we'll have, will come first. Always."

She rested her head on his chest and said, "I swear you must have taken a ten-year course in how to woo Reese Nicholson."

He kissed the top of her head. "I spent ten years figuring out how to *love* Reese Nicholson."

Chapter Twenty-Five

THERE WAS SO much commotion at Shelley's Café when Reese drove by on her way to Bay's Edge the next morning that she couldn't resist stopping by and taking a peek at what was going on. When she and Trent had left for work earlier that morning, he'd mentioned that they were putting the final touches on the café for the grand opening, and she was excited to see them. She was still on the sidewalk, standing just at the edge of the bushes out front, when she heard male voices.

"I've got this, Ethan." Derek stood atop a ladder holding a big oval sign that read Shelley's Café. The *a* was fashioned like a coffee mug with steam rising from it. The rustic wooden sign had dark green letters, accented with pastel-colored flowers along the border, matching the flowers in the garden beside the brook. It fit the appearance of the old mill perfectly.

Derek's biceps strained against his long-sleeved shirt. Beside him, Ethan was climbing up a second ladder with a wide grin.

"I can do it," Ethan insisted.

Both men were so focused on their staring contest from the top of their ladders that neither had noticed her standing there yet. *Boys will be boys*, she mused.

Trent walked out the front door, and Reese's heart did a little tap dance. "Are we really going to argue over who gets to hang the sign?" He always had been the mediator among his siblings.

"It's not about who gets to hang it. We have other stuff that needs to be done," Derek explained. "Ethan can go get the tables set up on the patio."

Ethan reached for the sign and said, "I want to help so you don't fall and need more stitches. I'd hate for Didi to have to stitch you up again," which made Trent and Ethan both laugh and Derek scowl.

Derek finally relented and shifted the sign so Ethan could take half of the weight. Trent held the ladders as his brothers climbed down. Reese couldn't hear what they said, but they all roared with laughter, which brought Sierra and

Shelley outside to see what was going on. They, too, began laughing. Quinn came around the side of the building and swooped Shelley into his arms, spinning her around as he kissed her.

Reese had forgotten how fun it was to be around Trent's family. They were so naturally loving and playful. Trent draped one arm over Sierra's shoulder, the other around Ethan's, showing the protective side of himself that she'd always loved.

Everything he did made her fall deeper in love with him.

"Reese!" The second Trent spotted her, he was out on the sidewalk with her, his arms around her and his mouth lowering to hers for a kiss. "You should have told us you were here."

Her head was spinning from his kiss just enough that it took her a few seconds to stop staring into his eyes like a lovesick fool and say, "I didn't want to distract anyone from the work you're all doing."

His eyes immediately smoldered with heat. "I'm *always* up for being distracted."

But before either of them could further distract each other, Sierra was calling out Reese's name, then saying, "I'm so glad you're here. Shelley and I needed another hand with the curtains. You can spare fifteen minutes, right?"

Moments later, she was working just as

hard as everyone else. The Rockwells had always made her feel like family. She had missed being a part of their family terribly after she and Trent had split up. But thankfully, even though it was ten years later, being with all of them again felt just as right as it always had.

* * *

AFTER WORKING WITH his family at Shelley's, Trent went directly to Chandler's office. He was prepared for his grandfather to unleash his fury at Trent for not dropping everything and rushing back from Boston the day before. But as he stood across the desk from his grandfather, it wasn't disappointment or anger he saw in Chandler's dark eyes. Instead, there was an emotion coursing through the old man that was entirely unfamiliar.

"Didi, would you mind giving us a moment alone?" Chandler asked his private nurse.

"Of course." She smiled at Trent as she walked out of the office, then closed the door behind her.

"I'm sorry that I couldn't return to the island when you had Darla call yesterday afternoon," Trent said. "I'm making changes in my life, and part of those changes is setting my priorities in a way that will ensure that my relationship with Reese comes first."

"I've always believed that family should come first, Trent. Do you think you're telling me something new or doing something unique?" Chandler's tone was stern.

You have a strange way of showing it. "No, sir. But I am telling you something that is new to *me*."

Chandler stared at Trent for a long moment before saying, "I'm glad to see you're finally taking control the way a Rockwell should. I was sorely disappointed when your marriage ended, and now I am glad to see that my faith in you to fix the things you broke has not been misplaced."

Trent barely managed a nod, too stunned by his grandfather's praise—and his thoughts on his marriage to Reese—to speak.

Chandler opened his desk drawer and set an envelope between them on the desk. "I've made some arrangements, and I expect you'll be able to handle sharing the news with the others."

Trent removed the documents and quickly scanned them. He was so stunned by what he was reading that he had to sink down to the chair behind him to reread them more carefully.

"Grandfather, legal ownership of the resort is not supposed to change hands until after you're... after you are no longer with us. But this assigns the deed to me and my siblings and our father effective immediately." Trent looked at his grandfather, and his stomach sank. "Is your health getting worse?"

"No. I'm planning to hang on for a few more years, at the very least. I can't let you young people run around unattended." Chandler's eyes softened as he continued, saying, "You have all proven to me that you can handle the responsibilities of running the resort. It should be yours."

"I don't know what to say," Trent admitted, feeling his throat thicken as it had the other day.

"Just promise me you won't make the same mistakes I did with my Caroline."

Trent hadn't heard his grandfather mention his grandmother since the summer she'd passed away, and even then Chandler had moved out of the house they'd shared and into the resort so fast—even before his private wing was constructed—and spoken of her so rarely, that it was almost as if he'd filed her away like a business deal.

"I'm sure she knew you loved her," Trent said, feeling uncomfortable and yet thankful at the same time for his grandfather's opening up to him. He wasn't completely sure why Chandler had chosen to suddenly show this side of himself, but Trent suspected it had to do with his clearer view of his own mortality.

Or maybe he had finally grown tired of being so unhappy all the time—a man truly on an island.

"Caro knew I loved her," his grandfather said. "But that doesn't excuse how I treated her. And I would also like you to know that I think Reese is doing a fine job on the mural. You should take her to that dance we're hosting this weekend." His eyes went slightly misty as he said, "Caroline always loved dressing in something pretty and being twirled around the dance floor." A moment later, however, he cleared his throat and waved his hand in the air. "Now get out of here and run this resort."

For the second time that week, Trent left his grandfather's office without being chased by tension. He pulled out his phone and sent a group text to his siblings and parents, requesting a meeting at the Hideaway as soon as possible. He knew Reese was at Bay's Edge, and as much as he wanted to share what had just happened with her before he told anyone else, he didn't want to disturb her while she was teaching.

And he couldn't wait to see her beautiful eyes light up when he asked her to the dance. Just the way his grandmother's eyes must have lit up whenever Chandler took her somewhere special and showed her that she was important to him.

Chapter Twenty-Six

REESE WAS PLEASANTLY surprised by how far Tilly, Morris, and Norma had come with their paintings in only one week. When she'd first begun teaching them, Morris had had a difficult time getting perspective into his paintings. But although he was in his late eighties, he was smart as a whip and equally as determined. When she'd assured him that painting wasn't about perfection, he'd told her that there was nothing he couldn't master if he put his mind to it. And he'd been right.

"That looks beautiful, Morris," she said as she came around behind him.

Tilly coughed, and Reese's eyes lifted at the sound. "You still sound a little wheezy. Have you seen the doctor?"

She waved her hand. "I saw the doctor this

morning. It's a cold, and as my mother always said, it'll last seven days or a week, whichever comes first."

Reese smiled at that, but it didn't alleviate her concern. She loved Tilly like a grandmother, and she hated to see her not feeling well. "Would you like some water, or is there anything else I can get you?"

"No, sweetie. I'm fine, and with any luck, I'll get these leaves done today, too." She went back to brushing green paint on the leaves on the tree they'd started painting the other day.

"Maybe if you brought that nice fellow Trent Rockwell in for another visit, it would cheer her up," Norma said, making everyone chuckle.

"He was sure sweet on you, Reese," Morris added. "He looked at you the same way I look at Norma."

"Do you want to know how you looked at him, Reese?" Norma asked.

Reese was pretty sure she already knew, but she humored them by saying, "How?"

"Like he was a big, juicy steak."

Reese couldn't help but laugh, even as Tilly grinned mischievously and said, "You have to admit, Reese, he is awfully handsome."

Carin and Martha walked in before Reese could reply, and Carin immediately said, "Did you bring that hunka hunka burnin' love with you again today, Reese?"

"Oh my gosh, what have I done?" Reese was only half teasing. "Trent is *not* here today. We're here to paint, but I'm glad you all liked him so much."

"Liked him?" Martha sighed dreamily. "You are one lucky lady. He seems to be really taken with you."

"Trent *is* wonderful. He's attentive and caring, and—"

"Handsome. Don't forget handsome," Carin added.

"Did you see his hair? He's never going to lose it," Morris said as he rubbed his bald head.

"How long have you been seeing him?" Norma needed to know.

"They dated a long time ago," Carin said as she sat down beside Norma. "But he's never stopped loving her."

Reese had to pick her jaw up off the floor. "He told you that?"

"Well...not exactly," Carin admitted. "He simply said the two of you had dated a long time ago, but then I asked my granddaughter, who went to school with his brother Quinn. And she told me how the two of you were famous for never being able to keep your hands off of each other."

"Carin!" Tilly chided, even though she was clearly delighted with the information. "You gossip worse than a high school girl."

"How else are we going to figure out what's what?" Carin said. "If I were you," she said to Reese, "I'd swoop that man back up and never let him go."

Reese had a feeling that Carin's granddaughter had shared much more, but Carin was kind enough not to mention the rest of the details about her relationship with Trent. She ushered Carin and Martha out of the classroom on the premise of getting the class back on track, and for the remainder of the hour, the group focused on painting.

After class, Norma and Morris went to the game room, but Tilly stayed behind while Reese packed up her supplies. "Is Trent the reason why you were so flustered the other day?"

"Yes," Reese admitted.

"Then I'm guessing he must also be responsible for bringing out that special spark in your eyes today."

"He is." Reese knew she should have told her friend all about Trent a long time ago, but she'd been so intent on pretending the past didn't matter anymore. "I was married to him ten years ago."

She had expected Tilly's brows to lift with surprise. But her friend simply nodded as if all the pieces were finally fitting together. "He's the one who was everything to you, isn't he?"

"Yes. I was nineteen years old when I fell head over heels in love with him—and now I can't seem to stop falling again. Just as you said, love *is* like a boomerang. But it's all happening so fast again, and I..."

Tilly reached over and squeezed Reese's hand. "Love doesn't always appear in its final form. I know you're the teacher and I'm only just learning to paint, but it seems like love and painting aren't all that different. Our hearts start out open, just waiting for love to find us, like canvases waiting for that special image to bring them to life. And just like you show us how to tweak our colors and bring more life into our paintings by using different brushes and different strokes, or applying shading to temper some areas and bring out others, love is the same way. Two people bring together their personalities, wants, needs, hopes, fears—and hope to come out with something beautiful that inspires each of them, helps them grow— together and individually. Love takes tweaking." She looked away, and Reese knew she was thinking about the man she'd lost. "Really, that tweaking never stops, because we grow, and change, and bring babies into the mix." She turned a thoughtful gaze back to Reese. "But if it's meant to be, and you're both trying to please the other as much as yourselves, it's all worth it in the end."

Reese gave Tilly a long hug. Or maybe it was Tilly hugging her. Either way, Tilly's words of wisdom and their warm embrace were just what she needed to help settle the nerves that were trying to pop back up inside of her.

* * *

TRENT SAT BETWEEN Sierra and Quinn at their usual table in the Hideaway, where they were holding the family meeting he'd requested. Derek and Ethan took the heads of the table, while his parents sat side by side, just the way they did at the dinner table, as well. It was yet another reinforcement of how they'd always put their relationship first.

"Trent," his father said, "I'm glad you called us all together. I've been wanting to touch base and see if any of you are having trouble managing your own business alongside your responsibilities at the resort. Would you mind if we discussed that before we tended to your news?"

"No, Dad. That's fine," Trent agreed.

"It's been a big pain in the rear for me," Derek said, obviously still itching to get back to his *real* life in Boston. "I've got a client I need to visit sometime soon to go over some extensive patio designs. I can't close the deal over Skype, so I'll need a few days off."

"That's not a problem," Trent said. "Just tell us what needs to be covered while you're gone."

"I know you can deal with my absence on this one," Derek said, "but nine more months of this juggling is going to be a nightmare."

Sierra sighed. "Derek, if you would just let yourself enjoy the island again, you'd figure it all out and you wouldn't want to run back to Boston. Look at Quinn and Trent. They love it here now."

"She's right," Quinn agreed. "I definitely love it here, and I have no interest in going back to Annapolis."

Trent nodded in agreement.

"If you two are any indication," Derek said, "it seems to me that staying on the island is a surefire way to be sucked into a heavy-duty relationship."

"Obviously that's not true," Sierra said. "Look at me."

"And me," Ethan added. "Come out with me on the boat, Derek, and I'll remind you how much fun island life really is."

"Why don't we all give Derek a break." Abby smiled warmly at her third-eldest son. "We all know the island isn't for everyone, and Derek has a successful business that he shouldn't feel pressured to leave behind."

"Thanks, Mom."

"Speaking of businesses, I've taken steps to sell my practice." Trent watched his family's eyes widen. "I want to make a life here with Reese...if she'll have me." Even though Trent knew Reese still needed time to be absolutely sure, he reveled in the knowledge that every day was bringing them closer together.

"That would be wonderful," Abby said with a huge smile.

"Trent, I think that's very wise." Griffin's dark eyes were warm as he said, "I'm proud of you. That must have been a very difficult decision."

"Actually, once I realized what I really wanted, all the things that had been standing in my way became crystal clear. Speaking of which..." He pulled out the legal documents from Chandler and handed them to Griffin. "Grandfather must have had his own revelation recently. He's deeding the resort to us, effective as soon as the paperwork is processed."

Griffin looked stunned as he read the document. "I can't believe it." He lifted his eyes to Trent. "How did this come about?"

Derek held his hand out for the papers, and after reading them, he passed them around the table to their other siblings. "It's got to be a game of some kind."

"No game," Trent assured him. "And he actually thanked me for my hard work, too."

Their eyes widened again with disbelief.

"Chandler thanked you?" Ethan asked. "You sure you weren't in the wrong office?"

Trent laughed at that. "I couldn't believe it either. He also gave me a bit of advice about Reese, and then he said that Grandma Caroline's love for him didn't dismiss his rotten behavior toward her."

"He'd never say something like that," Derek grumbled. "I'm not buying it."

Griffin's brows knitted together, as well. "Is there any way you misunderstood any of this, Trent?"

After Trent shook his head, Quinn said, "Remember what I overheard him saying to Didi in his office when we first came back to the island? How he's proud of us and respects our determination. I think the heart attacks might have rocked his brain—in a good way."

"Well, I don't care what caused it," Sierra said. "I think it's wonderful. I have always hated how cold he was. Maybe we'll see another side of him in our lifetimes after all."

"You know what I think?" Abby's eyes trailed lovingly over each of her children. "I think he brought you all back to the island because he needed us all here. He may seem cold in many ways, but he is also a loyal man who was married to the same woman his entire life. I believe he does know what love is. He just has a hard time showing it."

"And he definitely has a hard time allowing himself to feel loved by others," Griffin added. "When his first love turned down his proposal, I think he shut part of himself off in order to protect himself. But if we continue to treat him like we'd like to be treated, then hopefully he'll come around more and more."

"I'm still not buying a word of it," Derek said.

Sierra shot Derek a narrow-eyed glare. "You don't have to buy it. Just try to be nice. Heck, maybe you should ask Didi to the dance. We all know you want to, and if she actually says yes, maybe that will make you sweeter, too."

"Speaking of sweet," Ethan said before Derek could jump down Sierra's throat for egging him on, "the mural is incredible. I see Reese out there most mornings when I'm heading down to the marina. She always looks so intent on painting that I'm afraid to interrupt her, but she's doing a fantastic job."

"I'll pass that along," Trent said, damn proud of the woman he loved. "She's really thankful that she was chosen for the project."

Abby and Sierra exchanged a smile before his sister said, "She was really the only person we could have chosen for the job."

Reese is the only person I could have chosen

for me, too.

Trent looked at his watch and told his family, "If we're done here, I've got to get going."

"I've got to head back to work, too," Derek muttered as he pushed away from the table.

"I'm not heading back to the office," Trent told his brother. "I'm going to go see Reese."

Something that looked like envy passed over Derek's face before he quickly covered it up with a smirk. "Two down, two to go."

"You really think you're going to dodge love's arrow, don't you?" Trent said.

"If I ever found a woman who could keep up with me and my adventures, I might change my mind," Derek said. "But I'm pretty sure she's not out there, so I'm happy going solo. In fact, what the hell. I'm going to fit in some rock climbing before I chain myself to my desk for the rest of the night."

How, Trent wondered as his brother headed for the rocks, could Derek not get that falling in love with a great woman made everything so much better?

Then again, Trent knew all too well just how easy it was to keep the blinders on where true love was concerned. And he also knew it was something he would never make the mistake of doing again.

Chapter Twenty-Seven

REESE'S WHOLE FACE lit up when Trent walked into her gallery. She seemed more beautiful every time he saw her, and yet again he wondered how he could have ever wanted to climb a corporate ladder instead of coming home to her. He'd been young, driven, and blind. So damn blind.

"Hi," Reese said as she stepped around the counter and lifted her mouth to his. Their kiss went from zero to sixty in the span of a heartbeat and would have definitely turned into even more if Jocelyn hadn't walked by and cleared her throat.

Trent and Reese were both laughing as they drew back. "I thought we were alone," Trent said.

"You were. I was in the ladies' room."

Jocelyn was laughing, too, as she said, "Go ahead; get out of here to kiss or whatever you want to do. Just don't tell me about it. Well...not *too* many details, anyway."

Reese and Trent headed out of the gallery, and as they began to walk down Old Mill Row, Trent couldn't wait to fill Reese in on the shocking developments with his grandfather. "Chandler just deeded over the resort to me and my siblings."

She stopped dead in the middle of the sidewalk. "No way."

"He said we've proved ourselves to him and that we deserve to own it. But there's more."

"More? My world is already spinning. I'm not sure I can handle more," she said with a laugh.

"He also started talking about his regrets over how he treated Grandma Caroline. And then he warned me not to make the same mistakes with you."

"Oh, Trent..." She squeezed his hand. "That's so sweet of Chandler."

"I never thought I'd hear the words 'sweet' and 'Chandler' in the same sentence."

"I knew he was a softie at heart."

"Only you saw that, Reese. Only you."

"There have been so many changes recently," she mused. "First with Quinn. And then with us."

"All good changes," he said as he pulled her into his arms to kiss her again in front of the whole world. "*Great* changes."

"I know one thing that's still the same, though," Reese said. "How great the fried calamari at Charley's Pub is. Have you been there since you've been back?"

"Not yet." Because it had reminded him too much of Reese. When they were first dating they'd gone to Charley's Pub every week, sometimes alone and sometimes with Trent's siblings or their friends. They'd often stayed for hours, talking and laughing. "We should go there for dinner."

Charley's was located on the corner of West and Main, beside Island View Pharmacy. Trent pulled open the heavy wooden door. "Mm," they said in unison as the scent of seafood wafted toward them. They claimed the table in the corner that they used to call their own. Trent slid in beside Reese and draped an arm over her shoulder. She snuggled against him as the waitress took their orders.

Two televisions were mounted behind the bar, one set to ESPN, the other to CNN. A handful of guys sat at the bar drinking, but the pub wasn't very busy otherwise. There were a few couples sitting in the tables around them, but sitting in the booth with Reese like they used to felt to Trent like they were all alone in their own little world.

"Does it feel like no time has passed?" Reese asked. "Or like we haven't been here in forever?"

"So much of what we do feels familiar," he told her. "But at the same time, it's all brand-new. What about for you?"

"Being here throws me back to when we were first dating, but just like you said, it doesn't feel the same as it did then. At nineteen, I had no idea I was so young. That we were both so young. I thought we had it all figured out, that nothing could stop us." She looked pensive as she said, "I've been thinking a lot about things. About the past...and the future, too. The truth is that ten years ago neither of us really knew what we wanted out of life. The problem wasn't just that we weren't good communicators—it was that even if we had been, we didn't *know* ourselves well enough yet back then to be able to honestly tell each other what we needed to be happy. But if we had met a few years later, once we were older and wiser..."

"No matter when we met, I would have fallen in love with you." He kissed her before adding, "But what you're saying makes a lot of sense. I loved you when you were nineteen, I love you now at twenty-nine, and I'll still be loving you just as much at eighty-nine."

She picked up her wineglass. "To new and old coming together."

"And to building a love that will last."

* * *

BY THE TIME Charley's had their last call, they were both a little tipsy, and Reese was sure she looked like she was swooning over Trent as much as he looked like he was desperately in love with her.

She'd been giddy when he'd asked her to come to the dance at the resort. Dancing with Trent had always been one of her favorite things. Her whole life was brighter since he'd been back, and now she had even more wonderful things to look forward to.

Trent paid the bill and then they made their way down the sidewalk toward home. He shrugged off his sweater and turned her toward him as he helped her put it on.

"You're cute when you're tipsy." He kissed the tip of her nose.

"You're hot all the time."

She went up on her toes and mashed her lips against his in a messy, needy kiss. His strong arms circled her, bringing their bodies flush against each other. He buried his hands in her hair, tilting her head, angling her just the way he liked, and she immediately surrendered to their passion. The kiss was warm and wonderful, sharing oxygen as he loved her mouth with all he had. Reese's insides were humming with need, and every kiss, every urgent touch, brought her desire for him even closer to the surface.

A car drove around the corner, putting them momentarily in a spotlight, and they came away breathless. They hurried several blocks in the chilly evening air, until Trent pulled Reese into an alley between two shops, where it was pitch-dark and they were blocked from the bay breezes.

He pressed his body to hers as he kissed her again, his hands traveling up and down her hips as she rocked into him, feeling the strength of his arousal, the ache of his lust in every stroke of his tongue. She couldn't resist palming him through his jeans. He moaned as he slid his lips to her neck, kissing and sucking as his hand slid between her legs.

"Reese," he whispered against her lips. "You've turned me into a teenage boy. I want to take you right here, right now."

"Take me," she urged him. "Here. *Now.*"

He cupped her face between his hands and kissed her. It was a rough kiss. A kiss that matched the urgency rushing through her and drove her hand to the button of his jeans.

"Yes," he said between kisses. *"Now."*

She didn't stop unbuttoning his pants as they stumbled deeper into the alley, away from the road. She managed to get his zipper down, pulling a groan from deep within his lungs. She could barely see in the dark alley, but she could feel his heart thundering in his chest and could feel each heavy breath against her cheeks, her lips, her neck, ratcheting up her fervor.

She tugged his pants down, and he lifted her up and claimed her mouth, groaning as he shoved her skirt up above her waist, lifted her legs to wrap around his hips, and shoved her panties to one side.

She sank down upon his hard shaft, both of them beyond words as the breath whooshed from their lungs and their bodies ground together.

His strong arms guided her up and down. She used his shoulders for balance, digging her nails into his muscles.

"Faster...harder...*Trent*..." She barely comprehended what she was saying as he took her up, up, up, and higher still. When he sealed his lips over the crest of her shoulder and bit down as he thrust into her, they both cried out, spiraling over the edge.

He silenced her passionate moans with kisses as they rode out their orgasms, thrusting and clawing for more. Finally, Trent backed them against the wall, holding her close, until their bodies began to calm.

"You're shaking," he said as he helped her straighten her clothes a short while later.

"Aftershocks." She fisted her hands in his shirt to stabilize her shaky legs.

"Jesus, Reese. I didn't mean to do that here," he whispered. "When I'm with you, I forget everything except how much I have to have you."

"I loved every single second of it," she said as she went up on her toes and kissed him again. "And even though some things have changed between us, I'm glad we still need each other just as much as we always did."

"More, Reese. I need you even more."

He was right. Even their desire for each other was bigger now. Bigger and better than before. And maybe it was that knowledge that helped her cautious worries stay settled for the first time as they took yet another step toward their second chance at forever.

Chapter Twenty-Eight

THE NEXT FEW days flew by in a blur of laughter and loving. Morning, noon, and night, Reese tumbled faster and faster over the edge of lust and into a love that was deeper and truer than she'd ever known love could be.

By Friday afternoon she was so excited to dance with Trent that she could barely concentrate on the mural. She was debating walking down to Annabelle's boutique to look for a new dress to wear, when she spotted a group of teenagers heading her way.

"That's awesome," said a guy who looked to be in his late teens, with long dark hair that hung over his eyes as he admired the mural.

"Thank you." Reese smiled at them. The other guy wore his hair cropped short. Each of the two girls with them had long hair, one blond, one brunette, both wearing cutoffs and sweaters.

Reese remembered how fun it had been to be so young and carefree. Then again, she was extremely pleased to realize that it was turning out to be even *more* fun—and much sexier—to be older and wiser and to have an even deeper connection.

"Did you paint this whole mural?" the slim blond girl asked.

"Yes, but it's not finished," Reese explained.

The short-haired guy studied the cottage she'd painted. "We're art students at the Rhode Island School of Design. I don't suppose you'd let us help?"

"We're visiting my aunt, Kathleen Torrence," the blonde with the high-tops said.

"I know your aunt. It's nice to meet you. I'm Reese Nicholson."

"I'm Stephanie, and this is Cory"—she pointed to the short-haired boy—"and Michael and Elise."

How could Reese say no to such a group of eager faces?

"Well, it is a community project. Why not?" Actually, now that she thought about it, she really loved the idea of *truly* making this a community project and bringing their creativity to the mural. In fact, she decided not to show them the drawing. "What would you like to paint?"

"I'd love to paint a guy with a surfboard down here at the edge of the water." Michael pointed to the far left of the mural.

"Can I paint a little boy playing with a ball over here?" Elise pointed to the grassy knoll between the cottages.

"Absolutely. Both of those ideas sound great."

"Can Cory and I paint one of those planes pulling a banner?" Stephanie asked. "We could have the banner read 'Welcome to Rockwell Island.'"

"I couldn't have thought up a more perfect idea."

As Reese handed them each brushes, Cory asked, "Do you mind if I play music? I like to listen while I paint. Classical's my jam, if that's okay with you." When she told him it sounded great, he pulled speakers out of a backpack that Michael had set on the grass and connected them to his cell phone. Classical music filled the air around them.

"That's an interesting choice for a guy your age," Reese said as she picked up her brush and began painting again.

"His father's a violinist," Elise explained.

The kids energized the air around them. They laughed and joked and talked about how cool the island was. Every so often, Cory leaned down and kissed Elise, and every single time, she sighed with pleasure as if she couldn't get enough of their kisses.

Isn't it lovely, Reese thought, *that at twenty-nine, I'm still doing that with Trent?*

Stephanie swung her hips to the music even though there wasn't a real dance beat. And when she caught Michael looking, she just laughed and rolled her eyes before turning her focus back to the mural.

A short while later, when Stephanie sat down beside her, Reese told the girl, "You're really talented. Have you thought about what you're going to do once you graduate?"

"I've spent each of the last few summers working to save money, and over my school breaks I also work full-time, so the first thing I'm going to do is backpack through Europe for a summer to see everything I can." Stephanie's big green eyes were wide with excitement and anticipation. "After that, I'm moving to Boston, where my parents live, and I'm hoping to find a job in graphic design."

"Wow. You really have it all planned out." When Reese had been her age, while she'd had lots of hopes and dreams, she'd had no concrete plans for achieving them until Trent had planted the seed of opening her own gallery.

"You kind of have to these days. There are so many college grads now without jobs. I'm planning to send out a bunch of applications a few weeks before I return from Europe. That way I can start interviewing right away. I had a paid internship last summer at a big firm that offered me a part-time job while I'm at school, but I want to focus on my grades."

Just then Trent came around the corner, and Reese didn't even try to control her urge to leap up into his arms. They'd taken so many wonderful steps toward building their new relationship that she was feeling more confident about it every day.

He kissed her dizzy in front of the teenagers before finally drawing back to ask, "Did you do some recruiting?"

It took her a few long seconds to get her synapses to fire properly again so that she could tell him, "They're art students. Aren't they doing a wonderful job?"

"Amazing. You've made this a real community project, Reese." Trent smiled at the teens and offered his hand in greeting to the teenagers.

After they'd all introduced themselves, Trent said, "The resort is hosting a dance tonight with a great live band. Are you all going?"

Elise grabbed Cory's shirt. "We should go!"

"Whatever you want." He leaned down and kissed her again.

BELLA ANDRE & MELISSA FOSTER

"Steph? Want to go?" Michael's eyes were so full of hope that even Reese found herself hoping Stephanie would say yes.

Stephanie shrugged. "Sure. Why not?"

The scene was so different from what she and Trent had been like when they were younger. She'd practically jumped up and down when he'd asked her out. Every. Single. Time.

Actually, she thought with a wide grin, she still did.

"It's on the lower patio around eight," Trent told the group before turning back to Reese and lowering his voice. "Do you want to listen to the music from our favorite overlook and have our own private dance?"

"I can't think of anything more perfect."

Besides us.

Chapter Twenty-Nine

TRENT HELD REESE'S hand as they made their way to what he'd always thought of as their spot, weaving through thick brush and trees and guided by the shimmering light of the moon slicing through the foliage.

"I always love how good it smells here, like pine trees and salty sea air," Reese said as they neared the overlook where they'd first met and she loved to paint. Trent had set out a blanket, candles, and a basket of wine and cheese and crackers. Reese's eyes widened with surprise as she stepped onto the blanket, looking radiant in her pretty blue dress, with a cardigan overtop and the moonlight at her back. Music played in the distance, providing a perfect hint of magic and romance.

"When did you do all of this?"

He bent to light the candles as he answered. "While you were working on the mural." He rose and circled her waist with his arms, drawing her in close. "I wanted you all to myself tonight. I hope you don't mind."

"I would always rather be with you than with a crowd of people."

As they sat on the blanket and Trent poured them each a glass of wine, he said, "Remember how we used to talk about buying this property and building a house?"

"I always thought it would be the most amazing place for kids to play."

"A few years ago, when I was home for the holidays, I came here and spent hours admiring the view of the bay and the lighthouse. And all the while, I thought of you, Reese."

"I'm surprised I didn't bump into you, since I was always doing the same thing and thinking of you. But wait, didn't a corporation buy this spot two years ago?"

"Yes," he said with a smile. "Trent Rockwell Enterprises bought it."

She turned with a huge smile and surprise in her beautiful eyes. "You bought it? But you couldn't have known we'd get back together. We were both fighting our feelings so hard back then. No one could have known."

"No, I couldn't have. But it was so special to us that I couldn't let it go, either. I guess even though I tried to bury my love for you in order to get through every day and move forward, deep down I always knew that loving you was the best thing that ever happened to me."

Which was why he had one more surprise for Reese, waiting in a black velvet bag he'd slipped into his pocket earlier, in the hopes that tonight would be the perfect night to finally give it to her.

* * *

REESE'S HEART FELT like it was going to burst from her chest, not just because he'd bought one of their favorite spots on earth, but because of what he'd just said, which resonated so strongly with her that she could have said the exact same thing.

"That's exactly what I feel like. Like I never let you go. You've always been right here with me. Because loving you is the best thing that ever happened to me, too." She pressed her lips to his, and it took all her focus to pull back from their sweet kiss and say, "I have a confession to make. The other day, after I bumped into you at Shelley's Café the first time, I came here. It was like I was driven here, totally inspired, of course, because you have always been my very best muse, one that I can't ever escape. And I saw you running down the beach toward the stairs."

"That was the first time I'd run that route since I returned to the island," Trent admitted. "I felt driven by you, too."

Never in her life had she felt like destiny was at work as strongly as she felt it right then. It was even stronger than when they'd first met, strong enough to bring them back together after they'd both rebuilt their lives and lived a lifetime in ten years without each other.

"I didn't see you that morning, Reese. How did I miss you?"

"I left before you could see me, because from the second I touched you again, when you looked into my eyes that night in front of Shelley's Café, all the walls I'd erected around my heart started crumbling."

"For me, too."

"It was unsettling, how quickly it happened. After we broke up, I always felt like I needed to be in control. For ten years, I've had a schedule that I've followed with work, teaching at Bay's Edge, and seeing my parents. But then, in one collision of our bodies, one whisper of my name from your lips, the safe, comfortable world I'd created for myself shattered."

His eyes turned serious. "Don't you feel safe with me, Reese? I've tried not to move forward too fast again, because I didn't want to scare you away, but it's been hard, really hard, to hold anything back at all."

"Even though we have moved forward really fast, I know you would never hurt me on purpose. And I *know* you'd never let anyone else hurt me." She hated the thought of his holding anything back from her, which was why she wouldn't hold anything back from him now.

"What's been really scary isn't that you shattered my safety—it's that you shattered my self-control. And then I couldn't stay safe from my feelings for you anymore."

"Do you need to be safe from them?"

"Now that we're sitting here beneath the stars talking honestly about everything? I'm almost positive I don't need to be safe from those feelings anymore. But all those years apart, deep down I must have known that if we spent time together again, I wouldn't be able to keep from loving you again."

He embraced her, holding her against his chest as he pressed a kiss to the top of her head.

"I can understand why you'd be scared about falling back in love with a man who hurt you."

She shifted slightly so that she could look into his eyes. "I was, but I was also worried about hurting you again by not being the partner you needed me to be, or the partner I wanted to be *for* you."

"Are you still worried about that?"

"We've both grown. We've both accepted our faults. And we're working on having an amazing relationship." She paused before adding, "You said it's been really hard to hold anything back from me, but I don't want you to do that, Trent. I don't want either of us to hold back anymore."

"I don't want either of us to hold back anymore, either. But if you still need more time before we officially take the next step and decide to move in together, I want you to know that I'm here and I'm yours, no matter how long it takes."

He cupped her face between his hands the way she loved and took her in a sensual kiss that made her head spin and her heart go crazy. Then he rose to his feet and reached for her hand.

"Dance with me."

He drew her in close and they swayed to the music. With the stars shining down upon them and the music in the distance, surrounded by candlelight and the sweet sounds of the bay, they danced and kissed and danced some more. Reese had never been so happy, and she didn't want this magical night to end.

"I love you, Trent," she whispered against his chest.

She felt his heartbeat quicken against her

own as he gazed deeply into her eyes and said, "I want to give you something I've held on to for so long and dreamed about giving to you. But if it's too much too fast, or if it brings back bad memories, I'll understand if you don't want it." He reached into his pocket, and when he opened his hand, nestled in the center of his palm was a black velvet bag. She could tell by the way his eyes moved between her and the bag that he was nervous, just as she was. With a shaky hand, she withdrew the most gorgeous diamond bracelet.

"Trent," she whispered, too emotional to say anything more. It was an elegant strand of canary diamonds, and each sparkling yellow diamond was surrounded by a circle of white diamonds, creating beautiful florets. Each of those florets was separated by a cluster of four chocolate diamonds. "I've never seen anything so exquisite."

He took it from her hand and fastened it around her wrist. Then he lifted her hand to his lips and pressed a kiss to it.

"I had it designed for our six-month wedding anniversary. I was going to give it to you the night I found your note." He ran his finger over the beautiful bracelet. "I wanted it to emulate dandelions."

"I love it." She tried to swallow past the lump forming in her throat. "This is so beautiful and thoughtful, and I'm so sorry. You must have been so upset..."

He gazed openly and lovingly into her eyes. "We were both hurting back then, but now we can start fresh. No more apologies. This is our new beginning, made better, richer, by the scars of our past."

She pressed her hands to his chest as he sealed his lips over hers, their bodies still moving in time to the music, their hearts dancing in the same frantic rhythm and their lives intertwining even more powerfully.

As he removed her sweater and lowered her to the blanket, blocking the bay breeze with his own body, they didn't rush to come together the way they usually did. He kissed her forehead, the corners of her mouth, the dip beneath her ear. The slow loving was even more intense than their fevered unions. He ran his hand up her thigh, beneath her dress, caressing her skin, heightening her anticipation as his mouth made a slow path across her shoulders.

And then their bodies came together and the music fell away as the sweet sounds of the sea whispering through the leaves gave way to their tender and passionate whispers of love.

Chapter Thirty

THE NEXT DAY Trent didn't go to work at the resort and Reese didn't paint. Instead, they spent half of the day in bed making love, then reading passages to each other from the books she'd given him.

He'd missed these moments with her. So damn much. Hindsight really was twenty-twenty. Never, ever would he make the same mistake again.

It was almost dinnertime by the time they decided to shower and dress and venture out for a walk down to the water to kick off their shoes. They followed the residential streets out to Main and walked sidewalks they knew by heart, stopping to talk to friends along the way.

"When we first met," Reese said, "I was floored by how many people you knew. It was

337

like no matter where we were, people singled you out."

"That's part of the Rockwell curse."

"But isn't it a blessing, too, because everyone on the island has always watched out for you and your family?"

"You're right, it is a blessing. Although," he added with a slightly crooked smile, "it means I usually have to budget an hour in when I'm running an errand that should only take five minutes."

"You handled it so well, Trent, even back then. You were always polite and you never got annoyed at all of the interruptions."

"I think it was worse than ever that summer because they'd never seen me date anyone seriously before, and then suddenly I was desperately in love with my girlfriend, who I couldn't stop kissing and dragging into alleys and behind bushes to have my way with her."

"I'm glad you didn't date every pretty girl on the island before me."

"And I wouldn't have blamed you for dating all the single guys who wanted to be with you after our divorce, but honestly, I'm glad you didn't."

"None of them were right for me."

"That's because they weren't me."

"No, they weren't," she agreed as she rested her head against Trent's shoulder. She wrapped her hands around his arm and he pulled her in closer. Always closer.

As they rounded the corner and walked down the hill, the lights of the resort shone brightly in the distance and sounds of laughter grew louder as they reached the beach.

Chugger, Ethan's golden retriever, bounded up to Trent, whining for attention. Trent and Reese both crouched to love him up. Chugger licked Trent's chin as they petted him.

"I wonder where Ethan is," Reese said.

Trent looked around and spotted Chandler sitting in his wheelchair facing the water. When Didi spotted them, she waved.

"Chugger must be here with Chandler and Didi," Trent guessed. "Are you up to saying hello to them?"

"Of course I am." Once they were out on the beach, she immediately reached out her hand to Didi. "I'm Reese. And it's such a pleasure to meet you."

"It's wonderful to meet you, too, Reese." Didi smiled warmly.

Chandler turned, and as his eyes trailed over Reese and Trent holding hands, his lips curved up in a smile. But just as quickly as the smile had appeared, he pressed his lips into a firm line.

Trent suddenly wondered how many other times he had missed Chandler's flashes of emotion.

"Hello, Reese," Chandler said in his characteristically sober tone. "It's very nice to see you again."

After Chandler's earlier reference of *that Nicholson girl*, Trent was delighted by his grandfather's kind greeting.

Reese beamed at his grandfather. "Hi, Mr. Rockwell. It's lovely to see you again, too."

Chugger stepped between Chandler's knees to be petted, and Chandler automatically pressed a kiss to the top of his head. Even though Chandler had lavished Chugger with attention since the first week Ethan brought him home, given the standoffish way he usually acted toward people, it still surprised Trent to see him give so much affection to the pup.

Now that they'd had a nice, brief encounter, he didn't want to chance it turning sour. "Enjoy your time on the beach," he said as he took a step away, pulling Reese along with him.

"Good night." Chandler nodded curtly.

As they walked farther down the beach, Trent heard Didi say, "Your grandson seems very happy," to which Chandler replied, "As well he should be."

"You're right," Reese said in a low voice that only Trent could hear. "Your grandfather did seem happy for us, and Didi seems really nice."

Reese truly had seen something good in his grandfather, long before anyone else did. "She seems to have really bonded with him, which is weird considering he fired so many nurses before her."

As Reese and Trent kicked off their shoes and rolled up their jeans, she mused, "That just goes to prove that there's someone special to fill every role in a person's life. You're my special person, and I'm yours."

Carrying her shoes, Reese walked toward the water as if she hadn't just sent his heart into a spin.

"Are there any roles that I don't fill?" he asked.

She tapped her chin, as if she were really thinking it over, then said, "You're a best friend, but you can't fill the space of a best girlfriend."

"I would be everything for you if I could."

"You very nearly are," she said with a smile, "although I'm going to go out on a limb and guess that you wouldn't enjoy girls' spa days, getting mani-pedis and catching up on island gossip."

A moment later, Reese dipped her toes in the water, then immediately ran back up to the dry sand. "Cold! Cold! Cold!"

"It's September in New England. What did you expect?" He laughed as he scooped her up into his arms and pressed his lips to hers. "I'll keep you warm."

"I need to store some of the coldness in my body for later, because you don't keep me warm, Trent. You make me scorching hot, all the time." She twined her arms around his neck and kissed him back. But too soon she was wriggling out of his arms and running down the beach, dragging him alongside her.

"Where are you taking me?"

"Here." She stopped and took both his hands in hers, with a wide grin. "Do you recognize this spot?"

It was dark now, save for the light of the moon dancing across the water, and in the distance, the beam of the lighthouse split the inky sky.

"This is where we exchanged our vows," he said softly.

"This is where I gave you my heart, Trent, and where you gave me yours."

"You were so beautiful in your wedding gown, with your hair falling over your shoulders. And when you looked at me with so much trust and love as you said your vows...I know we said no more apologies, but I wish I could erase the hurt of the past."

She cupped his face, in the same way he always touched hers, and gazed into his eyes so intently it was like she could see through to his soul. "You know what? I don't want to erase the hurt or any of the past. I'm glad I remember what it felt like when I left and that I know what you felt like when you came home to an empty apartment. That hurt is what drove us both to better ourselves, and it deepened our love for each other, which enabled us to be so much better this time. We're more giving, more aware of our own faults and of each other's needs. Our love *is* inescapable *and* unbreakable. It's totally consuming, and fast, and crazy, and too darn wonderful to even try to deny. All this time we've spent together has been like a dream come true. My parents are expecting me to come to their house for breakfast tomorrow, and I want you to come with me this time to share our joy with them."

"Reese..." He gathered her in his arms as he tried to slow his racing heart. He hadn't realized how desperately he'd longed to hear her complete and utter acceptance of their relationship. "There's no place else I'd rather be than by your side."

Chapter Thirty-One

THEY FOUND REESE'S parents outside in the backyard. A sparse forest of pitch pine trees separated their house from the neighbors' on either side. Their yard was lined with Knock Out roses, forsythia, and hydrangeas, as well as pretty flower beds that were past their spring and summer blooms. Beside the patio there was a rose garden, and it looked as though the trellis had come unsecured from the deck. Reese's father was standing thigh-deep in the center of a cluster of rosebushes, trying to simultaneously hold the roses back and nail the trellis into place.

Judith opened her arms as they approached. "Honey. Trent. I'm so glad you both made it." She embraced Reese, and then Trent stepped in for a warm hug.

"Thanks for having me over." Trent kissed Reese's forehead. "I'm going to help your father before he ends up with prickles all over."

"Okay." Reese waved to her father.

"Thank you," Judith said. "He's having a heck of a time with that trellis."

"We'll get it fixed up." Trent crossed the patio. "Hi, David. What can I do to help?"

Reese's father had one hand on the wooden trellis and the other on the rosebush. He grimaced and said, "If you have a trick for making the thorns on the rosebush not poke me every few seconds, that would be great."

"Here, let me get in there." Trent moved beside him and held back the thick rosebushes. "I spent years helping my father with our gardens. I'm used to being poked by these buggers. I'll hold them back while you nail up the trellis."

They worked in silence for a few moments before David said, "Reese seems happier than she's been since she came back to the island a decade ago."

"So am I, David. I'm glad we have a few minutes alone to talk." Trent took a deep breath as David lowered the hammer and turned to face him with a serious gaze.

"I know that Reese needs more time before we move forward, and I will give her all the time and space she needs. But she's the woman

I love and cherish, and I want to have a family with her. I'd like your blessing to ask her to marry me again when the time is right."

When David didn't respond immediately, Trent said, "I also want you to know that I'm selling my practice and staying on the island for good."

"That's good to hear, Trent. But my earlier warnings still apply. Don't hurt my daughter again. Do absolutely everything you can to make your relationship work. Forever, this time."

"I will, sir."

David smiled and scrubbed his hand down his face. "I know you will, but as her father, I still need to hear it. It's a dad thing. You'll understand when you have children of your own someday."

"I already understand, because we both have a common goal—loving and protecting Reese."

David put a hand on Trent's shoulder and said, "When you're ready, know that Judith and I are overjoyed that the two of you have found your way back together."

He pulled Trent into a warm embrace, and the scent of fresh-baked muffins wafted out the screen door. "Now, let's get this thing fixed so we can go eat some of my beautiful wife's, and your beautiful girlfriend's, down-home cooking."

* * *

REESE FILLED FOUR mugs with coffee, working shoulder to shoulder with her mother in the kitchen. She couldn't have been happier to be spending Sunday morning with her three favorite people. Watching Trent and her father work side by side made her feel good all over.

Her mother glanced at her for the hundredth time in the last ten minutes, smiling like she could barely stand to hold in whatever happy thoughts were going through her mind, and finally Reese couldn't hold back her curiosity any longer.

"What is it, Mom?"

"Nothing." She turned back to the eggs she was making and began humming a tune. She hadn't seen her mother with so much energy in a long time. It made her look several years younger, though that might have also had something to do with the cute new jeans and sweater she was wearing.

"You're humming, Mom. You only hum when you're super happy."

"Then I'm super happy," her mom said with a grin. "Aren't you?"

"Yes. I'm happier than I ever expected I would be again. I never dreamed Trent and I would get back together, or that if we did, it would happen in a whirlwind."

"Oh, honey. I think you did."

"How can you say that?" She set the mugs on a tray and glanced toward the sounds of her father and Trent laughing in the backyard.

"You never really gave anyone else the time of day since your divorce."

Reese held out the plates one at a time as her mother put eggs, bacon, and a freshly baked muffin on each one, then added a sprig of berries.

"I gave them the time of day. They just weren't"—she smiled as she thought about what had been wrong with the men she'd dated—"Trent."

"You don't look nervous anymore, like you did when you told me you were first starting to date him again. Are you?"

"Not anymore. We've talked about everything. I mean, *really* talked, in ways that I don't think we ever even tried to back then, or would have known how to. I feel like I know him so much better now. And I also feel like I know myself better now, too."

Her mother touched her hand. "All your father and I have ever wanted was for you to be happy, and I can see that you are." She leaned in close and said with a grin, "I have to thank you, too, Reese. Your happiness has rubbed off on me."

"What do you mean?" Reese asked as the men walked up to the deck.

"After you and I talked about wiggle room the other night, I thought, *you know, there's no reason we can't have wiggle room*. The past doesn't have to mark our future."

They picked up the plates to carry outside as her mother explained, "Your father and I are shaking things up a bit. We danced the night away at the resort the other night, and your father even signed up for a cooking class."

"Dad signed up for a cooking class?" Her parents had such a traditional marriage that she couldn't imagine her father cooking.

Her mother lowered her voice again. "I know. Can you believe it? I really do love cooking and making dinners, but now we'll do it together. I'm delighted about it. Oh, and we're going to take sailing lessons, too. I guess it really is never too late to make things even better."

"I'm so glad, Mom," Reese said as Trent came inside.

"Let me help." He took a plate from each of them. "This looks delicious."

"Thank you, sugar." Her mother took the remaining plate from Reese's hand and said, "I'll take these out to your father."

"I'll go get the coffee." Reese heard Trent

come back inside as she set cream and sugar on the tray. His arms snaked around her waist and his stubble tickled her neck. She turned toward him. "Frisky, aren't we?"

"Always. And I'm just so happy to be part of your life again." He pressed his lips to hers, and it took all of her restraint not to disappear into that kiss and revel in the happiness that rushed through her entire body.

And as they joined her parents out on the deck, Reese knew they had just taken another huge step closer to putting the past where it belonged...and building a beautiful future together.

Chapter Thirty-Two

MONDAY MORNING TRENT stopped by Shelley's Café to see if Quinn needed any last-minute help before the grand opening later that afternoon. The bushes had been trimmed, the lawn was freshly manicured, and with the tables and bright umbrellas that complemented the colors in the sign, the old mill looked revitalized and ready for business.

Inside, the wood floors had been refinished and the shelves Trent had built on the right side of the rear wall were now filled with fresh flowers, coffee mugs with the SHELLEY'S CAFÉ emblems, and several bags of the delicious organic coffee that Shelley was already becoming known for around the island. Tables were set up throughout, and the counter on the left rear of the room sparkled in the sunny overhead lights. Trent touched the old millstone as he passed by on his way to the stairs, thinking about the night he and Reese had bumped into each other after so long and all of his dreams had started to come true again.

He stepped up the first riser and looked out the front windows. Without the bushes in the way, he had a clear view of Reese's gallery and the shops on Old Mill Row. He gazed at the sign above her gallery door, thinking about how good their relationship was now and how far they'd come. Building their new strong foundation step by step, piece by piece.

The sound of Shelley giggling pulled him from his reverie, and he mounted the stairs.

"Quinn? Shelley?" he called up.

"Don't come up here!" Quinn said. Then Shelley giggled again, kicking Trent's brain into gear. He heard them shuffling around and quickly realized he'd interrupted a private moment.

"I'm leaving," he said with a chuckle. "Carry on."

As he made his way outside, he was struck by how envious he'd been of Quinn and Shelley's connection a few weeks ago. Now he realized it wasn't envy that he'd felt. It was longing for what—for *whom*—he'd lost.

When he reached the sidewalk, Reese's car

sped around the corner and came to a screeching halt in front of him. She jumped out, her eyes filled with despair as she flew into his arms.

"Tilly's in the hospital."

* * *

REESE SQUEEZED TRENT'S hand and clutched the flowers they'd bought for Tilly against her chest as they rode the elevator up to the third floor. Reese hated hospitals, from the sterile smell to the too-white walls and the looks of sadness that seemed to be etched into every face. She hadn't been in the hospital since her grandmother passed away when she was younger.

It seemed to her that the world that existed inside hospital walls was completely separate from life outside. Outdoors, birds sang as they sailed through the sky, flowers bloomed, and the wind blew off the bay. The shore changed with every wave, leaving behind seaweed and snails and clams that dug underground. *Life* was everywhere, being nurtured by the elements, whereas within the hospital walls, it felt like life was slowly slipping away. At least on this floor.

She knew hospitals were also the place where new life was brought into the world and lives were saved on a daily basis. As they walked down the wide hallway, passing the nurses' desk, where heads were bent over charts and phones were pressed to ears, all she could think was:

Please let Tilly be okay. Please let Tilly be okay.

When they reached Tilly's room, Trent took Reese by the shoulders and gazed into her eyes.

"She's not in the ICU, Reese. That's a good sign."

"But they said she has pneumonia."

"I know, and that's pretty common among elderly folks, as Kathleen told you when she called. I'm sure Tilly's in good hands, but I'm worried about you. What can I do to help you get through this?"

Reese pressed her body against his, hugging him close and soaking in his comfort.

"You've already helped me. Just being here with me makes me feel better. I just wish her daughter had come to visit. Last I heard, she's waiting until the end of the day to make a decision about coming out from Los Angeles." She gazed up at Trent, so thankful that he was there with her, putting her first without a second's hesitation.

"I'm sure her daughter will make the right decision. Take a deep breath, sweetheart, and I'll be right here by your side."

Reese walked into Tilly's room with her heart in her throat. The blinds were partially drawn, and the room was silent, save for the sounds of the monitors and Tilly's breathing. Tilly's eyes were closed, her head turned to the side. A clear oxygen tube snaked beneath each nostril. Without her carefully applied makeup and her headband securely in place, against the sterile white sheets and among the tubes running from her veiny arms, she looked much less like the upbeat woman who had become like family to Reese and more like Reese's frail grandmother before she passed away. The cold reality hit Reese in the center of her chest.

She set the flowers on the bedside table, and as she sat in the chair beside the bed, with Trent right there with her, Tilly opened her eyes.

She blinked several times, and her lips curved up in a smile as she said, "Reese."

Taking Tilly's warm hand in her own, Reese said, "Hi, Tilly. How are you feeling?"

"Oh, I'm okay. I have a really sweet doctor and a nurse who has been bringing me anything I need." She lifted her hand to her hair and patted it. "I just wish I could have made it through my morning regimen. It's a little embarrassing to be seen like this."

"You look beautiful, Tilly," Trent said with a smile. "Is there anything we can bring you from home that would make you more comfortable?"

"You are a doll, aren't you?" Tilly shifted her eyes to Reese, then back to Trent. "No, thank you, dear. They said I would only be here for a day or two."

"A day or two? Oh, that's great news!" Relief washed through Reese. "Do you want us to pick up a book for you? Can I come see you tonight? Can I bring you soup for dinner?" She wanted to do something—anything—to help Tilly heal.

"Honey, you take better care of me than my own daughter," Tilly said warmly. "Thank you, but the food here is just fine, and you have enough going on in your life. You don't have to come visit me. I'll be back home before you know it."

Trent settled a hand on Reese's shoulder. "That may be, but we'll still come by and visit tonight. We can always make time for the people we love."

Reese felt her throat thicken, at both the relief that Tilly would be okay and at Trent's words. He was so markedly different from the man she'd left in New York.

They visited with Tilly until the nurse came to shoo them out so that Tilly could rest. When Reese gave Tilly a kiss on her cheek, Tilly held tightly to her hand and said, "Reese, honey, you have your whole life ahead of you, but when you get to the end of it, it doesn't feel like it was long enough. Live every minute as if it's your last, so when you're my age, you have no regrets."

Reese glanced up at Trent, whose dark eyes were full of love as he waited patiently beside her. He hadn't rushed her through their visit, despite it being a workday, and she knew he would be totally supportive and loving when they walked out that door. She turned back to Tilly, leaned in close, and said, "A few weeks ago I might have needed that reminder, but not anymore."

As she walked to the parking lot, tucked safely beneath Trent's arm, knowing that later this evening he'd accompany her to check on Tilly again, the sadness that had swallowed her when she'd first seen Tilly in the hospital slipped away with the afternoon breeze.

Time wasn't a given; it was a gift. Life wasn't something that Reese or anyone else could accurately anticipate, and as they drove back toward town, she knew she wouldn't have changed a second of her past even if she had the power to.

She had this one life, and from now on she was going to make it everything she'd ever hoped for.

Chapter Thirty-Three

THEY COULDN'T HAVE asked for a more perfect evening for the grand opening of Shelley's Café. It was an unusually warm evening for September, which brought even more residents out to enjoy the event. Luckily, the café had a large yard to accommodate so many people. By the right side of the café there was a clown making balloon animals and entertaining the children. More balloons hung from the iron railings beside the brook on the opposite side of the café, where Eleanor, who ran the tourist information booth, was talking to a handful of shop owners and residents. Eleanor could keep them engaged for hours with her friendly demeanor and knowledge of the town's history.

Shelley had set large leafy plants on the

corners of the patio, which was also bustling with visitors. Music played from speakers that Derek had installed in the exterior walls, and there were tables strewn around the yard with finger foods and punch and several different types of Shelley's flavored organic coffees.

Shelley had been grinning ear to ear ever since her best friend and cousin, Taryn, had arrived. Taryn was a clothing designer, and she'd hit it off with everyone. She was currently chatting with Brandi, the owner of Savory Delights. Trent was enjoying watching his brother Ethan check Taryn out almost as much as he was enjoying watching Reese laughing with his mother, Sierra, Jocelyn, and his cousin Annabelle.

A heavy arm landed across his shoulder, and he knew without looking that it belonged to his father. His woodsy aftershave and familiar strength gave him away.

"They couldn't have asked for a better turnout." His father smiled at Trent, then held up his coffee cup. "Shelley sure brews a good cup."

"You're not kidding. Mine is something with hazelnut, and it's definitely addicting."

"The café renovations are gorgeous. Sometimes I forget how much each of you is capable of." Griffin lifted his chin toward Quinn, who was walking toward Shelley. "Did you ever think you'd see him settle down?"

"Actually, no, I didn't. And I never thought I'd see him take time off work, either." The fact that the same could once have been said about Trent didn't escape him. He'd learned so much about communication and honesty from these past weeks with Reese, and now he knew he needed to be just as up-front with his father. "Can you spare a minute, Dad? There's something I'd like to talk with you about."

"Of course."

"When Chandler brought us all back to the island, while Derek and Quinn fought the move tooth and nail, I had actually been contemplating moving back for a very long time. But the thing was, I always felt that I needed to live up to the Rockwell name. And I knew you didn't want me to be under Chandler's thumb if I came back."

"Trent, you more than live up to the Rockwell name in every respect. Being a Rockwell means being loyal to your family, giving to others, and being true to yourself and your heart." Griffin looked across the yard at Abby. "Your mother and I have been discussing the recent changes we've seen in you and Quinn, and I think I owe you both, and probably the rest of the kids, too, an apology. As the eldest, you probably felt more pressure than the others, but I believe my efforts to get you all to follow your own paths and move out from under Chandler's control might have backfired. I ended up just applying a different type of pressure, and for that I'm truly sorry."

"Dad, your mentorship helped me in more ways than I can count. You gave me the drive to succeed and the confidence to know that I could. I should have been man enough to look past my own fears and take charge of my life. And I've finally done just that. I've started the process of selling my practice so I can have more time to focus on Reese and, hopefully someday, a family of our own."

He pulled his father into a hug, and over his shoulder, he could see Reese and Sierra laughing together. Reese looked so happy, and so beautiful, and when he caught her eye, he blew her a kiss.

"You know what, Dad? You and Mom taught me the most important thing of all. How to love. It just took me a while to figure out how to combine my competitive instinct with loving Reese the way she deserves."

Just then Didi pushed Chandler's wheelchair over the crest of the hill. Chandler was clinging to the arms of the chair as it rolled over the bumpy grass. He was dressed in a sweater and slacks, looking far less stoic in the more casual attire. Happier, too, than he had in a very long time.

* * *

THE DIN OF the crowd quieted as Shelley and Quinn stood on the front steps of the café. Shelley looked beautiful in a peach-colored cotton skirt and an off-white sweater, which highlighted her gorgeous, thick dark hair. Quinn gazed at her with pride and love in his eyes.

Reese had closed the gallery during the grand opening and finally spotted Jocelyn across the lawn flirting with some cute guy standing by the coffee table. Trent joined Reese and wrapped an arm around her waist as they waited for Shelley to address the friends who had gathered to wish her well.

"Just got the call," he said with a big smile. "My partner's agreed to buy me out. Now I'll have even more time for us."

Butterflies took flight in her stomach. He was living up to all of his promises, and every single thing he did was for them. "Are you sure you want to do that?"

"Totally sure. About everything, Reese, especially us." He pressed his lips to hers just as Shelley began speaking.

"Thank you all for coming out to celebrate the opening of my café. I fell in love with Rockwell Island the moment I set foot on it, and you've all made me feel so welcome that I've come to love it even more than I ever thought possible. Griffin, Abby, Trent, Derek, Sierra, and Ethan...You have all welcomed me into your family, your homes, and your hearts, and you've given so freely of your time and energy to help me renovate the mill and make all of my dreams come true. I can't thank you enough. And, Taryn, you're my best friend and I love you like a sister. Without your endless encouragement, I may never have come on my solo honeymoon and discovered not only this amazing island and community, but the love of my life, too. Rest assured, Taryn, I *will* get you to move here someday!"

Everyone laughed at that and gave Shelley a round of applause. She made her way through the crowd, accepting hugs and kind words, and when she finally joined Reese, Taryn, and the Rockwells, Reese could tell that she was overwhelmed with emotion. Which was exactly the way Reese felt at the moment. She was standing with the man of her dreams, among lifelong and new friends.

"I can't believe it's open," Shelley said. "Three months ago I was living and working in Maryland, and now..."

"Now you're engaged to the best guy around," Quinn said as he pulled her against him. "And you have a terrific new café and a cute cottage overlooking the bay."

"You pretty much live in paradise," Taryn

agreed.

"But I'll debate the best guy around part," Reese teased as she snuggled closer to Trent. "I think that title belongs to my man."

"What am I?" Ethan said on a laugh. "Chopped liver?"

"If that's what chopped liver looks like," Taryn said in a very flirtatious tone, "serve it up."

"You have a boyfriend," Shelley reminded her.

"Yes, and he's a really great guy." Taryn waved a hand in the air. "I was just making an observation."

"Things on the island always seem to happen fast." Derek ran a hand through his hair. "Look at Trent and Reese. They didn't talk for ten years, and now suddenly they're an item again. My head is still spinning. I just hope that this time it lasts."

Trent froze next to Reese. And when she looked up at him, his eyes were serious, as if he was ready to give Derek a piece of his mind.

Derek clearly must have seen the same thing in his brother's eyes, because he said, "I'm sorry, guys. I didn't mean anything by that. I'm so glad you two are together. I meant it as a joke. Honestly, I didn't mean to upset either of you."

"You didn't upset me," Reese said. What

was she doing, trying to hold herself back from Trent at all? She'd been giving her body wholly to the man she loved but still trying to protect her heart, when it so clearly didn't need protecting. Not from this man. Not from the one person who had proven that he'd move heaven and earth to be with her after all these years. "In fact, I'm glad you said that, because I want Trent—and everyone he loves—to know exactly how I feel about him."

She took Trent's hand in hers, and then she dropped to one knee. All the love she'd held in for ten years came tumbling out. "Trent, there's no denying our love. We *are* a whirlwind, and I'm not ashamed of it. Our love is more real than anything I've ever known—*inescapable and unbreakable*." She was only vaguely aware of the *awws* coming from the crowd that had gathered around them. "When I'm with you, I'm the happiest girl in the world, and for the first time since I returned to the island, I know I'm exactly where I am supposed to be—where I *want* to be. Right here by your side—forever. Marry me, Trent. I promise to make you the happiest man in the world. I'll love you, cherish you, and most of all, communicate with you until you're sick of hearing my voice. Be mine, Trent. Father my children and love me forever, because I have never stopped loving you."

Trent dropped to his knees with a wide

smile on his lips. "Reese, you are my love, my life, and my inspiration to be a better man. And I have never, ever stopped loving you either. I would be honored to be your husband."

"Oh my God!" Sierra squealed as Reese fell into Trent's arms and he sealed his lips over hers.

"I love you, Dandelion," Trent said against her lips. "And I always will. *Forever.*"

He kissed her again, and as they rose to their feet, Sierra barreled in between them and hugged Reese. "You proposed! You're getting married! We're going to be sisters again! Now I'll have two sisters!" She pulled Trent into the hug. "I'm so happy!"

Trent laughed as he lifted his sister off her feet. "I am, too."

"That's the most romantic thing I've ever seen!" Taryn hugged Reese. Then she hugged Shelley. "I just want to hug everyone."

Abby and Griffin moved in for hugs and congratulations next. "I am so pleased for you both," Abby said as she hugged Trent, then folded Reese into her arms as well. "I can't say welcome *back* to the family, because you've always been right here in our hearts. We love you, sweetie."

Reese barely held tears of joy at bay. "I love you, too."

Griffin embraced Trent and then hugged

Reese. "Congratulations. We're so happy for you both."

Reese turned, surprised to see her mother patting her eyes with a tissue. She hadn't seen her parents arrive. They both embraced her in a group hug.

"Oh, honey! I'm so happy," her mother said through fresh tears. "You two belong together."

"Congratulations, Reese," her father said.

She drew back and kissed them both on the cheek in time to see Trent leaning down to hug Chandler and Chandler's arms wrapping around his grandson. Tears streamed from her eyes at the look of love on Chandler's face as he said, "I wish Caro had been here to see this."

"Me too," Trent said as he pressed a hand to Reese's lower back.

Reese wanted to rush in and hug Chandler, too, but she also wanted to respect his personal boundaries. So when he lifted his arms and motioned for her to come forward, she felt her heart crack wide open. He held her close and patted her back. "Welcome back to the Rockwell family, Reese."

"Thank you, Mr. Rockwell," she managed.

After hugging Derek, Ethan, and about half of the Rockwell Island community, Trent took Reese by the hand and guided her over to the brook. Water trickled down the rocks, and the sweet scent of Shelley's coffees filled the air around them. She gazed up at the man she would soon marry as he touched his forehead to hers.

"This time all of our Cape Cod promises are going to last forever."

And as they kissed, she knew that forever was just the beginning...

* * *

Four weeks later...

SO MANY PEOPLE showed up for the unveiling of Reese's mural that they spilled over from the grass into the parking lot and beyond. They had arranged for a drape to be hung over the mural and rigged it so that when Reese cut the red ribbon running across the front, the drape would fall, revealing the mural.

Reese and Trent stood at the front of the crowd, both elated as they gazed into each other's eyes. Trent had taken Reese's old engagement ring and had it reset, and now, as he lifted her hand to his lips, the diamonds glistened against the October sun. Trent stepped up to the microphone. "Thank you all for coming out today to celebrate the reveal of the Rockwell Resort mural, which was painted by none other than my beautiful fiancée, Reese Nicholson." He glanced at Reese with love and adoration as the crowd began to clap.

That was when Reese cut the ribbon and unveiled the final piece of her mural—at the top of the mural she had painted the beautifully scripted words *Cape Cod Promises.*

—The End—

Love Bella's and Melissa's writing?

Find more of **Bella's books** at your favorite retailer, including **THE LOOK OF LOVE**, the first book in her *NYT* bestselling series about the Sullivans.

Find more of **Melissa's books** at your favorite retailer, including **LOVERS AT HEART (currently FREE in ebook format)**, the first book in her bestselling series about the Bradens.

More about Bella and Melissa

BELLA ANDRE

Bella Andre is the *New York Times, USA Today,* and *Publishers Weekly* bestselling author of **"The Sullivans"** and **"The Morrisons"** series.

Having sold more than 4 million books, Bella Andre's novels have been #1 bestsellers around the world and have appeared on the *New York Times* and *USA Today* bestseller lists 23 times. She has been the #1 Ranked Author at Amazon (on a top 10 list that included Nora Roberts, J. K. Rowling, James Patterson, and Steven King), and *Publishers Weekly* named Oak Press (the publishing company she created to publish her own books) the Fastest-Growing Independent Publisher in the US. Known for "sensual, empowered stories enveloped in heady romance" (*Publishers Weekly*), her books have been *Cosmopolitan* Magazine "Red Hot Reads" twice and have been translated into ten languages. Winner of the Award of Excellence, The *Washington Post* called her "One of the top writers in America" and she has been featured by NPR, *Entertainment Weekly*, *USA Today*, *Forbes*, The *Wall Street Journal,* and *TIME* Magazine. Bella also writes the *New York Times* bestselling "Four Weddings and a Fiasco" series as **Lucy Kevin**.

MELISSA FOSTER

Melissa Foster is a New York Times and USA Today bestselling and award-winning author of the Love in Bloom series which includes the "Snow Sisters," "The Bradens," "The Remingtons," and the "Seaside Summers" series.

Melissa writes sexy and heartwarming, award-winning contemporary romance novels with emotionally compelling characters that stay with you long after you turn the last page. Her books have been recommended by *USA Today's* book blog, *Hagerstown* magazine, *The Patriot*, and *Mensa Bulletin*. Melissa is the founder of the World Literary Café and Fostering Success. When she's not writing, Melissa helps authors navigate the publishing industry through her author training programs on Fostering Success. Melissa is also the author of the *New York Times* and *USA Today* bestselling, and award-winning historical fiction novel Have No Shame, as well as several other award-winning suspense and women's fiction titles. Melissa enjoys discussing her books with book clubs and reader groups and welcomes an invitation to your event.

26665711R00234

Made in the USA
San Bernardino, CA
02 December 2015